KT-199-861

Bestselling author **Tess Gerritsen** is also a doctor, and she brings to her novels her first-hand knowledge of emergency and autopsy rooms.

But her interests span far more than medical topics. As an anthropology undergraduate at Stanford University, she catalogued centuries-old human remains, and continues to travel the world, driven by her fascination with ancient cultures and bizarre natural phenomena.

Now a full-time novelist, she lives with her husband in Maine.

For more information about Tess Gerritsen and her novels, visit her website at **www.tessgerritsen.co.uk**

www.**rbooks**.co.uk

HAVE YOU READ THEM ALL?

The thrillers featuring Jane Rizzoli and Maura Isles are:

THE SURGEON

Introducing Detective Jane Rizzoli of the
Boston Homicide Unit
In Boston, there's a killer on the loose. A killer who
targets lone women and performs ritualistic acts of
torture before finishing them off . . .

'If you've never read Gerritsen, figure in the price of electricity
when you buy your first novel by her, 'cause, baby, you are going
to be up all night'
Stephen King

THE APPRENTICE

The surgeon has been locked up for a year, but his chilling legacy
still haunts the city, and especially
Boston homicide detective Jane Rizzoli . . .

'Gerritsen has enough in her locker to seriously worry Michael
Connelly, Harlan Coben and even the great Dennis Lehane.
Brilliant'
Crime Time

THE SINNER

Long-buried secrets are revealed as Dr Maura Isles and detective
Jane Rizzoli find themselves part of an investigation that leads to
the awful truth.

'Gutsy, energetic and shocking'
Manchester Evening News

BODY DOUBLE

Dr Maura Isles has seen more than her share of
corpses. But never has the body on the autopsy table been her
own . . .

'It's scary just how good Tess Gerritsen is. This is crime writing at
its unputdownable, nerve-tingling best'
Harlan Coben

VANISH

When medical examiner Maura Isles looks down at the body of a
beautiful woman she gets the fright of her life. The corpse opens its
eyes . . .

'A horrifying tangle of rape, murder and blackmail'
Guardian

THE MEPHISTO CLUB

Can you really see evil when you look into
someone's eyes? Dr Maura Isles and detective Jane Rizzoli
encounter evil in its purest form.

'Gruesome, seductive and creepily credible'
The Times

KEEPING THE DEAD

She's Pilgrim Hospital's most unusual patient and when she is
brought in for scanning Maura Isles is there because the patient is
a mummy thought to have been dead for centuries. And then the
scan shows the image of a very modern bullet . . .

'A seamless blend of good writing and pulse-racing tension'
Independent

Have you read Tess Gerritsen's stand-alone thrillers?

THE BONE GARDEN

Boston 1830: A notorious serial killer preys on his victims, flitting from graveyards and into maternity wards. But no one knows who he is . . .

'Fascinating . . . gory . . . a fast-paced novel that will leave you with a real appreciation of just how far medicine has come in the past century'
Mail on Sunday

HARVEST

How far would you go to save a life? A young surgical resident is drawn into the deadly world of organ smuggling.

'Suspense as sharp as a scalpel's edge. A page-turning, hold your breath read'
Tami Hoag

LIFE SUPPORT

A terrifying and deadly epidemic is about to be unleashed . . .

'If you like your crime medicine strong, this will keep you gripped'
Mail on Sunday

GIRL
MISSING

TESS GERRITSEN

BANTAM BOOKS

LONDON • TORONTO • SYDNEY • AUCKLAND • JOHANNESBURG

TRANSWORLD PUBLISHERS
61–63 Uxbridge Road, London W5 5SA
A Random House Group Company
www.rbooks.co.uk

GIRL MISSING
A BANTAM BOOK: 9780553824421

First published in the US
in 1994 by HarperPaperbacks
a division of HarperCollins Publishers
under the title *Peggy Sue Got Murdered*

First published in Great Britain
in 2009 by Bantam Press
an imprint of Transworld Publishers
Bantam edition published 2009

Copyright © Tess Gerritsen 1994

Tess Gerritsen has asserted her right under the Copyright, Designs and
Patents Act 1988 to be identified as the author of this work.

This book is a work of fiction and, except in the case of historical fact, any
resemblance to actual persons, living or dead, is purely coincidental.

A CIP catalogue record for this book
is available from the British Library.

This book is sold subject to the condition that it shall not,
by way of trade or otherwise, be lent, resold, hired out,
or otherwise circulated without the publisher's prior
consent in any form of binding or cover other than that
in which it is published and without a similar condition,
including this condition, being imposed on the
subsequent purchaser.

Addresses for Random House Group Ltd companies outside the UK
can be found at: www.randomhouse.co.uk
The Random House Group Ltd Reg. No. 954009

The Random House Group Limited supports The Forest Stewardship
Council (FSC), the leading international forest certification organisation. All
our titles that are printed on Greenpeace approved FSC certified paper carry
the FSC logo. Our paper procurement policy can be found at
www.rbooks.co.uk/environment

Typeset in 11.5/14.5pt Sabon by
Falcon Oast Graphic Art Ltd.
Printed in the UK by CPI Cox & Wyman, Reading, RG1 8EX.

6 8 10 9 7

GIRL
MISSING

An Introduction
From the Author

Years before I built my reputation as a thriller writer, I had another life – as a romantic suspense author. Fans of my crime novels may be surprised to learn that I launched my career by writing stories in which romance shared equal billing with murder, where characters struggle with both fear and sexual tension. At the time, I was working as a doctor in a hospital, a job in which I saw far too much pain and heartbreak at work. At the end of the day, I drew comfort from reading – and writing – romance novels.

But over the course of writing nine of those novels, I found that the thriller elements began to dominate my plots. I was evolving into a crime writer, and in *Girl Missing* (first published in 1994 under the title *Peggy Sue Got Murdered*), that evolution is well underway. Yes, it's a romance. But it's also a crime novel, featuring a female medical examiner who must track down the cause of an epidemic of mysterious deaths. I consider it my 'bridge' novel, a moment in time when I was poised to step from one genre into the next.

Recently updated for today's readers, *Girl Missing* will give you a glimpse of the thriller writer I would one day become. I hope you enjoy the look back!

Tess Gerritsen
May 2009

1

An hour before her shift started, an hour before she was even supposed to be there, they rolled the first corpse through the door.

Up until that moment, Kat Novak's day had been going better than usual. Her car had started on the first turn of the key. Traffic had been sparse on Telegraph, and she'd hit all the green lights. She'd managed to slip into her office at five to seven, and for the next hour she could lounge guiltlessly at her desk with a jelly doughnut and today's edition of the *Albion Herald*. She made a point of skipping the obituaries. Chances were she already knew all about them.

Then a gurney with a black body bag rolled past her doorway. *Oh Lord*, she thought. In about thirty seconds, Clark was going to knock at her door, asking for favors. With a sense of dread, Kat listened to the gurney wheels grind down the hall. She heard the autopsy room doors whisk open and shut, heard the distant rumble of male voices. She counted ten seconds, fifteen. And there it was, just as she'd anticipated: the sound of Clark's Reeboks squeaking across the linoleum floor.

He appeared in her doorway. 'Morning, Kat,' he said.

She sighed. 'Good morning, Clark.'

'Can you believe it? They just wheeled one in.'

'Yeah, the *nerve* of them.'

'It's already seven ten,' he said. A note of pleading crept into his voice. 'If you could just do me this favor . . .'

'But I'm not here.' She licked a dollop of raspberry jelly from her fingers. 'Until eight o'clock, I'm nothing more than a figment of your imagination.'

'I don't have time to process this one. Beth's got the kids packed and ready to take off, and here I am, stuck with another Jane Doe. Have a heart.'

'This is the third time this month.'

'But I've got a family. They expect me to spend time with them. You're a free agent.'

'Right. I'm a divorcee, not a temp.'

Clark shuffled into her office and leaned his ample behind against her desk. 'Just this once. Beth and I, we're having problems, you know, and I want this vacation to start off right. I'll return the favor sometime. I promise.'

Sighing, Kat folded up the *Herald*. 'Okay,' she said. 'What've you got?'

Clark was already pulling off his white coat, visibly shifting to vacation mode. 'Jane Doe. No obvious trauma. Another body-fluid special. Sykes and Ratchet are in there with her.'

'They bring her in?'

'Yeah. So you'll have a decent police report to work with.'

Kat rose to her feet and brushed powdered sugar off her scrub pants. 'You owe me,' she said, as they headed into the hall.

'I know, I know.' He stopped at his office and grabbed his jacket – a fly-fisherman's version, complete with a zillion pockets with little feathers poking out.

'Leave a few trout for the rest of us.'

He grinned and gave her a salute. 'Into the wilds of Maine I go,' he said, heading for the elevator. 'See you next week.'

Feeling resigned, Kat pushed open the door to the autopsy room and went in.

The body, still sealed in its black bag, lay on the slab. Lieutenant Lou Sykes and Sergeant Vince Ratchet, veterans of the local knife and gun club, were waiting for her. Sykes looked dapper as usual in a

TESS GERRITSEN

suit and tie – a black homicide detective who always
insisted on mixing corpses with Versace. His partner,
Vince Ratchet, was, in contrast, a perpetual candidate
for Slim-Fast. Ratchet was peering in fascination at a
specimen jar on the shelf.

'What the hell is that?' he asked, pointing to the jar.
Good old Vince; he was never afraid to sound stupid.

'That's the right middle lobe of a lung,' Kat said.

'I would've guessed it was a brain.'

Sykes laughed. 'That's why she's the doc and you're
just a dumb cop.' He straightened his tie and looked
at her. 'Isn't Clark doing this one?'

Kat snapped on a pair of gloves. 'Afraid I am.'

'Thought your shift started at eight.'

'Tell me about it.' She went to the slab and gazed
down at the bag, feeling her usual reluctance to open
the zipper, to reveal what lay beneath the black
plastic. *How many of these bags have I opened?* she
wondered. A hundred, two hundred? Each one contained its own private horror story. This was the
hardest part, sliding down the zipper, unveiling
the contents. Once a body was revealed, once she'd
weathered the initial shock of its appearance, she
could set to work with a scientist's dispassion. But the
first glimpse, the first reaction – that was always pure
emotion, something over which she had no control.

'So, guys,' she said. 'What's the story here?'

Ratchet came forward and flipped open his

14

notebook. It was like an extension of his arm, that note-book; she'd never seen him without it. 'Caucasian female, no ID, age twenty to thirty. Body found four A.M. this morning, off South Lexington. No apparent trauma, no witnesses, no nothing.'

'South Lexington,' said Kat, and images of that neighborhood flashed through her mind. She knew the area too well – the streets, the back alleys, the playgrounds rimmed with barbed wire. And, looming above it all, the seven buildings, as grim as twenty-story concrete headstones. 'The Projects?' she asked.

'Where else?'

'Who found her?'

'City trash pickup,' said Sykes. 'She was in an alley between two of the Project buildings, sort of wedged against a Dumpster.'

'As if she was placed there? Or died there?'

Sykes glanced at Ratchet. 'You were at the scene first. What do you say, Vince?'

'Looked to me like she died there. Just lay down, sort of curled up against the Dumpster, and called it quits.'

It was time. Steeling herself for that first glimpse, Kat reached for the zipper and opened the bag. Sykes and Ratchet both took a step backward, an instinctive reaction she herself had to quell. The zipper parted and the plastic fell away to reveal the corpse.

It wasn't bad; at least it appeared intact. Compared to some of the corpses she'd seen, this one was actually in excellent shape. The woman was a bleached blond, about thirty, perhaps younger. Her face looked like marble, pale and cold. She was dressed in a long-sleeved purple pullover, some sort of polyester blend, a short black skirt with a patent leather belt, black tights, and brand-new Nikes. Her only jewelry was a dime-store friendship ring and a Timex watch – still ticking. Rigor mortis had frozen her limbs into a vague semblance of a fetal position. Both fists were clenched tight, as though, in her last moment of life, they'd been caught in spasm.

Kat took a few photos, then picked up a cassette recorder and began to dictate. 'Subject is a white female, blond, found in alley off South Lexington around oh four hundred . . .' Sykes and Ratchet, already knowing what would follow, took off their jackets and reached into a linen cart for some gowns – medium for Sykes, extra large for Ratchet. The gloves came next. They both knew the drill; they'd been cops for years, and partners for four months. It was an odd pairing, Kat thought, like Abbott and Costello. So far, though, it seemed to work.

She put down the cassette recorder. 'Okay, guys,' she said. 'On to the next step.'

The undressing. The three of them worked together to strip the corpse. Rigor mortis made it difficult; Kat had to cut away the skirt. The outer clothing was set aside. The tights and underwear were to be examined later for evidence of recent sexual contact. When at last the corpse lay naked, Kat once again reached for the camera and clicked off a few more photos for the evidence file.

It was time for the hands-on part of the job – the part one never saw on *House*. Occasionally, the answers fell right into place with a first look. Time of death, cause of death, mechanism and manner of death – these were the blanks that had to be filled in. A verdict of suicide or natural causes would make Sykes and Ratchet happy; a verdict of homicide would not.

This time, unfortunately, Kat could give them no quick answers.

She could make an educated guess about time of death. Livor mortis, the body's mottling after death, was unfixed, suggesting that death was less than eight hours old, and the body temperature, using Moritz's formula, suggested a time of death of around midnight. But the cause of death?

'Nothing definitive, guys,' she said. 'Sorry.'

Sykes and Ratchet looked disappointed, but not at all surprised.

'We'll have to wait for body fluids,' she said.

'How long?'

'I'll collect it, get it to the state lab today. But they've been running a few weeks behind.'

'Can't you run a few tests here?' asked Sykes.

'I'll screen it through gas and TL chromatography, but it won't be specific. Definitive drug ID will have to go through the state lab.'

'All we want to know,' said Ratchet, 'is whether it's possible.'

'Homicide's always possible.' She continued her external exam, starting with the head. No signs of trauma here; the skull felt intact, the scalp unbroken. The blond hair was tangled and dirty; obviously the woman had not washed it in days. Except for post-mortem changes, she saw no marks on the torso either. The left arm, however, drew her attention. It had a long ridge of scar tissue snaking down it toward the wrist.

'Needle tracks,' said Kat. 'And a fresh puncture mark.'

'Another junkie,' sighed Sykes. 'There's our cause of death. Probable OD.'

'We could run a fast analysis on her needle,' said Kat. 'Where's her kit?'

Ratchet shook his head. 'Didn't find one.'

'She must've had a needle. A syringe.'

'I looked,' said Ratchet. 'I didn't see any.'

'Did you find anything near the body?'

'Nothing,' said Ratchet. 'No purse, no ID, nothing.'

'Who was first on the scene?'

'Patrolman. Then me.'

'So we've got a junkie with fresh needle marks. But no needle.'

Sykes said, 'Maybe she shot up somewhere else. Wandered into the alley and died.'

'Possible.'

Ratchet was peering at the woman's hand. 'What's this?' he said.

'What's what?'

'She's got something in her hand.'

Kat looked. Sure enough, there was a tiny fleck of pink cardboard visible under the edge of her clenched fingers. It took two of them to pry the fist open. Out slid a matchbook, small and pink with raised gold lettering: 'L'Etoile, fine nouvelle cuisine. 221 Hilton Avenue.'

'Kind of out of her neighborhood,' Sykes remarked.

'Hey, I hear that's a nice place,' said Ratchet. 'Not that I could ever afford to eat there myself.'

Kat opened the matchbook. Inside were three unused matches. And a phone number, scrawled in fountain pen ink on the inside cover.

'Think it's a local number?' she asked.

'Prefix would put it in Surry Heights,' said Sykes. 'That's still out of her neighborhood.'

'Well,' said Kat. 'Let's try it out and see what happens.' As Sykes and Ratchet stood by, she went to the wall phone and dialed the number. It rang, three times, four. An answering machine came on, the message spoken by a deep male voice:

'I'm not available at the moment. Please leave your name and number.'

That was all. No cute music, no witty remarks, just that terse request, and then the beep.

Kat said, 'This is Dr. Novak at the Albion medical examiner's office. Please call me back, in regards to a . . .' She paused, unwilling to reveal that she had a corpse whom he might know. Instead she said, 'Please call me. It's important,' and left her number. She hung up and looked at the two cops. 'We'll just have to wait and see who calls back. In the meantime, do you both want to stick around for the autopsy?'

It was probably the last thing the men wanted to do, but they remained stoically by the table, wincing as she stabbed various needles into the corpse, collecting blood from the femoral vein, vitreous fluid from the eye, and urine from a puncture through the lower abdominal wall. After watching a needle pierce an eyeball, a blade does not hold nearly as many horrors. Kat picked up the Henckel knife and this time neither man flinched, even as her blade sliced into the torso. Even as she snapped apart ribs and lifted off the sternum, releasing the odor of blood and offal.

Inside the chest, organs glistened.

Kat put down her knife and picked up a far more delicate scalpel. Reaching into the cavity, her gloved hands registered the neutral temperature of those organs. Neither warm like the living, nor chilled like a refrigerated corpse. As Goldilocks would have said, *Not too hot, not too cold, but just right* – this description suitable for a corpse that had been lying exposed on a spring night. She sliced through the great vessels, freeing the heart and lungs, which she lifted out of the chest cavity.

'These lungs feel pretty heavy,' she noted. She set them on the scale and watched as the dial confirmed her judgment.

'What would cause them to be heavy?' asked Ratchet.

She noticed the fleck of froth that had leaked from the bronchi. 'There's foamy edema. The lungs are filled with fluid.'

'Meaning what? She drowned in an alley?'

'In a sense, she did drown. But the fluid came from her own lungs. Foamy edema can be caused by any number of things.'

'Like a drug OD?' asked Sykes.

'Absolutely. This could certainly happen after an overdose of narcotics.'

She sliced open the heart, examined the chambers. Except for the soggy lungs, the organs appeared grossly normal. The coronary vessels were healthy, the liver and pancreas and intestines undiseased. Cutting open the stomach, she found no food remnants, only 20cc of bilious fluid.

'Died with an empty stomach,' said Kat.

'Look at how skinny she is,' said Sykes. 'When you're shooting crap into your veins, I'd guess eating takes second priority.'

Kat moved on to the vagina and rectum. It was one aspect of the postmortem that made her uncomfortable, but only because two men were in the room. As she inspected the external genitalia, as she inserted swabs to collect body fluids, they were watching intently, and it was more than just Jane Doe's privacy that felt violated. 'I don't see any evidence of sexual assault,' she said.

She turned her attention to the head. Of all the parts of a corpse, the face is the most personal, and the most disturbing to contemplate. Until that moment, Kat had avoided looking at it too closely, but now she was forced to. In life, the young woman might have been pretty. Shampoo her hair, animate those facial muscles into a smile, and she would probably have caught the eye of more than a few men. But death had made her jaw droop, her mouth gape open, revealing coffee-stained teeth and a tongue dried out from exposure. It was a blank face, revealing no secrets.

Neither did her cranium provide any answers. Kat

sawed open the skull and the brain within showed no signs of hemorrhage or stroke or trauma. It was a healthy-looking brain, a young brain, and it should have given its owner many more years of service. Instead that brain, with its lifetime of memories, was now dropped into a bucket of formalin. And the body – what was left of it – would go into a refrigerated drawer, dubbed with the name shared by far too many other unidentified women who had come before her.

Jane Doe.

Kat was sitting at her desk later that morning when her phone rang. She picked it up and answered: 'Dr. Novak, Assistant ME.'

'You left a message,' said a man. She recognized at once the voice from the answering machine. Its deep timbre was now edged with anxiety. 'What's this all about?' he demanded.

Kat at once reached for pen and paper. 'Who am I speaking to?' she asked.

'You should know. You called *me*.'

'I just had your telephone number, not a name—'

'And how did you get my number?'

'It was written on a matchbook. The police brought a woman into the morgue this morning, and she—'

He cut in: 'I'll be right there.'

'Mister, I didn't catch your—'

She heard the click of the receiver, then a dial tone. *Jackass*, she thought. What if he didn't show up? What if he didn't call back?

She dialed Homicide and left a message for Sykes and Ratchet: 'Get yourselves back to the morgue.' Then she waited.

At noon, she got a buzz on the intercom from the front desk. 'There's a Mr. Quantrell here,' said the secretary. 'He says you're expecting him. Want me to send him down?'

'I'll meet him up there,' said Kat. 'I'm on my way.'

She knew better than to just drag a civilian in off the street and take him straight down to the morgue. He would need a chance to prepare for the shock. She pulled a white lab coat over her scrub suit. The lapel had coffee stains, but it would have to do.

By the time she'd ridden up the basement elevator to the ground floor, she'd rearranged her hair into a semblance of presentability and straightened her name tag. She stepped out into the hallway. Through the glass door at the end of the corridor she could see the reception area with its couch and upholstered chairs, all in generic gray. She could also see a man pacing back and forth in front of the couch, oblivious to her approach. He was nicely dressed, and didn't seem like the sort of man who'd be acquainted with a Jane Doe from South Lexington. His camel-hair jacket was perfectly tailored to his wide shoulders.

He had a tan raincoat slung over his arm, and he was tugging at his tie as though it were strangling him.

Kat pushed the glass door open and walked in. 'Mr. Quantrell?'

At once the man turned and faced her. He had wheat-colored hair, perfectly groomed, and eyes a shade she'd never seen before. Not quite blue, not quite gray, they seemed as changeable as a spring sky. He was old enough – his early forties perhaps – to have amassed a few character lines around those eyes, a few gray hairs around his temples. His jaw was set with tension.

'I'm Dr. Novak,' she said, holding out her hand. He shook it automatically, quickly, as though to get the formalities done and over with.

'Adam Quantrell,' he said. 'You left that message on my answering machine.'

'Why don't we go down to my office? You can wait there until the police—'

'You said something about a woman,' he cut in rudely. 'That the police brought in a woman.' No, it wasn't rudeness, Kat decided. He was afraid.

'It might be better to wait for Lieutenant Sykes,' she said. 'He can explain the situation.'

'Why don't *you* explain it to me?'

'I'm just the medical examiner, Mr. Quantrell. I can't give out information.'

The look he shot her was withering. All at once she

wished she stood a little straighter, a little taller. That she didn't feel so threatened by that gaze of his. 'This Lieutenant Sykes,' he said. 'He's from Homicide, right?'

'Yes.'

'So there's a question of murder.'

'I don't want to speculate.'

'Who is she?'

'We don't have an ID yet.'

'Then you don't know.'

'No.'

He paused. 'Let me see the body.' It wasn't a request but a command, and a desperate one at that.

Kat glanced at the door and wondered when the hell Sykes would arrive. She looked back at the man and realized that he was barely holding it together. *He's terrified. Terrified that the body lying in my refrigerated drawer is someone he knows and loves.*

'That's why you called me, isn't it?' he said. 'To find out if I can identify her?'

She nodded. 'The morgue is downstairs, Mr. Quantrell. Come with me.'

He strode beside her in silence, his tanned face looking pale under the fluorescent lights. He was silent as well on the elevator ride down to the basement. She glanced up once, and saw that he was staring straight ahead, as though afraid to look anywhere else, as though afraid he'd lose what control he still had.

When they stepped off the elevator, he paused, glancing around at the scuffed walls, the tired linoleum floor. Overhead was another bank of flickering fluorescent lights. The building was old, and down here in the basement one could see the decay in the chipped paint, the cracked walls, could smell it in the very air. When the whole city was in the process of decay, when every agency from Social Services to trash pickup was clamoring for a dwindling share of tax dollars, the ME's office was always the last to be funded. Dead citizens, after all, do not vote.

But if Adam Quantrell took note of his surroundings, he did not comment.

'It's down this hall,' said Kat.

Wordlessly he followed her to the cold storage room.

She paused at the door. 'The body's in here,' she said. 'Are you . . . feeling up to it?'

He nodded.

She led him inside. The room was brightly lit, almost painfully so. Refrigerated drawers lined the far wall, some of them labeled with names and numbers. This time of year, the occupancy rate was running on the high side. The spring thaw, the warmer weather, brought the guns and knives out onto the street again, and these were the latest crop of victims. There were three Jane Does. Kat reached for the drawer labeled 373-4-3-A. Pausing, she glanced at Adam. 'It's not going to be pleasant.'

He swallowed. 'Go ahead.'

She pulled open the drawer. It slid out noiselessly, releasing a waft of cold vapor. The body was almost formless under the shroud. Kat looked up at Adam, to see how he was holding up. It was the men who usually fainted, and the bigger they were, the harder they were to pull up off the linoleum. So far, this guy was doing okay. Grim and silent, but okay. Slowly she lifted off the shroud. Jane Doe's alabaster-white face lay exposed.

Again, Kat looked at Adam.

He had paled slightly, but he hadn't moved. Neither did his gaze waver from the corpse. For a solid ten seconds he stared at Jane Doe, as though trying to reconstruct her frozen features into something alive, something familiar.

At last he let out a deep breath. Only then did Kat realize the man had been holding it. He looked across at her. In an utterly calm voice, he said, 'I've never seen this woman before in my life.'

Then he turned and walked out of the room.

2

Kat shut the drawer and followed Adam into the hall. 'Wait. Mr. Quantrell.'

'I can't help you. I don't know who she is.'

'But you *thought* you knew. Didn't you?'

'I don't know what I thought.' He was striding toward the elevator, his long legs carrying him at a brisk pace.

'Why did she have your phone number?'

'I don't know.'

'Is it a business number? One the public might know?'

'No, it's my home phone.'

'Then how did she get it?'

'I told you, I don't know.' He reached the elevator and stabbed the Up button. 'She's a total stranger.'

'But you were afraid you knew her. That's why you came down here.'

'I was doing my civic duty.' He shot her a look that said, *No more questions*.

Kat asked anyway. 'Who did you think she was, Mr. Quantrell?'

He didn't answer. He just regarded her with that impenetrable gaze.

'I want you to sign a statement,' she said. 'And I need to know how to reach you. In case the police have more questions.'

He reached into his jacket and pulled out a card. 'My home address,' he said, handing it to her.

She glanced at it. *11 Fair Wind Lane, Surry Heights*. Sykes had been correct about that phone prefix.

'You'll have to talk to the police,' she said.

'Why?'

'Routine questions.'

'Is it a homicide or isn't it?'

'I don't know yet.'

The doors slid open. 'When you make up your mind, call me.'

She slipped into the elevator after him, and the doors shut behind her. 'Look,' she said. 'I have a dead body with no name. Now, I could just call her Jane Doe and leave it at that. But somewhere, there's someone who's missing a sister or a daughter or a wife. I'd like to help them out, I really would.'

'Fingerprints.'

'I've done that.'

'Dental X-rays.'

'I've done that, too.'

'You sound capable. You don't need my help.' The doors slid open and he stepped out. 'It's not as if I don't care,' he said, leading her on a brisk chase down the hall, toward the reception area. 'But I don't see why I should get dragged into this, just because my number happens to be written in some – some restaurant matchbook. She could've gotten it any-where. Stolen it—'

'I never told you it was from a restaurant.'

He halted and turned to her. 'Yes, you did.'

'No, I didn't. I *know* I didn't.'

He fell silent. Their gazes locked, both of them refusing to yield ground. *Even a guy as smooth as you are can slip up*, she thought with a dart of satisfaction.

'And I'm sure you're wrong,' he said evenly. He turned and went into the reception area.

Sykes and Ratchet were standing by the front desk.

Sykes turned to Kat and said, 'We got your message . . .' His gaze shifted to the man with her, and he reacted with surprise. 'Mr. Quantrell. What brings you down to . . .' Suddenly he glanced back at Kat.

'It was his phone number, Lou,' said Kat. 'But Mr. Quantrell says he doesn't know the woman.'

31

'Talk to her, Lieutenant,' said Adam. 'Maybe you can convince Dr. Novak I'm not some ax murderer.'

Sykes laughed. 'Novak giving you a hard time?'

'Since I can see you two already know each other,' said Kat in irritation, 'I'll just take Mr. Quantrell at his word.'

'I'm so relieved,' said Adam. 'Now, if you'll excuse me . . .' He gave Kat a brief nod. 'Dr. Novak, it has been . . . interesting.' He turned to leave.

'Excuse me, Mr. Q.?' called Sykes. 'A word, please.'

As the two men moved to a far corner of the room, Kat caught Adam's glance. It said, *This has nothing to do with you.*

'We'll see you downstairs, Lou,' Ratchet said. Then he gave Kat a nudge. 'C'mon. You got any more of that god-awful coffee?'

She could take a hint. As she and Ratchet walked to the elevators, she looked over her shoulder. The two men were still in the corner, talking in low voices. Adam was facing her, and over the head of the shorter Sykes, he caught sight of her backward glance and he returned it with a look of cool acknowledgment. The tension in his face was now gone; he was back in full control.

In the elevator she said, 'Okay, Vince. Who is he?'

Ratchet shrugged. 'Owns some pharmaceutical company. Cyrus, something or other.'

'Cygnus? He owns the *Cygnus* Company?'

'Yeah, that's it. He's always in those society pages. You know, this or that black-tie affair. Surprised you haven't heard of him.'

'I don't read the society pages.'

'You should. Your ex was mentioned in them the other day. He was at some campaign benefit for the mayor. Had a nice-looking blond on his arm.'

'That's why I don't read the society pages.'

'Oh.'

They got out of the elevator and headed to Kat's office. The coffee machine was doing overtime today. The glass pot had already been emptied twice, and what was left in it now looked positively vile. She poured out a cup and handed it to Ratchet.

'How does Lou know Mr. Society?' she asked.

Ratchet frowned at the evil brew in his mug. 'Some private thing. Quantrell asked Lou for a little police assistance. Something to do with his daughter.'

'Quantrell has a daughter?'

'That's what I hear.'

'He didn't strike me as the daddy type. Not a guy who'd let sticky little hands anywhere near his cashmere coat.'

Ratchet took a sip from the mug and winced. 'Your coffee's improved.'

'What sort of help did Lou give him?'

'Oh, the girl dropped out of sight or something.

You'd have to ask Lou. It happened a while back, before we got paired up.'

'Was he working South Lexington?'

'Been on that beat for years. That's where his partner went down. Drive-by. Then I lost mine in Watertown, and Lou got stuck with me. The rest, as they say, is history.' He took another sip of coffee.

'Adam Quantrell doesn't live anywhere near South Lexington.'

Ratchet laughed. 'That's for sure.'

'So why did he tap a South Lexington cop for help?'

'I don't know. Why don't you ask Lou?' Ratchet's cell phone rang. Automatically he glanced down at the number on the display and sighed. 'Ratchet here,' he said. 'Yeah, what have you got for us now?'

Kat turned her attention to the stack of papers on her desk. They were the request forms to be sent with the body fluid samples to the state lab. If she wanted to make the three o'clock pickup, she'd have to fill them out now. She sat down and began checking the appropriate boxes: Gas chromatography/UC; immunoanalysis. Every test that might possibly identify the drug that had killed Jane Doe.

She looked up at the sound of footsteps. Sykes walked in. 'Sorry to brush you off,' he said. 'It was sort of a personal matter for Mr. Quantrell.'

'So I heard.' She resumed filling out the forms.

He noticed the papers. 'Is that for Jane Doe?'

'Courier comes by at three. I know you want quick answers.' She gathered up the slips, wrapped them around the test tubes, and stuffed it all in a lab envelope. 'So here it is, off to the races.' She dropped the bundle into the basket marked *Pick up*.

'Thought you were going to run some tests here.'

'I'll do them when I do them. First, I've got deadlines on a few autopsy reports. Court dates coming up. And my ex has already sent me nasty messages over voice mail.'

Sykes laughed. 'You and Ed still at each other's throats?'

'Lou, love is fleeting. Contempt is forever.'

'I take it you're not going to vote for him.'

'Actually, I think Ed's got the right temperament for a DA. Don't you agree he's got that striking resemblance to a Doberman pinscher?' She went to the filing cabinet and began rummaging for papers. 'Besides, Ed and the mayor deserve each other.'

'Hell,' grunted Ratchet, snapping shut the phone. 'Now we'll miss lunch.'

'What is it?' asked Sykes.

'We just got a call. They found another one. Female, no signs of trauma.'

Kat looked up from the file drawer. Ratchet was already scribbling in his notebook. 'Another OD?' she asked.

'Probably. And my stomach's already growling.' He kept writing in that matter-of-fact way of his. *Too many corpses, too many deaths, and this is what it does to us*, Kat thought. *A dead body means nothing more to us than a canceled lunch.*

'Where's the vic?' she asked.

'South Lexington.'

'What part of South Lexington?'

Ratchet shut his notebook and looked up. 'Same place we found the other one,' he said. 'The Projects.'

Adam Quantrell walked briskly across the street, his shoulders hunched against the wind, his hands thrust deep into the pockets of his raincoat. It was April already, but it felt like January. The wind was cutting, the trees skeletal; people on the street wore their winter pallor like masks.

He unlocked his Volvo, slid into the driver's seat, and shut the door.

He sat there for a moment, safely hidden behind tinted glass, relieved to be in a place where no one could read his face, divine his thoughts. It was cold inside; his breath misted the air. But the real chill came from within.

It wasn't her. At least I should be thankful for that.

He started the engine and guided the Volvo into city traffic. His first inclination was to head for Surry Heights and home. He should call his secretary and tell her he wouldn't be in the office today. What he needed was a chance to regain his composure, something he'd lost when he'd first heard that doctor's voice on his answering machine.

What was her name again? Novak. Yes, that was it. Vaguely he wondered what Dr. Novak's first name was, thought it had to be something blunt and to-the-point, like the woman. She was a straight shooter; he appreciated that. What he hadn't appreciated were her sharp eyes, her keen antennae. She'd seen far more than he'd intended to reveal.

He merged onto the freeway. Still a half hour to Surry Heights. He wanted out of the city, out of all this gray and gloomy concrete.

Then he passed a highway sign that said: *South Lexington, exit ½ mile.*

What came next was a snap decision, a crazy impulse that rose purely out of guilt. He turned onto the ramp and followed the curve until it eased into South Lexington Avenue. Suddenly he was driving through a war zone. The area around the ME's office had been shabby, but at least the buildings were occupied, the windows intact.

Here, on South Lexington, it was hard to imagine anything but rats residing behind all this red brick and shattered glass. He drove past empty warehouses and dead businesses, reminders of the city's better days. Two miles south, beyond the abandoned

Johan Weir tannery, he came to the Projects. He could see them from blocks away, those seven gray towers propped up against an equally gray sky.

They were relics from an earlier age, born of good intentions, but doomed by location and design. Built miles from any jobs, constructed of monolithic concrete, they looked more like prison towers than public housing. Even so, they remained occupied. He saw cars parked on the road, clumps of people gathered on corners, a man huddled on his front stoop, a kid shooting baskets in an alley hoop. They all glanced up as Adam drove past, every pair of eyes taking note of this territorial incursion.

Adam drove another block, pulled over to the side, and parked in front of Building Five.

For an hour he sat in his car, watching the sidewalks, the alleys, the playground across the street. Mothers shuttled babies in strollers across broken glass. Young kids played hopscotch on the pavement. *Even here*, he thought, *life goes on*. He knew people were watching him; they always did.

Someone tapped on his window. He glanced out through the lightly tinted glass and saw a young woman. She had a wild mane of uncombed black hair, dark eyes, a white face heavily caked with makeup. Upon closer scrutiny, he realized it was just a young girl under all that rouge and powder.

Once again, she tapped on the window. He rolled it down a few inches.

'Hey, honey,' she said sweetly. 'You lookin' for me?'

'I'm looking for Maeve,' he said.

'Don't know any Maeve. What about me?'

He smiled. 'I don't think so.'

'I'm open to anything. Indulge your fantasies.'

'I'm really not interested. Thank you.' He rolled up the window.

At once her smile transformed to a scowl. She muttered an obscenity, audible even through the closed glass, then she turned and walked away.

He watched her blue jean-clad hips sway as she headed down the street, saw her pause by a gathering of young men. Automatically she tilted her head up in a smile. No interest there either. With a shrug, she kept walking.

Something about that young woman – her raven-colored hair, perhaps, or that walk, announcing to the world: *I can take care of myself* – reminded him of someone. Dr. Novak, the woman with no first name. She had hair that color, a thick and glossy black, just long enough to lap at her shoulders. And her gait, what he'd seen of it in the dim basement corridor, had that confident spring to its step. He suddenly wished he'd told her the truth, about the matchbook, about Maeve. He knew she knew he'd been lying. It was necessary to hide the truth, but he felt uneasy about it. And it troubled him that Dr. Novak now considered him some sort of miscreant, whose word was not to be trusted.

Why should it bother me? I'll never see the woman again.

At least he hoped he wouldn't. A trip to the city morgue wasn't the sort of experience he cared to repeat. He wondered how she could stand it, dealing every day with death, probing the contents of those ghastly refrigerated steel drawers. How did one live with the images? He himself was having trouble dealing with just one image he'd confronted an hour ago – the dead woman, the one who'd been clutching the matchbook.

Thank God it wasn't Maeve.

He reached for the car phone, dialed his office, and told Greta he wouldn't be coming in. She sounded surprised; it was unlike him to skip work, even for a day. 'Let Hal hold the fort,' he told her. After all, what were senior vice presidents for?

Outside, a police car slowly cruised by and continued down South Lexington. Children, just out of school, skipped along the pavement, kicking glass. Adam told Greta he'd see her in the morning, and hung up the phone. Then, grim-faced, he settled back against the seat and resumed watching the street.

*　　*　　*

Dr. Davis Wheelock, the chief medical examiner, had an office on the fourth floor, in a distant corner of the facility. It was about as far as one could get from the grim day-to-day business of the morgue and still work in the same building. The brass plaque on his door was a gift from his wife, who had been distressed by the cheap plastic version provided by the city of Albion. If one must be a public servant, so her reasoning went, at least one could do so in style.

Dr. Wheelock shared his wife's view, and his office was a reflection of his expensive and eclectic taste. In various places of honor were displayed Kenyan masks, Egyptian papyruses, Incan statuettes, all acquired during his travels. The office faced east, toward the river. On this overcast day it was an unremittingly depressing view. The gray light through the window seemed to cloak Wheelock and all his primitive artwork in gloom.

'Drug ODs are a fact of life in this town,' said Wheelock. 'We can't chase them all. Unless you're sure it's something new, I can't see getting distracted—'

'That's just it,' said Kat as she sat down in the chair across from him. 'I don't *know* if it's something new. But I think you should notify the mayor. And maybe the press.'

Wheelock shook his head. 'Aren't you overreacting?'

'Davis, in the last twenty-four hours, I've had two come in, young women, no signs of trauma. Both found in the South Lexington area. Since they both had tracks on their arms and recent needle punctures, I was ready to call them ODs.'

'Heroin?'

'That's the problem. I can't identify it. I've sent blood, urine, and vitreous to the state lab for immunoassay, but that'll take a week.'

'What have you run here?'

'Thin layer and gas chromatography. Subject One had a positive ethanol. Subject Two turned up salicylates, probably just aspirin. Both subjects had the same peak on gas chromatography – it looks like a narcotic.'

'There's your answer.'

'Here's the problem. It's a weird peak, biphasic. Not quite an opiate, not quite cocaine. I've never seen it before.'

'Impurities. Someone cut two drugs together.'

'Maybe.'

'Wait till the state IDs it. It'll just take a week.'

'And in the meantime?'

'You've only got two victims.'

She leaned forward on his desk. 'Davis, I don't *want* any more victims. And I'm afraid we're about to get more.'

'Why?'

'After the second woman rolled in, I got on the phone. Called around town to all the hospitals. I found out Hancock General admitted three ODs yesterday. Two were obviously suicide attempts. But the third was a young man brought in by his parents. He had a cardiac arrest in the ER. They managed to pull him back. He's in the ICU now, still unconscious and critical.'

'Hancock's a busy ER. You'd expect ODs to show up there.'

'I spoke to the hospital lab. They ran a routine gas chromatography on the man's blood. It turned up a biphasic peak on the narcotics screen. Not quite an opiate, not quite cocaine.'

Wheelock said nothing. He simply sat there, frowning at her.

'Davis,' she said, 'we're seeing the start of an epidemic.'

3

Wheelock shook his head. 'It's too early to call,' he said. 'Too early to go to the press. You've only got three vics—'

'Guess where the young man lived? South Lexington. Within five blocks of where the two women were found. I'm telling you, there's something new, something that's killing off junkies. And South Lexington seems to be its point of origin. Here's what I think you should do, Davis. Get on the phone to the mayor. Call a joint press conference. Get the news out before we get more John and Jane Does cluttering up my basement.'

'I don't know.'

'What don't you know?'

'It could be a single batch. Maybe that's all it is.'

'Or maybe there's a whole ton of the stuff sitting in some pusher's warehouse.'

Agitated, Wheelock sat back and ran his hand through his gray hair. 'All right. I'll talk to the mayor. It's a bad time to be bringing this up, what with the city bicentennial and all. He's launching his campaign this week—'

'Davis. People are *dying*.'

'All right, all right. I'll call him this afternoon.'

Satisfied that she'd made her point, Kat left Wheelock's office and headed down to the basement. In the corridor, two of the overhead fluorescent lights flickered like a strobe flash. Everything seemed to be wearing down, wearing out. The building. The city.

And there they were, celebrating the bicentennial. *What are we celebrating exactly, Mr. Mayor? Two hundred years of decline?*

Back in her office, Kat considered drinking the last dregs of the coffee pot. No, she wasn't that desperate. Two files lay on her desk, files she couldn't complete, perhaps would never be able to complete. One was Jane Doe's. The other was for Xenia Vargas, the second woman from South Lexington. She, at least, had been found with ID in her purse, though they hadn't yet confirmed Vargas was really her name. Nor had they been able to contact any relatives.

Two dead women. And no one who could tell her how – or why – they had died.

On a corner of her desk was a notepad, with the name *Dr. Michael Dietz* scribbled on it. He was the ER doctor she'd spoken to earlier, the one who'd admitted the male overdose victim at Hancock General.

It was five o'clock; she could hear the evening morgue attendants laughing in the prep room, enjoying the brief and blessed lull before the madness of nightfall.

Kat changed into her street clothes, pulled on her coat, and left the building.

She didn't drive home. Instead, she drove to South Lexington, to Hancock General Hospital.

It sat like a fortress in a war zone, its parking lot surrounded by a barbed-wire fence, the front entrance overhung by surveillance cameras. The ER clerk was sitting behind glass – bulletproof, Kat surmised. He spoke through a microphone; the tinny voice coming through the speaker made Kat think of a McDonald's drive-through. 'How can I help you?' he asked.

'I'm Dr. Novak,' she said. 'ME's office. I want to see a Dr. Michael Dietz. It's about a patient of his.'

'I'll page him.'

Dr. Dietz emerged a few minutes later, looking like some weary veteran of the trenches. A stethoscope was looped around his neck, and his scrub pants were splattered with blood. 'You just caught me,' he said. 'I was going off shift. You're from the ME?'

'We talked earlier. About that overdose.'

'Oh, yeah. He's up in Intensive Care. I can't remember his name . . . '

'Can we go up to the Unit?' she asked. 'I'd like to look over his chart.'

'I guess it's okay. Seeing as you're official and all.'

They headed to the elevators. The hospital looked the same as Kat remembered it, dingy linoleum floors, halls painted a bizarre aqua color, gurneys shoved up against the walls. Through the doorway on the right was the cafeteria, with its echoes of clinking dishes and scraping chairs. On the overhead paging system, a bored voice read out a list of doctors' names and extension numbers. Dr. Dietz moved like a sleepwalker in tennis shoes.

'I see the place hasn't changed any,' said Kat.

'Did you use to work here?'

'No. I did my residency over at St. Luke's. But I knew a patient here. A relative.'

He laughed. 'I'm not sure I'd want any of *my* relatives here.'

'Didn't matter to her. She didn't know where she was, anyway.'

They stepped into the staff elevator and crowded in beside nurses and orderlies. Everyone stared straight ahead, as though mesmerized by the changing floor numbers.

'So are you from the city?' asked Dietz.

'A native. And you?'

'Cleveland. I'm going back.'

'Don't like it here?'

'Let's put it this way. Compared to this town, Cleveland is the Garden of Eden.'

They got off on the third floor and headed into Intensive Care.

The Unit was set up like a giant stable, with stalls marked out by curtains. Only two beds were empty, Kat noted; not much preparation for an unexpected disaster. And there was a full moon. That was always a harbinger of a busy night.

The patient was in bed thirteen. Only comatose patients went into that bed, Dietz said. Why scare some conscious patient? When you're fighting for your life, even dumb superstitions take on frightening significance.

The man's name was Nicos Biagi. He was a husky fellow, about twenty, with biceps and pectorals that had obviously done time in the weight-rooms. There were seven tubes snaking out of various parts of his body – a grim prognostic indicator. He lay utterly flaccid. According to the chart, he was unresponsive to even the most intense of stimuli.

'Twenty-four hours and not a twitch,' said the nurse. 'Plus, we're having trouble stabilizing his pressure. It goes haywire on us, shoots up, then bottoms out. I'm going crazy, juggling all these meds.'

Kat flipped through the chart, quickly deciphering

the hurried notes of the ICU resident. The patient had been found unconscious in his car, parked outside his parents' apartment. He'd been sprawled on the front seat. Beside him on the floor had been his kit: a tourniquet, syringe and needle, spoon, and cigarette lighter. Somehow, during the frantic rush to stabilize the patient and transport him to the ER, the EMTs had lost track of the syringe. They thought the family might have it; the family claimed the EMTs had it. The police said they'd never even seen it. In any event, the blood toxicology screen would provide the answers.

At least, it should.

They'd found out a few things. A 0.13 ethanol level proved the man was legally drunk. Also, he'd been pumped full of steroids – something Kat could have guessed, judging from those bulging biceps. What the tests hadn't answered was the primary question: Which drug had put him into the coma?

All the usual medical steps had been taken. Despite a treatment of glucose, Narcan, and thiamine, he hadn't awakened. The only therapeutic strategy left was supportive: maintain his blood pressure, breathe for him, keep his heart beating. The rest was up to the patient.

'You have no history at all?' asked Kat. 'Nothing about what he shot up? Where he got it from?'

'Not a thing. His parents are in the dark. They had

no idea their kid was a junkie. That's probably why
he did it in the car. So they wouldn't know about it.'

'I've got two women in the morgue. Both with the
same biphasic peak on gas chromatography. Like
your man.'

Dietz sighed. 'Terrific. Another wonder drug hits
our streets.'

'When will your final tox report be done?'

'I don't know. It's been twenty-four hours already.
If this is something new, it may take weeks to identify.
These pharmaceutical whizzes out there crank out
drugs like new shoes. By the time we catch up with
the latest fad, they're on to something else.'

'You agree, then? That it's something new?'

'Oh, yeah. I've seen it all come down the pike. PCP,
tropical ice, fruit loops. This is something different.
Something *bad*. I think the only reason this guy's still
alive, and your two women aren't, is that he's a big
dude. All that muscle mass. Takes a bigger dose to kill
him.'

It still might kill him, thought Kat, gazing at the
comatose patient.

'If this goes to the media, can I use you as a
source?' she asked.

'What do you mean?'

'I think a warning ought to go out on the streets.
That there's bad stuff making the rounds.'

Dietz didn't answer right away. He just kept

looking at Nicos Biagi. 'I don't know,' he said at last.

'What do you mean, you don't know? It'd just be to voice your opinion. To confirm my statement.'

'I don't know,' he said again. He was gripping the IV pole. 'It's not as if you need me. You've got the authority.'

'I could use the backup.'

'It's just . . . the press. I'm not crazy about talking to them.'

'Okay, then just let me cite you by name. Would that be okay?'

He sighed. 'I guess so. But I'd rather you didn't.' Abruptly, he straightened and glanced at his watch. 'Look, I have to get going. I'll catch you later.'

Kat watched him walk out of the ICU, his shoulders hunched forward as though his whole body was straining to break into a sprint. What was he afraid of? she wondered. Why wouldn't he talk to the press?

She was on her way out of the ICU when she spotted the Biagis, coming in to visit their son. She guessed at once who they were, just by the grief in their faces. Mrs. Biagi was dark-haired, dark-eyed, and her face was seamed with worry. Mr. Biagi was much older and bald; he looked too numb to be feeling much of anything at the moment. They went to Nicos's bedside, where they stood for a moment in silence. Mrs. Biagi stroked her son's hair and began to sing softly, something in Italian. A lullaby, perhaps. Then she faltered, dropped her head to her son's chest, and began to cry.

Mr. Biagi didn't say a word.

Kat walked out of the ICU.

In her haste to leave behind that scene, she took a wrong turn in the hallway. Instead of heading to the elevators, she found herself in a different wing, a part of the hospital she hadn't seen before. White walls and gleaming linoleum told her this was a new addition, constructed only recently. Behind a glass case on the wall were displayed various mementoes of the wing's opening: photographs of hospital officials at the ribbon cutting. Shots of a celebrity black-tie dinner. A bronze plaque, engraved with *The Georgina Quantrell Wing*. And a newspaper article with the headline: *Cygnus president dedicates multimillion-dollar drug rehab addition*. The accompanying photograph showed a sober-faced Adam Quantrell, posing beside the plaque.

For a long time, Kat stood by that case, studying the photos, the news articles. Drug rehab? A surprising crusade for a man who made his fortune from drugs. Her gaze traveled the length of the case, paused at a teaching display of commonly abused drugs. Mounted on the board was a multicolored variety of capsules. And below it was the label: *Display courtesy of the Cygnus Company.*

Something clicked in Kat's head. Dead junkies. A new drug on the street. Cygnus Pharmaceuticals.

And a matchbook with Adam Quantrell's phone number.

She reached for her cell phone, and called Sykes in Homicide.

He was just leaving for home and did not seem particularly eager to prolong his work day.

'Let me put it this way, Novak,' he said. 'In the grand scheme of things, drug ODs are not high on my list of priorities.'

'Think about it, Lou. What's an addict doing with Quantrell's personal phone number? Why was Quantrell so eager to look at the body? He's hiding something.'

'No, he's not.'

'I think he is.'

'They were junkies, Novak. They lived on the edge, they fell off. It's not homicide. It's not suicide. It's stupidity. Social Darwinism, survival of the smartest.'

'Maybe that's what you think. Maybe that's what Quantrell thinks. But I've still got two dead women.'

'Forget Quantrell. The man's into drug rehab, not drug pushing.'

'Lou, this is a new drug. I spoke to an ER doctor here who says he's never seen it before. To cook up a brand new drug, you need a biochemist. And a lab. And a factory. Cygnus has it all.'

'It's a legitimate company.'

'With maybe an illegitimate branch?'

'Christ, Novak. I'm not going to hassle Quantrell.'

'I heard you did a favor for him. On the side.'

There was a pause. 'Yeah. So what?'

'So what were you doing for him out in South Lexington?'

'Look, you want to hear the details?' Sykes snapped. 'Then you talk to *him*.' He hung up.

Kat stared at the phone. Well, maybe she *had* pushed Lou too far on this one. *My big mouth*, she thought. *One of these days it's going to get me into trouble.*

Slipping her cell phone into her pocket, she saw Mr. and Mrs. Biagi coming out of the ICU. They were leaning on each other, holding each other up, as though grief had sapped all their strength.

Kat thought of their son Nicos, with the seven tubes in his body. She thought of Jane Doe and Xenia Vargas, both relegated to the approximate level of primordial muck in Sykes' scale of social Darwinism. Something was killing these people, something that had sunk its evil roots into the Projects.

Her old neighborhood.

On her way back to the freeway, she drove up South Lexington. In the last few years, nothing had changed. The seven Project buildings still looked like prison towers, the playground still had a bent basketball hoop, and teenagers still hung out on the corner of Franklin and South Lexington. But the faces were different. It wasn't just that these were different people. There was a new hardness to their gazes, a wariness, as they watched her drive by. Only then did the thought strike her.

To them she was an outsider. Someone to be watched, someone to be guarded against. Someone not to be trusted.

They don't know I'm one of them. Or I was.

She continued up South Lexington and took the freeway on-ramp.

Traffic was still heavy moving north. It was the evening exodus to the suburbs, a daily hemorrhage of white-collar types to Bellemeade, Parris, Clarendon, and Surry Heights. Those who could afford to flee, fled. Even Kat, a city girl born and bred, now called the suburbs home. Just last year, she'd bought a house in Bellemeade. It seemed a logical move, financially speaking, and she'd reached the point in life when she had to make a commitment – any commitment, even if it was only to a three-bedroom cape. Bellemeade was a hybrid neighborhood, close enough to town to make it feel like part of the city, yet far enough away to put it squarely in the safety of the suburbs.

On impulse, she bypassed the Bellemeade turnoff and stayed on the freeway. It took her a half hour to drive to Surry Heights.

Along the way, the traffic thinned out, the scenery changed. Cookie-cutter houses gave way to trees and rolling hills, newly green from those proverbial April showers. White fences and horses appeared – a sure harbinger of old money. She took the Surry Heights exit onto Fair Wind Lane.

Two miles down the road she came to the Quantrell residence. There was no mistaking the place. Two stone pillars flanked the driveway entrance; the name *Quantrell* was spelled out in wrought iron lettering mounted on one of the pillars. The gate hung open to visitors. Kat drove through, and followed the curving driveway to the house.

There were three cars parked out front, a Jaguar and two Mercedes. She parked her five-year-old Subaru next to the Jag and climbed out. *Nice paint job*, she thought, eyeing the Jag's burgundy finish. The interior was spotless, with not a clue to its owner's personality in sight. No bumper stickers, either, though one that said *Let them eat cake* would have been appropriate.

She went to the front door and rang the bell. It pealed like a church chime in a cavern.

The door opened, and a man wearing a butler-type uniform gazed down at her. 'Yes?' he said.

Kat cleared her throat. 'I'm Dr. Novak. Medical examiner's office. I wonder if I could speak to Mr. Adam Quantrell.'

'Is Mr. Quantrell expecting you?'

'No. But I'm here on official business.'

For a moment the man seemed to consider her request. Then he opened the door wider. 'Come in.'

Surprised at how easy that was, she stepped inside. In wonder, she gazed up at a crystal chandelier. It was just a modest little entry hall, she thought. Nothing you wouldn't find in a typical castle. The floor was gleaming terrazzo, and a massive banister traced a staircase to a second-floor gallery. Paintings – mostly modern, vaguely disturbing, wild blots of color – hung in various places of honor.

'If you'll wait here,' said the butler.

He disappeared through a side door. She heard the distant sound of a woman's laughter, the strains of classical music. *Oh, great. He's got a party going*, she thought. *Terrific timing, Novak.*

She turned as she heard footsteps. Adam Quantrell emerged from a side room, quietly shutting the door behind him. He was dressed formally, black tie, ruffled white shirt. He did not look pleased to see her.

'Dr. Novak,' he said. 'Is this urgent? Or can it wait till some other time?'

'I think it's urgent.'

'More questions?' he asked.

'And another body.'

She watched for his reaction and was not at all

surprised to see his face flinch. After a pause he said, 'Whose?'

'A woman. They found her not too far from where they found the first one. In a stairwell off South Lexington. It looks like another drug OD.'

He still looked stunned. 'Do you . . . want me to come down and look at her?'

'Not necessarily. But maybe you'll know the name. She had her purse with her. The driver's license said Xenia Vargas. I assume it's hers because the photo matched the corpse. Does that name ring a bell?'

He let out a breath. She wondered if it was a sigh of relief.

'No,' he said. 'I don't know that name.'

'What about the name Nicos Biagi?'

'I don't know that name either. Why?'

'Just curious.'

Adam reacted with a snort of disbelief. 'You show up at my door and assault me with the names of corpses, just to see how I react. And all because you're curious?'

'Who said Nicos Biagi was a corpse?'

'I don't know who the hell he is! I just assumed. Everyone else you mention seems to be a corpse!' His voice seemed to echo off the terrazzo floor and bounce around the far reaches of the vast entrance hall. At once he regained his composure, his face settling into an expression of cool unreadability. 'So,' he said. 'Who *is* Nicos Biagi? And is he or is he not a corpse?'

'Nicos happens to be alive – barely,' she said. 'He's a patient at Hancock General. A drug OD. We're worried about the drug. It seems to be something new, and it's already killed Jane Doe and Xenia Vargas. It's left Nicos Biagi critically ill. I wondered if you knew something about it.'

'Why would I?'

'A hunch.'

To her annoyance, he laughed. 'I hope this isn't the way the ME's office usually conducts business. Because if it is, our criminal justice system is in big trouble.'

The side door opened again. A woman appeared, looking quizzical. And gorgeous. Her evening dress, shot through with gold thread, seemed to glitter in the chandelier light. Her hair, an equally brilliant gold, fell in ripples to her shoulders. She glanced at Adam's visitor, a look that Kat recognized at once for what it was – a feminine sizing-up, then a curt dismissal. 'Adam?' she asked. 'Is something wrong?'

'No,' he said, his gaze still fixed on Kat. 'It's just – business.'

'Oh.' The woman smiled sweetly. 'Pearl just brought out the soup. And we didn't want to start without you.'

'Sorry, Isabel. Why don't you all just go ahead with supper? Dr. Novak and I aren't finished yet.'

Again, her gaze shifted to Kat. 'We can set another place, if you'd like. For your visitor.'

There was an awkward silence, as though Adam were hunting for a graceful way to avoid inviting this unwelcome guest.

'That won't be necessary,' said Kat, and thought she saw a look of relief cross Adam's face. 'I'll be leaving, as soon as we're done with our . . . business.'

Isabel smiled again, as though equally relieved. 'Join us when you can, Adam,' she said, and withdrew into the side room.

Adam and Kat regarded each other for a moment.

'Let's talk in the study,' he said, and abruptly turned and opened another door. She followed him inside.

It was a characteristically masculine space, dark and clubby, with a fireplace and wood paneling, the sort of room in which one smoked pipes and drank cognac. She sat on the leather couch. He didn't sit at all, but paced in front of the fireplace. The longer she watched him, the more annoyed she felt. It was irrational, of course, but she was insulted that *he* hadn't offered her a place at the supper table. She would have turned it down, of course; you didn't just drop into a formal supper, and judging from Isabel's evening gown, this was no potluck they were serving.

But at least she would have had the pleasure of turning him down. It was a matter of pride.

'So what's the basis for this hunch of yours?' he demanded. 'Why do you think I would know anything about it?'

'Because of that matchbook.'

'Not much of a reason.'

'Because this is a new drug, never seen before.'

He shrugged. 'So?'

'And because you're president of Cygnus Pharmaceuticals. A company known for its R and D in painkillers. A company that just released a new class of opiates.'

'We also make drugs for athlete's foot.'

'Oh, and one more thing.'

'Yes?' When he tilted his head his blond hair caught the glow of the table lamp.

'Until you saw the body, you thought Jane Doe was someone you might know.'

At once he fell silent, all trace of mockery gone from his face. He sat down, his gaze avoiding hers.

'Who did you think she was, Mr. Quantrell?'

'Someone . . . close to me.'

'What's the secret here? Why can't you just say who you thought she was?'

'These are things I don't wish to discuss. Not with a stranger.'

'Then can you discuss the drug? It's something new.

61

A narcotic with a biphasic peak on gas chromatography. Could it be something that leaked out of Cygnus? Something you're developing?'

'I wouldn't want to speculate.'

Of course he wouldn't. Because then he'd be vulnerable to all sorts of accusations. The manufacture of lethal drugs. The slaughter of junkies.

Slowly he looked up. 'You said you had another body in the morgue. A woman.'

'Xenia Vargas.'

'Is she . . . young?'

'About twenty.'

'Describe her for me.'

'You think you might know her?'

'Please. Just tell me what she looks like.'

Something about the tone of his voice, the stifled note of anxiety, made her feel sorry for him. 'She's about five foot four, on the thin side. Dark brown hair—'

'Could it be dyed?'

Kat paused. 'It's possible, I guess.'

'What about her eyes? What color?'

'Hazel.'

Another silence. Then, with sudden agitation, he rose to his feet. 'I think I'd better see her,' he said.

'You mean – now?'

'If we could.' He met her gaze. 'If you'd be so kind.'

She too stood up and followed him into the main hall. 'What about your dinner guests?'

'They can feed themselves. Would you excuse me a moment, while I gracefully duck out?'

He went through the side door, but this time he left it open. Kat caught a glimpse of a formal dining room and a half-dozen guests seated around the table. Some of them glanced curiously in Kat's direction. She heard Isabel ask, 'Should I wait for you, Adam?'

'Please don't,' he said. 'I don't know how long I'll be.'

'This is really quite naughty of you, you know.'

'It can't be helped. Good night, everyone! You're free to have a go at my wine cellar, but leave me a few bottles, will you?' He clapped one of the men on the shoulder, waved farewell, and came back into the hall, shutting the door behind him.

'That's done,' he said to Kat. 'Now. Let's go.'

4

The morgue elevator slid open. *Here we go again*, she thought.

The basement seemed calm tonight. The only noise was the morgue attendant's radio, playing in a side office. Something mean and gritty and tuneless. She and Adam passed the open door, where they could see the attendant sitting with his feet propped up on the desk, his gaze focused on a girly magazine.

'Hey, Willie,' said Kat.

'Hey, Doc,' he said, grinning at her over the cover. 'Not much action coming down tonight.'

'I can tell.'

'You mean this?' He waved the magazine and laughed. 'Man, I get tired of looking at *dead* chicks. I like mine live and sassy.'

'We're going into the cold room, okay?'

'Need any help?'

'No. You just stay with your sassy chicks.'

She and Adam walked on down the hall, beneath the bank of fluorescent lights. The bulb that had been flickering earlier that day was now dead; it left a patch of shadow on the linoleum floor.

They entered the storage room. She flicked on the wall switch and blinked at the painful blast of light on her retinas. The refrigerated drawers faced them from the opposite wall.

She moved to the drawer labeled *Vargas, Xenia*, and slid it open. Covered by the shroud, the body seemed shapeless, like a lump of clay still to be molded. She glanced up at Adam in silent inquiry.

He nodded.

She removed the shroud.

The corpse looked like a mannequin, not real at all, but plastic. Adam took one good look at Xenia Vargas, and all the tension seemed to escape his body in a single sigh.

'You don't know her?' said Kat.

'No.' He swallowed. 'I've never seen her.'

She replaced the shroud and slid the drawer shut. Then she turned and looked at him. 'Okay, Mr. Quantrell, I think it's time for you to fess up. Who, exactly, are you looking for?'

He paused. 'A woman.'

'I know that. I also know she's got hazel eyes. And

the chances are, she's either a blond or a redhead.
Now I want to know her name.'

'Maeve,' he said softly.

'Now we're getting somewhere. Maeve who?'

'Quantrell.'

She frowned. 'Wife? Sister?'

'Daughter. I mean, stepdaughter. She's twenty-
three. And you're right. She's blond. Hazel eyes. Five
foot five, a hundred fifteen pounds. At least, that's
what she was when I saw her last.'

'And when was that?'

'Six months ago.'

'She's missing?'

He shrugged one tuxedoed shoulder. 'Missing,
hiding. Whatever you want to call it. She drops out of
sight whenever she feels like it. Whenever she can't
face up to life. It's her way of coping.'

'Coping with what?'

'Everything. Bad grades. Love affairs. Her mother's
death. Her lousy stepfather.'

'So you two didn't get along.'

'No.' Wearily he raked his fingers through his hair.
'I couldn't handle her. I thought I could shape her up.
You know, a firm hand, some good old-fashioned
discipline. The way my father raised me. I even got her
a job, thinking that all she needed was some
responsibility. That at a minimum she could show up
on time, do the job right, and pay for her own damn

groceries.' He shook his head. 'She went to work one day, two hours late, her hair dyed purple. She had a screaming match with her supervisor. Then she walked off the job.' He let out a breath. 'She was fired.'

'And that was the last time she was seen?'

'No. I took her out to lunch. To try to patch things up. Instead, we had an argument. Naturally.'

'Let me guess,' said Kat. 'You took her to L'Etoile, on Hilton Avenue.'

He nodded. 'Maeve showed up in black leather and green hair. She insulted the maître d'. Lit up a joint in the nonsmoking section. And proceeded to tell me I had sick values. I told her she was sick, period. I also told her I was withdrawing all financial support. That if she shaped up, behaved like a responsible human being, she was welcome to come back to the house. I'd just changed my phone number – I was getting crank calls – so I wrote my new number in a matchbook and gave it to her. Just in case she wanted to get in touch with me. She never did.'

'And the matchbook?'

He shrugged. 'Maybe she passed it around to a friend, and somehow Jane Doe got it. I don't know.'

'You haven't seen her since the restaurant?'

'No.'

She paused. 'Where does Lou Sykes come in?'

'A private detective I hired told me Maeve was hanging around South Lexington. That's Lieutenant

Sykes' beat. I simply asked him to keep an eye out for her. As a favor to me. He thought he spotted her once, but that was it.'

It sounded believable enough, Kat thought, studying his pose, the elegant cut of his tuxedo. *So why do I get the feeling he's still hiding something?*

His gaze was focused elsewhere, as though he was afraid to let her see his eyes.

'What you're telling me, Mr. Quantrell, isn't exactly earth-shattering. Lots of families have problems with their kids. Why were you afraid to tell me about her? Why hide it from me?'

'It's a rather . . . embarrassing state of affairs.'

'Is that all?'

'Isn't that enough?' He swung around to look at her, the challenge plain in his aristocratic face. She felt trapped by the spell of that gaze. What was it about this guy?

She gave her head a shake, as though to clear it. 'No,' she said. 'It's not enough. So what if you had told me the truth this morning? I'm just a public servant. You don't get embarrassed in front of your servants, do you?'

He gave her a tight smile. 'You, Dr. Novak, I hardly consider a servant.'

'Is there something else about Maeve you don't want to tell me? Some minor detail you haven't mentioned?'

'Nothing of any relevance to your job.' He turned away, a sure sign that he wasn't telling the whole truth. His gaze focused on one of the body drawers.

'Then I'd say our business here is finished,' she said. 'Go on home to your guests. If you hurry, you might be able to make it back in time for brandy.'

'Who is this?' he asked sharply.

'What?'

'This drawer here. It says Jane Doe.'

Kat took a closer look at the label: #372-3-27-B. 'Another one. Dated seven days ago. Clark must have processed this one.'

'Who's Clark?'

'The other Assistant ME. He's on vacation right now.'

Adam took a breath. 'May I . . .' He looked up mutely at Kat.

She nodded. Without a word, she pulled open the drawer.

Wisps of cold vapor swirled out. Kat felt her old reluctance to lift the shroud, to reveal the body. This Jane Doe she hadn't laid eyes on. She steeled herself against the worst and slid off the shroud.

The woman was beautiful. Seven days of stainless-steel imprisonment couldn't dull the glow of her hair. It was a rich red, thick and tumbling about her shoulders. Her skin had the luster of white marble, and in life must have seemed flawless. Her eyes, revealed by partly opened, heavily lashed lids, were gray. Her torso was marred by a sutured Y-incision, the ugly aftermath of an autopsy.

Kat looked across at Adam.

He shook his head. 'You can close the drawer,' he murmured. 'It's not her.'

'I wonder who she is?' said Kat, sliding the drawer shut. 'She looks like the kind of woman who'd be missed. Not our usual Jane Doe type.'

'Would you know how she died?' The question was asked softly, but its significance at once struck Kat.

'Let's pull the file,' she said.

They found it in Clark's office. It was buried in a stack on his desk, waiting to be completed. On top were clipped a few loose pages, recent correspondence from the central identification lab.

'Looks like she's no longer a Jane Doe,' said Kat. 'They found a fingerprint match. Her name's Mandy Barnett. I guess Clark never got around to relabeling the drawer.'

'Why does she have fingerprints on file?'

Kat flipped to the next page. 'Because she has a police record. Shoplifting. Prostitution. Public drunkenness.' Kat glanced up at Adam. 'Guess she wasn't as sweet as she looked.'

'What was the cause of death?'

Kat opened the folder and squinted at Clark's

notes. He must have been in a rush when he wrote them; it was a typical doctor's scrawl, the *i*s undotted, the *t*s uncrossed. 'Subject found 3/27 at 02:35 in public restroom at Gilly's bar, off Flashner Avenue.' Kat looked up. 'That's in Bellemeade. I live there.' She turned to the next page. 'No injuries noted . . . tox screens pending. Police report empty bottle of Fiorinal pills found near body. Conclusion: cardio-pulmonary arrest, most likely due to barbiturate overdose. Awaiting tox screen from state lab.'

'Is the report back yet?'

Kat went to the courier box and riffled through the stack of pages. 'I don't see it here. It's probably still pending.' She closed the file. 'This case doesn't really fit with the others. Bellemeade's a different neighbor-hood, with a different class of drug users. Higher priced.'

'The others were all in South Lexington?'

'Within blocks of each other. Jane Doe was smack in the Projects. So was Xenia Vargas. Nicos Biagi was a little further out, on Richmond Street. Let's see, that'd make it somewhere near the old railroad tracks. But it's still the same neighborhood.'

'You seem to know the area well.'

'Too well.' She tossed Mandy Barnett's file on Clark's desk. 'I grew up there.'

He looked at her in surprise. 'You?'

'Me.'

'How did you...' He paused, as though not certain how to phrase the question with any delicacy.

'How did I happen to grow up there? Simple. That's where my mom lived. Right up until she died.'

'So you would know the people there.'

'Some of them. But the neighborhood's always changing. People who can get out, get out. It's like this giant pond. Either you float up and crawl out or you sink deeper into the mud.'

'And you floated.'

She shrugged. 'I got lucky.'

He studied her with new appreciation, as though he was really seeing her for the first time. 'In your case, Dr. Novak,' he said, 'I think luck had nothing to do with it.'

'Not like some of us,' she said, looking at his tuxedo and his immaculate shirt.

He laughed. 'Yes, some of us *do* seem to be rolling in it.'

They rode back up in the elevator and walked out of the building. It was chilly outside. The wind blew an empty can down the street; they could trace its progress by the tinny echoes in the darkness.

He had driven in his car, and she in hers. Now they paused beside their respective vehicles, as though reluctant to part.

He turned to her. 'What I was trying to say earlier – about your knowing people in South Lexington...'

He paused. She waited, feeling strangely breathless. Eager. 'I was trying to ask for your help,' he finished.

'My help?'

'I want to find Maeve.'

So it's my help he wants, she thought. *Not me in particular*. She wondered why that fact should leave her feeling so disappointed. She said, 'Lou Sykes is a good cop. If he can't find her—'

'That's just it. He's a *cop*. No one out there trusts cops. Certainly Maeve wouldn't trust him. She'd think he was out to arrest her. Or reel her in for me.'

'Is that what you're trying to do?'

'I just want to know she's alive and well.'

'She's an adult, Adam. She can make her own choices.'

'What if her choices are insane?'

'Then she lives with them.'

'You don't understand. I made a promise to her mother. I promised that Maeve would be taken care of. So far I've done a pretty deplorable job.' He sighed. 'At the very least, I should look for her.'

'What if she doesn't want to be found?'

'Then she should *tell* me that, face to face. But I have to find her first. And you're the only one I know who's familiar with South Lexington.'

Kat laughed. 'Yeah, I guess it's not the sort of neighborhood your dinner guests would frequent.'

'I would appreciate it. I really would. Just show me

the place. Put me in touch with some of the people. I'd reimburse you for your time, of course. You only have to say how much—'

'Wait a minute.' She moved closer to him, her chin tilted up in astonishment. 'You were going to *pay* me?'

'I mean, it's only appropriate—'

'Forget it. *Forget it*. I'm a doctor, Quantrell, okay? I'm not the butler. I'm not the cook. I'm a doctor, and I already get paid for what I do.'

'So?'

'Which means I *don't* need a moonlighting job. When I do a favor for a friend – and I'm not necessarily putting you in the category – I do it *as* a friend. Gratis.'

'You want to do it out of the kindness of your heart. You want me to feel grateful. And I do, I really do.' He paused, then added softly: 'I also really need your help.'

Kat wasn't philosophically opposed to helping her fellow man. And a devoted dad in search of his daughter, well, that was an appeal she could hardly refuse. But this particular dad was no charity case.

Still . . .

She walked over to her car and flung open the door. 'Get in, Quantrell.'

'Excuse me?'

'We're not taking your car, because a nice new

Volvo's an invitation to a chop job. So let's go in mine.'

'To South Lexington?'

'You want an intro to the place, I know some people you can talk to. People who'd know what's going on in the neighborhood.'

Adam hesitated.

'Listen,' she said. 'You want to live dangerously or not?'

He regarded her battered Subaru. Then he shrugged. 'Why not?' he said, and climbed into her car.

South Lexington was a different place at night. What by day had seemed merely drab and depressing had, by night, assumed new menace. Alleys seemed to snake away into nowhere, and in that darkness lurked all the terrible unknowns a mind could conjure.

Kat parked beneath a streetlamp, and for a moment she studied the sidewalk, the buildings. A block away, a dozen or so teenagers had gathered on the corner. They looked harmless enough, just a bunch of kids engaged in the adolescent rites of spring.

'It looks okay,' she said. 'Let's go.'

'I hope you know what you're doing.'

They got out of the car and walked up the sidewalk, toward Building Five. The teenagers, at once alerted to intruders in their territory, turned and stared. Automatically, Adam moved close beside Kat and tightly grasped her arm.

The building was unlocked, so they went inside. The lobby was as she'd remembered it: dingy walls, nutmeg-colored carpet to hide the stains, half the hall lights burned out. The graffiti was a little more graphic, and less poetic than she remembered; the artwork had definitely taken a slide for the worse.

The elevator, as always, was out of commission.

'I don't think it *ever* worked,' she muttered, noting the faded *Out of Order* sign. 'It's four flights up. We'll have to walk.'

They went up the stairs, stepping over broken toys and cigarette butts. The handrail, once smoothly burnished, was now scarred by a series of initials carved in the wood. Noises filtered out from the various apartments: crying babies, blaring TV sets and radios, a woman yelling at her kids. Floating above it all were the pure and crystalline tones of a girl singing 'Amazing Grace.' The sound soared like a cathedral above the ruins. As they ascended the stairs to the fourth floor, the girl's voice grew louder, until they knew it was coming from behind the very door where they stopped.

Kat knocked.

The singing stopped. Footsteps approached, and the door opened a crack. A girl with a silky face the color of mocha gazed out over the security chain with doe eyes.

'Bella?' said Kat.

The smile that appeared on the girl's face was like a brilliant wash of sunshine. 'Kat!' she cried, unlatching the door chain. She turned and called out: 'Papa Earl! It's Kat!'

'Don't rush me,' grumbled a voice from the next room. 'I don't go runnin' for no one.'

Bella gave Kat an embarrassed look as they stepped into the apartment. 'Those bones of his,' she murmured. 'Ache him real bad in this weather. He's in a foul mood . . .'

'*Who's* in a foul mood?' snapped Papa Earl, shuffling into the room. He moved slowly, his head tipped forward, his once jet-black hair now a grizzled white. How old he had gotten, thought Kat sadly. Somehow, she had never thought this man would be touched by the years.

Kat went forward to give him a hug. It was almost like hugging a stranger; he seemed so small, so frail, shrunken by time. 'Hi, Papa Earl,' she said.

'You got your nerve, girl,' he grumbled. 'Go two years, three, not even droppin' by.'

'Papa Earl!' Bella said. 'She's here now, isn't she?'

'Yeah, got good 'n' guilty, did she?'

Kat laughed and took his hand. It felt like bones

wrapped in parchment. 'How you been, Papa Earl? Did you get the coat I sent?'

'What coat?'

'You know,' sighed Bella. 'The down jacket, Papa Earl. You wore it *all* winter.'

'Oh. *That* coat.'

Bella gave Kat a weary *you know how he is* look and said, 'He *loves* that coat.'

'Papa Earl,' said Kat. 'I brought someone with me.' 'Who?'

'His name is Adam. He's standing right over here.'

Gently she turned the old man to face Adam. Papa Earl extended his arm, held it out in midair for the expected handshake. Only then, as the two men faced each other, did Adam notice the snowy cataracts clouding the old man's eyes.

Adam took the offered hand and grasped it firmly. 'Hello . . . Papa Earl,' he said.

Papa Earl let out a hoot. 'Makes you feel dumb, don't it? Big fella like you callin' a shrimp like me Papa.'

'Not at all, sir.'

'So what you got going with our Katrina here?'

'He's just a friend, Papa Earl,' said Kat.

There was a pause. 'Oh,' the old man said. 'It's like that.'

'I wanted you to meet him, talk to him. See, he's looking for someone. A woman.'

Papa Earl's grizzled head lifted with sudden interest. The blind eyes seemed to focus on her. 'What do I know?'

'You know everything that goes on in the Projects.'

'Let's sit down,' the old man said. 'My bones are killing me.'

They went into the kitchen. Like the rest of the apartment, the room was on the far side of used. Linoleum tiles had worked loose below the sink. The formica counters were chipped. The stove and refrigerator were straight from the *Leave It to Beaver* era. Papa Earl's other grandchild, Anthony, sat hunched at the table, shoveling spaghetti hoops into his mouth. He scarcely looked up as the others came in.

'Hey, Anthony!' barked Papa Earl. 'Ain't you gonna say hello to your old babysitter?'

'Hello,' Anthony grunted and stuffed in another spoonful of spaghetti hoops.

Their personalities hadn't changed a bit, Kat realized, watching Anthony and Bella, remembering all those evenings she had looked after them while Papa Earl worked. Back in the days when the old man still had his vision. These two might be twins, they might have the same mocha coloring, the same high, sculpted cheekbones, but their personalities were like darkness and light. Bella could warm a room with her smile; Anthony could chill it with a single glance.

Papa Earl shuffled about the familiar kitchen with all the sureness of a sighted man. 'You hungry?' he asked. 'You want something to eat?'

Kat and Adam watched Anthony noisily lap tomato sauce and they said, in the same breath, 'Nothing, thanks.'

They all sat down at the table, Papa Earl across from them, his cataracts staring at them eerily. 'So who's this woman you looking for?' he asked.

'Her name is Maeve Quantrell,' said Kat. 'We think she's living in the Projects.'

'You have a picture?'

Kat glanced at Adam.

'Yes. As a matter of fact, I do,' he said, and reached for his wallet. He placed a snapshot on the table.

Kat had been expecting to see a version of what he'd described to her, a hellion in black leather with Technicolor hair. What she saw instead was a fragile blond girl, the sort you'd find shrinking in the corner at a school dance.

'Bella?' said Papa Earl.

Bella reached for the photo. 'Oh, she's real pretty. Blond hair. Sort of shy looking.'

'How old?'

'She's twenty-three,' said Adam. 'She looks different now. Probably dyed her hair some crazy color. Wears more makeup.'

'Anthony? You seen this girl around?' asked Papa
Earl.

Anthony glanced at the photo and shrugged. Then
he rose, tossed his empty bowl in the sink, and
stalked out of the kitchen. A moment later, they heard
the apartment door slam shut.

'Like a wild animal, that boy,' Papa Earl said with
a sigh. 'Comes and goes when he wants. Don't know
what to do 'bout him.'

Bella was still studying Maeve's photo. Softly she
asked, 'Who is she?'

'My daughter,' said Adam.

Papa Earl sat back, nodding with instant understanding. 'So you lookin' for your girl.'

'Yes.'

'Why?'

Adam shook his head, puzzled by the question.
'Because she's my daughter.'

'But she run away. She don't want to be found. Girl
like that, you ain't never gonna find her 'less she
comes to *you*.'

'Then I suppose . . .' Adam looked down wearily. 'I
suppose I'd settle for just knowing she's all right.'

Papa Earl was silent a moment. It was hard to tell
what thoughts were going on behind those clouded
eyes of his. At last he said, 'You'll want to talk to
Jonah.'

'Jonah?' asked Kat.

'He's the big man now.'

'Since when?'

'Year ago. Took over when Berto went down. Anything you want round here, gotta go through Jonah.'

'Thanks,' said Kat. 'We'll follow up on that.' She was about to stand up when another question occurred to her. 'Papa Earl,' she said, 'did you know a boy named Nicos Biagi?'

The old man paused. 'I heard of him, yeah.'

'Xenia Vargas?'

'Maybe.'

'Did you hear she died?'

He sighed. 'Lotta people die 'round here. Don't stick in your mind much anymore, people dying.'

'They both took the same drug, Papa Earl. This drug, it's moved into the Projects and it's killing people.'

He said nothing. He just sat there, his sightless eyes staring at her.

'If you hear anything, anything at all about it, will you call me?' She took out her business card and laid it on the table. 'I need help on this.'

He touched the card, his bony fingers moving across 'Kat Novak, M.D.' printed in black. 'You still workin' for the city?' he asked.

'Yes. The medical examiner.'

'Don't understand you, Katrina. You a doctor now, and you takin' care of dead people.'

'I find out why they die.'

'But then it's too late. Don't do 'em no good. You should be in a hospital. Or open your own place out here. It's what your mama wanted.'

Kat was suddenly aware of Adam's gaze on her. *Damn it, Papa Earl*, she thought. *Save the lecture for another time.*

'I like my job,' she said. 'I couldn't stand it in a hospital.'

Papa Earl gazed at her with sad understanding. 'Those were bad times for you, weren't they? All those months with your mama . . .'

Kat rose to her feet. 'Thanks for your help, Papa Earl. But we have to leave.'

Bella and her grandfather escorted them through the living room. It never changed, this room. The chairs were set in precisely the same places they'd always been, and Papa Earl navigated past them like a bat with sonar.

'Next time,' he grumbled as Adam and Kat left the apartment, 'don't you wait so long before visits.'

'I won't,' said Kat. But it sounded hollow, that promise. *I don't believe it myself*, she thought. *Why should he?*

She and Adam headed back down the four flights of stairs, stepping over the same broken toys, the same cigarette butts. The smells of the building, the echoes of TV sets and babies' squalls, funneled up

83

the stairwell and unleashed a barrage of memories. Of how she used to play on these steps, used to sit outside her apartment door, her knees bunched up against her chest. Waiting, waiting for her mother to calm down. Listening to the crying inside the apartment, the sounds of her mother's anguish, her mother's despair. The memories all rushed at her as she walked down the stairwell, and she knew exactly why she'd waited three long years to come back.

On the third floor landing, she paused outside apartment 3H. The door was a different color than she'd remembered, no longer green. Now it was a weirdly bright orange, and it had a built-in peephole. It would be different inside as well, she realized. Different people. A different world.

She felt Adam's hand gently touch her arm. 'What is it?' he asked.

'It's just—' She gave a tired little laugh. 'Nothing stays the same, does it? Thank God.' She turned and continued down the stairs.

He was close beside her. *Too close*, she thought. *Too personal. Threatening to invade my space, my life.*

'So your name's Katrina?'

'I go by Kat.'

'Katrina's lovely. But it doesn't quite fit with Novak.'

'Novak's my married name.'

'Oh. I didn't know you were married.'

'Was. My divorce became final six months ago.'

'And you kept your ex-husband's name?' He looked surprised.

'Not out of affection, believe me. It just felt like a better fit than Ortiz. See, I don't *look* like an Ortiz.'

'Are you referring to your green eyes? Or the freckles on your nose?'

Again, Kat paused on the steps and looked at him. 'Do you always notice the color of women's eyes?'

'No.' He smiled. *What a lot of practice that smile must have had*, she thought. 'But I did notice yours.'

'Lucky me,' she said, and continued down the stairs to the ground floor.

'Could you explain something?' he asked. 'Who is this Jonah person you were talking about in there? And what's a "big man"?'

'The big man,' said Kat, 'is like a – a head honcho. The guy in charge of this territory. For years it was Berto, but I guess he's gone. So now it's a guy named Jonah. He watches over things, keeps out rival gangs. If you want any favors, have any questions to ask, you have to go through the big man.'

'Oh. A sort of unofficial mayor of the neighborhood.'

'You got it.'

They went outside, into a night that smelled of

wind and rain. She glanced up at the sky, saw clouds hurtling past the moon. 'It's getting late,' she said. 'Let's get out of here.'

They hurried down the steps. Two paces was all they managed to take before they both halted, staring in shock at the empty stretch of road beneath the streetlamp.

Kat let fly an oath that would have made a sailor cringe.

Her car had vanished.

5

Laughter drifted down the dark street, carried by the wind.

Kat spun around and saw the teenagers, still standing at the far corner. They were looking her way and grinning. *Damn punks*, she thought. *They think this is hilarious.* In fury she stalked toward them. 'Hey!' she yelled. '*Hey!*'

Adam grabbed her arm and dragged her to a halt. 'I think this is a bad idea,' he whispered.

'Let me go.'

'On further thought, it's a *terrible* idea.'

'I want my car back!' she said, and yanked her arm free. Rage was all the fuel she needed to propel her to the corner. The kids stood watching her, but they made no move. 'Okay,' she snapped. 'Where is it?'

'Where's what, lady?'

'My car, asshole.'

'You had a car?' a boy asked with mock innocence.

Kat ignored him. 'It's not worth a hell of a lot, that car. And it's sure not worth going to jail for. So just give it back to me. And maybe I won't call the cops.'

Some of the kids retreated and faded into the background. The rest – a half-dozen of them – began to fan out into a semicircle. Suddenly she realized that Adam was standing right beside her, shoulder to shoulder. *Amazing. He didn't turn tuxedo and run*, she thought. Maybe she had underestimated him.

The kids were watching her, waiting for signs of fear. She knew how their minds worked; she'd grown up with kids just like these. Turn your back, show a flicker of anxiety, and you were theirs.

She said, slowly, deliberately, '*I want my car.*'

'Or what?' one of the boys said.

'Or my friend here' – she nodded at Adam – 'gets nasty.'

All gazes turned to Adam. *Just a bluff, Quantrell*, she thought. *Don't fold on me.*

He stayed right where he was, solid as a wall.

Now two more of the boys backed down and slid away into the darkness. Only four were left, and they were getting edgy.

'No way you gonna get your wheels back,' one of them said.

'Why not?'

'Man, she's long gone. Wasn't us.'

'Who was it?'

'Repo dude. He's in and outta here. Your car, lady, she's chop.'

Damn. They were probably telling the truth, she thought.

'This is hopeless,' she muttered to Adam. 'Let's go.'

'I thought you'd never ask,' he hissed between his teeth.

Cautiously they eased away from the gang and quickly headed back toward Building Five. She would make her call to the police from Papa Earl's apartment. As for her Subaru, well, at least it was insured.

Kat was so worried about whether the boys were pursuing them that she scarcely noted the footsteps moving in the darkness ahead. Just as they reached the front steps of Building Five, two figures emerged from the darkness and barred their way.

'Let us through,' said Kat.

The boys didn't move.

'Just move aside,' said Adam calmly. 'And there won't be any trouble.'

They laughed, and Kat saw them glance past her, behind her.

She whirled around, just in time to spot the rear attack.

A figure flew at Adam's back, thudding into him so hard he staggered forward to his knees.

Now the two in front launched their assault. A fist

slammed into Adam's jaw. Grunting, he brought his arm up to fend off the second blow.

Kat leaped into the fight. With a cry of rage she threw a left hook at the nearest attacker. Her knuckles connected with cheekbone. Pain exploded in her hand, but the triumph of watching the punk stagger away was worth it.

By now Adam had hauled off and landed a blow on his forward attacker. The rear attacker was still pummeling him on the back. Adam flung him loose. The kid rolled a few feet, then leaped to a crouch. Something clicked in his hand – a switchblade.

'He's got a knife!' yelled Kat.

Adam's gaze instantly focused on the silvery blade. He was unprepared for the sideways tackle by the other punk. They both landed on the ground, the punk on top.

The boy with the switchblade moved in toward the struggling pair.

Kat let fly a kick, felt an instant thump of satisfaction as her shoe connected with the back of Mr. Knife's knee. He groaned and fell forward, but didn't drop the knife.

Something thudded into her from behind, made her stumble to her knees. *A fourth?* she thought in confusion as hands gripped her arms. How many were there?

Her hair was jerked back, her throat lay bare.

The boy with the knife crouched beside her.

'No!' yelled Adam. 'Don't hurt her!'

The blade touched her throat, lingered there a moment. She caught a peripheral view of Adam struggling to reach her, panic stamped plainly on his face. Two boys had him by the arms. A third kicked him soundly in the ribs. Adam doubled over, groaning. 'Leave her alone,' he gasped.

'We won't cut you,' whispered a voice in Kat's ear. 'Not now. But you stay away, you hear, lady cop? 'Cause she don't want to be found.'

'I'm not a cop,' rasped Kat.

The knife bit sharply into her flesh; she felt a drop of blood trickle down her neck. Then, suddenly, the knife was lifted away and her hair was released. Kat knelt on the ground, her heart thudding, her throat closed down by terror. She touched her neck, then stared at the blood on her fingers. 'I thought,' she said hoarsely, 'that you weren't going to cut me.'

'That?' the kid with the knife laughed. 'That's not a cut. That's just a little *kiss*.' He signaled to his buddies that it was time to leave. With startling efficiency, they picked Adam's wallet, stripped off his overcoat, relieved Kat of her purse.

'This time,' said the kid, 'you get off easy.' He gave Kat a kick in the shoulder, which sent her sprawling onto the glass-littered sidewalk.

*   *   *

'No goddamn car is worth it,' said Adam, gingerly holding an ice pack to his cheek. The left side of his face was swollen, and dried blood had caked in his eyebrow. His tuxedo, which had started the evening crisply immaculate, was now in tatters.

He fit right in with the other down-and-outers sitting in the Hancock Emergency Room waiting area. The benches were filled with a tired collection of the bruised and sick, coughing kids, wailing babies, all of them resigned to the long wait for a doctor.

'Anyone with a modicum of sense knows when to fight, and when to turn tail and run,' said Adam. 'You should've run.'

'I didn't see *you* running,' she shot back.

'How could I? I wasn't going to let you take them on by yourself.'

'Well, I do appreciate the gesture.'

'Let me tell you, I wasn't the least bit happy about getting killed over some old Subaru.'

'I liked that car,' muttered Kat. 'It was the first car I ever bought brand-new.'

'It could've been the *only* car you ever bought brand-new.'

A man staggered into the waiting room, rolled his eyes back, and fainted. He was quickly scooped up by two orderlies and wheeled into the inner sanctum. Everyone in the room gave a collective sigh of unhappiness. The wait would be that much longer.

'I tell you what,' said Adam. 'Next time this happens, I'll *buy* you a new car.'

'I can buy my own car,' said Kat. 'I just don't like getting ripped off.' She – as well as everyone else – looked up hopefully as the ER nurse came into the waiting area.

'Ripped off,' said Adam, 'is better than beaten to a pulp. I can't believe they did that to us. And all over something so trivial.'

'But it wasn't over the car,' said Kat. 'Don't you get it? My car had nothing to do with it.'

The nurse called out: 'Novak!'

Kat shot to her feet. 'Here.'

'Follow me.'

'Wait,' said Adam, tossing aside the ice pack. 'What do you mean, your car had nothing to do with it? Then what was that fight all about?'

'Your daughter,' Kat replied, following the nurse out of the waiting area.

Adam was right behind her as she went into the treatment room.

'You'll have to wait outside, sir,' said the nurse.

'He's with me,' said Kat.

The nurse looked at Adam's battered face, then at Kat's black eye. 'I think I can tell,' she said, and shook out a paper drape. 'Lie down and put this over your blouse. So it doesn't get blood on it.'

'It's already got blood on it,' said Kat as she settled

back on the treatment table. The nurse began to clean the knife slash; the sting of Betadine was almost worse than the blade itself.

'What makes you think Maeve had anything to do with this?' said Adam.

'Something our friend with the knife whispered in my ear.'

'Hold still,' snapped the nurse.

'He said, "Stay away, lady cop. Because she doesn't want to be found." Now, that tells me a couple of things. First, he's stupid. He can't tell a cop from a civilian. Second, he's warning us that *she* doesn't want to be found. Who do you suppose *she* is?'

'Maeve,' he said, looking stunned.

The ER doctor came in, a shaggy version of Dr. Michael Dietz, with the same look of battle fatigue. Kat wondered how many hours he'd been working, how many bodies he'd laid hands on. He glanced at her neck wound. His name tag said *Dr. Volcker*.

'How'd you get it?' he asked.

'Switchblade.'

'Someone try to kill you?'

'No, it was an accident.'

'Okay.' The doctor sighed. 'I'll skip the dumb questions.' He turned to the nurse. 'Suture set. She'll need about three stitches. And hand me the Xylocaine.'

Kat winced as the needle with local anesthetic pierced her skin. Then there was the moment's wait for the drug to take effect.

'I can't believe she'd do it,' said Adam. 'I mean, we've had our differences. But for Maeve to have her friends assault us . . .'

'She wasn't attacking you, specifically. She probably didn't know who the hell was asking about her. We might've avoided the whole scene if we'd just told Anthony right off that you were her father.'

'You're saying *Anthony* warned her?'

'He left the apartment while we were still there, remember? Before you said anything about her being your daughter. Probably went straight to Maeve.'

'And she had her friends jump us.'

'Well,' said the doctor, tying off the first stitch. 'You two lead exciting lives.'

They ignored him. 'Maeve must be scared of something,' said Kat. 'Why send the troops to attack at the first sign of strangers?' She glanced at Adam and saw his troubled look. 'What's she afraid of? What did you forget to tell me?'

He shook his head. 'She's in trouble.'

'What kind of trouble?'

He sank into a nearby chair and wearily ran his hands across his battered face.

'Does it have to do with Jane Doe?' asked Kat. 'With Xenia Vargas and Nicos?'

'Maybe.' His answer came out muffled, as though he wanted to bury the words in his throat.

'Or does it have to do with Cygnus? Some miracle drug you've got in development?'

He looked up in anger. 'Why blame it on Cygnus? None of your tests are back! You don't know what the hell those junkies were shooting up.'

'Do *you* know?'

He started to speak, then saw that both the doctor and nurse were watching them in fascination.

'Are you going to sew her up or what?' Adam snapped.

'I was hoping I could hear the end of the story,' said the doctor. He tied off the last stitch and snipped the thread. 'All done. Come back for suture removal in five days.'

'I can pull them myself, thanks,' said Kat. She sat up. The room seemed to sway around her like a boat. She waited for a moment for everything to stop moving.

'Last tetanus shot?' the doctor asked.

'Two years ago. I'm current.'

'Keep the wound dry for twenty-four hours. Clean it twice a day with peroxide. And call if it gets red or warm.' He gave her the ER sheet to sign, then he headed for the door. 'Come back any time,' he said over his shoulder. 'I can't wait for the next installment.'

Back in the hospital lobby, Kat waited for Adam to call his house. Collect, of course; the punks had done a thorough job of emptying their pockets. It was a helpless feeling, being penniless. When Kat had told the ER billing clerk she'd mail in her payment, the clerk had given her a *yeah, sure* look. No respect at all.

'Thomas is on his way,' said Adam, hanging up. 'We'll give you a ride home.'

'Who's Thomas?'

'Sort of my man Friday.' Adam glanced down at his soiled shirt. 'And he's not going to be pleased when he sees what I've done to his ironing job.'

Kat looked down at her own wrinkled shirt. 'Maybe I should borrow him sometime,' she said. 'Along with his iron.'

They sat down in the waiting area. A nurse walked by, carrying a cup of coffee from the vending machine. Kat would have loved a cup of coffee, but her pockets were empty. *Broke and in purgatory*, she thought.

A half hour passed, forty-five minutes. It was almost midnight, and things were still hopping at Hancock General. The next shift of nurses dribbled in from the parking lot, lugging umbrellas and lunch sacks. At the front door, an armed guard eyed everyone who entered. This was frontline medicine, and Hancock General was the equivalent of trench warfare. Every stabbing, every shooting that took place within a three-mile radius, anything on South Lexington, would roll in these ER doors. So would the drug ODs. Kat wondered if another Nicos Biagi or Jane Doe had been found.

'He's upstairs, you know,' she said. 'In the ICU.'

'Who?'

'Nicos Biagi. I came by to see him, earlier today.' She shook her head. 'He didn't look good. Whatever it was he shot up, it's fried his brains. And kidneys.'

Adam was silent. Coldly so.

'The ER doc says it's something new. Something he's never seen before . . .' She paused, as a chilling thought suddenly came to mind. She looked at Adam and saw that he was avoiding her gaze. 'You said you gave Maeve a job. Was it at Cygnus?'

He sighed. 'Yes.'

'Which department?'

'Really, this has nothing to do with Maeve—'

'Which department, Adam?'

He let out another breath, a sound of profound weariness. 'Research and Development,' he said. 'She was doing cleanup in the lab. Running the autoclave. Nothing vital.'

'What was the lab working on?'

'Various projects. Everything from antibiotics to hair restorers.'

'Morphine analogues?'

'Look,' he snapped. 'We're a pharmaceutical company. And pain relief is a big market—'

'You're cooking up something new in that lab, aren't you? Something no one else has developed yet.'

A pause. Then, reluctantly, he nodded. 'It's . . . a breakthrough. Or it will be, if we can iron out the kinks. It's a close relative to natural endorphins. Latches on to the same enzyme receptors as morphine does, holds on to those receptors like Krazy Glue. So it's very long-lasting. Which makes it perfect for terminal cancer patients.'

'Long-lasting? How long?'

'A dose will give pain relief for seventy-two hours, maybe longer. That's its advantage. And its disadvantage. If you overdose an animal, you'll put it in a long-term coma.' He looked up at her; what she saw in his eyes was worry, maybe guilt. And absolute honesty.

She rose suddenly to her feet. 'Come upstairs with me.'

'The ICU?'

'Nicos Biagi's tox screen might be back. I want you to look at it, tell me if it matches your miracle drug.'

'But I'm not a biochemist. I'd need confirmation from my staff—'

'Then take the report back to them. Have them confirm it.'

He shook his head. 'Hospital tox screens aren't specific enough.'

'Why are you so reluctant? Afraid to hear the truth? That it could be a Cygnus drug that's killing people?'

Slowly he rose to his feet. His height put her at a disadvantage. Now she was looking up at *him*, confronting the chilly silence of his eyes.

Up till now, she hadn't felt in the least bit intimidated by Adam Quantrell, not by his wealth or his power or his good looks. But his anger – this was something else. This she couldn't brush off, couldn't turn her back on. Their gazes held and all at once something new flared inside her, so unexpected she was stunned by its intensity. Suddenly she was unable, unwilling, to take note of anything else in the room.

It was a woman's voice, calling Adam's name, that finally broke the spell.

'Adam! What on earth did you *do* to yourself?'

Kat turned and saw Isabel, still in full evening dress. She'd just come through the ER doors and now was staring at Adam in dismay.

'Look at your clothes! And your face! What happened?' Isabel reached up and touched the bruise on his cheek.

He winced. 'We got into a little . . . trouble,' he said. 'What are you doing here, Isabel?'

'I heard Thomas say he was coming to fetch you. I told him I'd do it instead.'

'I'll have to talk to him about this—'

'No, I insisted. I thought you'd be glad to have me rescue you.' She flashed him a smile. '*Aren't* you glad?'

'You shouldn't be down here,' he said. 'Not at this time of night. It's not safe.'

'Oh, well.' Isabel glanced around in disbelief at the tired army of people waiting on the benches and she clutched her wrap more tightly around her shoulders. 'I can't imagine what you're doing in this part of town.' She looked at Kat's equally bruised face. 'It appears you both got into a little trouble.'

'Dr. Novak needs a ride home, too,' said Adam. 'Her car got stolen. And at the moment, we're penniless.'

There was a brief silence, then Isabel shrugged. 'Why not? The more the merrier, I say.' She turned toward the exit. 'Come on. Let's get out of here before *my* car gets stolen.'

'Wait.' Adam looked at Kat. 'There's something we need to do first.'

'What's that?' asked Isabel.

'We have to go upstairs. There's a patient we have to see. In the ICU.'

Kat gave him a nod of approval. So he was finally ready to hear the truth.

'I'll just come along,' said Isabel. 'You wouldn't leave me down here all by myself, would you?'

101

With Adam and Isabel in tow, Kat retraced the steps she'd taken earlier that day. Down the hallway with the tired aqua walls. Up the elevator. Down another hall. Isabel's high heels clacked across the floor.

The ICU was a hive of activity, nurses scurrying about, monitors beeping, ventilators whooshing. At the central nursing desk, two dozen heart tracings zigzagged across a bank of oscilloscopes.

The ward clerk glanced up in surprise at the trio of visitors. 'Are you visiting someone?' he asked.

'I'm Dr. Novak, ME's office,' said Kat. 'I was here earlier with Dr. Dietz, looking over Nicos Biagi's chart. Would you know if his tox screen came back?'

'I just came on duty. Let me check the reports.' The clerk turned to the in-box, riffled through the stack of newly delivered lab slips. 'There's no tox screen here for a Biagi.'

'How is he doing?'

'You'll have to talk to one of the nurses. Which bed is he in?'

'Bed thirteen.'

'Thirteen?' The clerk looked at the Cardex file and frowned. 'There's no one in bed thirteen.'

'That's his bed number, I'm sure of it.' Kat glanced at the oscilloscope, where every patient's heart rhythm wriggled across the screen. Number thirteen was blank.

A nurse walked past the desk, carrying an armful of charts. 'Excuse me, Lori?' called the ward clerk. 'There was a Mr. Biagi in bed thirteen. Do you know if he's been moved?'

Lori stopped, turned to look at the trio of visitors. 'Are you friends or relatives?'

'Neither,' said Kat. 'I'm from the ME's office.'

'Oh.' The look of caution eased from the nurse's face. 'Then I guess it's okay to tell you.'

'Tell me what?'

'Mr. Biagi died. Two hours ago.'

6

Jane Doe. Xenia Vargas. Nicos Biagi. They were all dead.

How many more would die?

Kat sat in the back seat of Isabel's Mercedes and stared out at the midnight scenery of South Lexington. She'd forgotten about her bruises, her empty stomach, the throbbing of her freshly sutured neck. She was numb now, shaken by the new addition to the death toll. Three in two days. It was lethal, this drug. It sucked the life out of its victims as surely as a dose of strychnine. Unless the word got out on the streets, there'd be more Jane Does checking into private drawers in the morgue. She only hoped Wheelock had stressed the urgency in his press conference. *Had* there been a press conference? She'd missed the evening news . . .

Exhausted, she sank back into the luxury of soft,

buttery leather. She'd never been in such a clean car. She'd never been in the back seat of a Mercedes, either. This she could learn to like. She could also learn to like the smooth ride, the sense of insulated safety. Maybe there was something to be said for money.

Isabel had stopped at a red light, and she brushed back Adam's hair with her manicured fingers. 'You poor thing! Look at those bruises! I'll have to get you all cleaned up when we get home.'

'I'm perfectly fine, Isabel,' Adam said with a sigh.

'What happened to your overcoat?'

'They took it. Along with my wallet.'

'Oh! And you got hurt trying to fight them off?'

'No, as a matter of fact, I got hurt trying to get away.'

'Don't say things like that, Adam. I know perfectly well you're not a coward.'

So do I, thought Kat.

Adam merely shrugged. 'Keep your illusions, then. I'll try not to shatter them.'

The red light changed to green. Isabel drove up the freeway on-ramp. 'We missed you at dinner, you know,' she said.

Adam looked out the window. 'Hope you left some wine in my cellar.'

'Enough for a nightcap.'

'I'm really pretty tired. I think I'll probably go straight to sleep.'

There was a silence. 'Oh,' said Isabel. 'Well, there's still tomorrow night. You *are* up for that, aren't you?'

'What's tomorrow night?'

'The mayor's dinner. Adam, how *could* you forget?'

'I just did.'

Isabel gave a laugh. 'You'll be a hit, you know. All those lovely bruises. Like some macho badge of honor.'

'More like a badge of stupidity,' said Adam.

'What is the matter with you?'

'Get off here,' said Adam. 'Bellemeade exit.'

'Why would I want to go to Bellemeade?'

'It's where I live,' said Kat from the back seat. Had Isabel forgotten she was there?

'Oh, of course.' Isabel took the exit. 'Bellemeade. That's a nice neighborhood.'

'It's close to town,' said Kat, a neutral response that could be taken in many different ways.

After a few blocks and a few turns, they pulled up in front of Kat's house. She was proud of that house. It had three bedrooms, a charming front porch, and a lawn that wasn't loaded with chemicals. It wasn't Surry Heights, but she was happy here. So why did she feel the sudden urge to apologize?

Adam got out and opened her door. To her surprise, he also offered his hand. She stepped out onto the sidewalk beside him. The streetlamp spilled light across his golden hair.

'Can you get into the house?' he asked.

'I keep an extra key under the flowerpot.'

'You don't have a car.'

'I'll catch the bus to work.'

'That's crazy. I'll arrange something.'

'I'm really okay, Adam. I've gone without wheels before.'

'Still, I feel responsible. You got into this mess because of me. So let me take care of it. A taxi to work, at least.'

She looked up at him, sensed how very much he wanted her to accept his help. 'Okay,' she said. 'Just for a day or two. Until I come up with a new car.'

She headed up the walkway to her front porch. Then she glanced back.

He was still watching, waiting for her to go inside.

Only when she'd entered the house and turned on the hallway light did he get back in the car. She looked out the front window and saw the Mercedes drive away.

Back to Surry Heights, she thought. *Back to his world.*

And Isabel's.

She locked the front door and wearily climbed the stairs to bed.

* * *

107

After he'd sent Isabel home, Adam holed up in his study and nursed a much-needed glass of brandy. His head ached, his eyes were bleary, and his ribs hurt like hell when he took a deep breath, but he couldn't quite drag himself off to bed yet.

He kept playing and replaying that terrifying image from tonight: Kat Novak, down on her knees, her hair yanked back, her throat bared. And the switchblade, pressing against her flesh. He closed his eyes and tried to shut it out, but couldn't. At the instant he'd seen it, he'd lost all fear for himself, had stopped caring what would happen to *him*. All he knew was that they were going to kill her, and there was nothing he could do to stop it, not a single damn thing.

He clutched the brandy glass and drained it in one neat gulp. *She came through it better than I did*, he thought.

But then, Kat Novak was something extraordinary. A true survivor who would land on her feet every time. Considering her roots, she *had* to be a survivor. He wondered what she saw when she looked at him.

He wasn't sure he really wanted to know.

Finally he set down the brandy glass and hauled himself out of the chair. On the way out of the room, he passed the photo of Maeve. It sat on the end table, a quiet portrait of his smiling stepdaughter. Was Maeve smiling much these days?

He should have known. He should have seen it coming.

He had no excuses, except that he'd felt over-whelmed, by his work, by single fatherhood, by a daughter who was so traumatized by her mother's death that she slipped into an eternally sullen adolescence. He couldn't talk to her; after a while he'd given up trying and had resorted to a father's tactic of last resort: asserting his authority. That hadn't worked, either.

By the time he'd realized Maeve was in trouble, it was too late. She was on a constant high – booze, pills, everything, anything.

Like Georgina.

Maybe it was in their genes, some cruel twist in their DNA that preordained their addictions. Maybe it was simply that they couldn't cope with life or stress.

Or was it him?

He turned away from the photograph and climbed the stairs. Once again, alone to bed. It didn't have to be this way. It had been clear tonight that Isabel was ready and willing – and frustrated by his lack of interest. They'd known each other for years, had been seeing each other on a regular basis for months. Shouldn't he be making *some* kind of move?

But tonight, when she'd driven him to his door, he'd taken a good look at her. She was perfect, of course – her hair, her dress, her smile – perfect in every way. And yet he felt no interest whatsoever in taking her to bed. He'd looked at her, and all he could see was Kat Novak, her face as bruised as a prizefighter's, grinning at him by the light of that Bellemeade streetlamp.

Wonderful, he thought. *After all these years I finally admit to the possibility of romance, and look who inspires it. A woman who almost gets me killed over some beat-up Subaru.*

Not at all a promising match.

Kat woke up with every muscle in her body aching. It took a massive infusion of willpower just to roll out of bed. She went into the bathroom and saw, in the mirror, the evidence of last night's brawl: three neat stitches on her neck and the bruises and scrapes on her face. So it hadn't been a nightmare after all.

She managed to wash around that painful minefield of facial cuts and sweep her hair back in a ponytail. Forget the makeup; she'd wear her bruises to work instead.

Downstairs, fueled by a cup of extra-strength Yuban, she started in on the tasks at hand: canceling her credit cards and her bank card, replacing her driver's license. When the punks had grabbed her purse, they'd made off with most of her financial identity. At least she still had her checkbook – that she'd left safely at home last night. She made one last call, begging a locksmith to come change her locks ASAP. Then she got up and poured herself another cup of coffee. The caffeine was having its blessed effect – she was feeling human again. And feisty. Getting beaten up and robbed wasn't good for her disposition.

So when she heard the footsteps on her front porch, she was expecting the worst. Were the punks there already to try out her house keys?

She scurried into the living room, grabbed the baseball bat out of the front closet, and stood poised by the front door. When she heard the clink of keys, she raised the bat, expecting the door to swing open any second.

Instead, the mail slot squealed open, and a set of car keys slid through and clattered to the wood floor. Kat stared at them. What the hell?

Whoever had dropped them off was now walking away. She yanked open the door and saw Adam Quantrell's butler climb into a car driven by another man.

'Hey!' Kat yelled, waving the keys. 'What's this?'

The butler waved back and called, 'Compliments of Mr. Quantrell!'

Bewildered, Kat watched them drive off. Then her gaze shifted to her driveway.

A lemon yellow Mercedes was parked there.

She looked down at the keys she was holding. Then

she went to the driveway and slowly circled the car. It was beautiful. Absolutely beautiful. *Regis Luxury Rentals*, said the license plate frame. She peered in the window – leather seats. *Clean.* She opened the door, climbed in behind the wheel, and just sat there for a moment. There was a note taped to the dashboard, addressed to Dr. Novak. She unfolded the slip of paper and read it.

Hope this will do. A.Q.

She sat back. 'Well, I just don't know, Mr. Quantrell,' she said aloud. 'Lemon yellow isn't *quite* my color. But I suppose it will have to do.' Then she threw her head back and laughed.

At work, she stopped laughing.

Davis Wheelock told her the mayor had vetoed the idea of any press conference.

'You can't be serious,' said Kat.

Wheelock looked genuinely apologetic. 'I explained the situation to the mayor and his staff. I told them we'd had two deaths—'

'Three, Davis. Nicos Biagi died. I've had it classified an ME case.'

'All right, three. I told them the trend was not good. But they felt a press conference was premature.'

'At what point does this crisis become mature?'

Wheelock shook his head. 'It's not in my power to

go around them. The line of authority's clear. When it comes to press releases, the mayor has final say.'

'Maybe you weren't persuasive enough.'

'Maybe we should ride this out a bit. See what develops.'

'I can tell you what'll develop. And it won't be good press.' She leaned across Wheelock's desk. 'Davis, we're going to come out of this looking incompetent. When all hell breaks loose, do you think the mayor's going to take the rap? We will. *You* will.'

Wheelock was looking more and more unhappy.

'Let me talk to them,' said Kat. 'I'll bring in Dr. Dietz from Hancock General as my authority. This news has to get out, and soon. Before South Lexington turns into a graveyard.'

For a moment, Wheelock said nothing. Then he nodded. 'All right. You take care of it. But don't be surprised if they slap you down.'

'Thanks, Davis.'

Back in her office, the first call she made was to the mayor's secretary. She learned that His Honor had a hole in his appointment book at one o'clock and she might be able to slip in then, but there were no guarantees.

The second call she made was to Hancock General. Unfortunately, Dr. Michael Dietz was not on duty in the ER.

'Is there any way I can reach him?' asked Kat. 'This is urgent. I've booked us into the mayor's office at one o'clock.'

'I'm afraid that's impossible,' said the ER clerk.

'Why?'

'Dr. Dietz has left town. He resigned from the staff. Effective yesterday evening.'

During his three and a half years in office, Mayor Sampson had presided over the worst economic slide in Albion's history. To be fair, it wasn't entirely his fault – across the country, cities were reeling from the recession. But with three major plant closings, a host of business bankruptcies, and an inner city rotting at its core, Albion had suffered worse than most. So it struck Kat as more than a little ironic that the bicentennial poster displayed behind the receptionist's desk showed a slick couple in evening dress, dancing before a view of the night skyline.

Albion – a city for all reasons.
Nolan Sampson, Mayor.

It was, of course, just your typical election year hype. How convenient for His Honor that the celebration just happened to coincide with the kick-off for his reelection campaign.

She approached the receptionist. 'I'm Dr. Novak,

ME's office. Is there a chance I could get in to see Mayor Sampson?'

'I'll check.' The receptionist pressed the intercom. 'Mayor Sampson? There's a doctor here from the ME's office. Are you free?'

'Uh, yeah. We just finished lunch. Send him in,' Kat heard from the speaker.

Him? He must think I'm Wheelock, she thought. She opened the door and masculine laughter spilled out. Just inside the office, she halted.

The mayor was behind his desk, puffing on a cigar. In a nearby chair sat the acting district attorney – Kat's ex-husband.

'Hello, Ed,' said Kat stiffly. 'Mayor Sampson.'

Both men looked surprised. 'It's you,' Ed said, for want of anything else to say. She noticed he'd spiffed up his wardrobe since their divorce. He had a new suit, Italian shoes, a shirt that looked like a hundred percent linen. *Just think of all those wrinkles. I wonder who he's got ironing his shirts these days.*

'Is this . . . official business?' asked the mayor, looking bewildered.

'Yes,' said Kat. 'Davis Wheelock spoke to you yesterday. About that press conference.'

'What? Oh.' Sampson waved his hand in dismissal. 'You mean the junkies. Yeah, we talked about it.'

'I think it's time to go to the press, sir,' said Kat. 'We've had three deaths.'

'I thought it was two.'

'Another OD died last night. At Hancock General.'

'Have you confirmed it's the same drug?'

'Let's just say my suspicions are running high.'

'Ah.' Sampson sat back, suddenly at ease. 'So you don't have confirmation.'

'Toxicology screens take time. Especially when the drug's an unknown. By the time we get a positive ID, we could have a full-blown crisis in South Lexington.'

Ed laughed. 'South Lexington *is* a crisis.'

Kat ignored him. 'All I'm asking for is a statement to the press. Call in the local news stations. Tell them we've got some bad stuff on the streets. Junkies are dying.'

The mayor glanced at Ed with an amused look. 'Some would say that's progress.'

'Sir,' said Kat, trying to stay calm, 'you have to let people know.'

'Now therein lies our problem,' said Mayor Sampson, shifting forward in his chair. 'Dr. Novak, in case you're not aware of it, we have a bicentennial celebration coming up. Parade, marching bands, the whole nine yards. We have the heads of eight major corporations coming to town to join in the fun. And to look us over, see if they like us. We're talking jobs they could bring to Albion. But they won't bring a *thing* to town if they start seeing headlines like *Junkie epidemic* or *Grim reaper stalks city*. They'll just move their companies to Boston or Providence instead.'

'So what do you suggest?' asked Kat. 'We sweep it under the rug?'

'Not exactly. We just . . . wait a while.'

'How long?'

'Until you've got more information. Next week, say.'

'A lot of people can die in a week.'

'Lighten up, Kat,' Ed cut in. 'These aren't the pillars of society we're talking about. These are the same folks who mug old ladies and hold up gas stations. The same folks I'm already sticking in jail.' He paused. 'The same folks who ripped off your car.'

'How did you hear about that?' Kat snapped.

Ed grinned. 'We hear a lot of things at the office. Like who's been filing stolen car reports.'

'Forget my car. I want to know when we can see some action on this.'

'I think I answered that question, Dr. Novak,' said Mayor Sampson.

'You're making a mistake.'

'Christ,' Sampson said with a sigh. 'You can't even prove to me these deaths are related. Why go and get the whole town panicked about it?'

Ed added, 'They're only junkies.'

She shook her head in disbelief. 'You know what, Ed?' she said with a laugh. 'It's a continuing source of wonder to me.'

'What is?'

'What the hell I ever saw in you.' She turned and walked out of the room.

Ed followed her, through the receptionist's office and into the hallway. 'Kat, wait up.'

'I'm going back to work.'

'Just love those stiffs, huh?'

'Compared to present company? Don't ask.' She got into the elevator, and he slipped in beside her.

'Looks like life's been rough since you left me,' he said, glancing at her bruised face with a grin.

'Not nearly as rough as it was *with* you. And you left *me*, remember?'

'You know, you really blew it in there with Sampson. Next time you should try a little honey, not so much vinegar. It'd be better for your career.'

'I see *your* career doesn't need any help,' she said, glancing at his tailored shirt.

He grinned. 'You heard that Sampson endorsed me? The campaign coffers are already loaded.'

'Be careful whose coattails you grab onto. Sampson's days are numbered.'

They stepped out of the elevator and left the building.

'It's just a stepping stone,' he said. 'Today, DA. Tomorrow – who knows? Are you coming to the campaign benefit? I could use you there. Show of support from the ME's office.'

'I've got better ways to spend my money.'

He reached in his pocket and produced an invitation. 'Here.' He dropped it in her purse. 'My compliments. Will you vote for me, at least?'

She laughed. 'What do *you* think?'

'I think you're gonna need a friend in high places. Especially with the rut your career seems to be—' He broke off and stared as Kat unlocked the door of the Mercedes. 'This is *your* car?' he asked.

'Nice, isn't she?' Kat slid into the driver's seat and slammed the door. She smiled sweetly out the window. 'Those of us in career ruts have to find *some* way to compensate.'

The look on his face was enough to keep her smiling for a block. Then the anger hit, anger at Ed and Sampson and Wheelock. And at herself, for acknowledging defeat. She could go around them all. Ignore the lines of authority, call up the news stations herself, and announce a crisis . . .

And promptly get herself fired.

She gripped the steering wheel, silently railing at herself, at election-year politics, at a system that made you park your conscience if you wanted to stay employed. She just didn't have the evidence to force the issue – not yet. What she needed was a pair of matching tox screens – just one pair, enough to link two of the deaths. Enough to go to the press and say, 'We have a trend here.'

The minute she got back to her office, she called the state lab. 'This is Dr. Novak, Albion Assistant ME. Do you have results yet on Jane Doe number 373-4-3-A?'

'I'll check,' said the technician.

A moment later, the tech came back on the line. 'I have a blood, urine, and vitreous on Jane Doe number 372-3-27-B.'

'That's a different number.'

'It was ordered by a Dr. Clark, Albion ME. Is this the one you want?'

'No, that's the wrong Jane Doe. I want 373-4-3-A.'

'I have no record of any such request.'

'I sent it in April third. Name's Dr. Novak.'

'My log for April third doesn't show any Jane Doe specimens from Albion. Or anything from you, Dr. Novak.'

Kat tugged at a loose hair in frustration. 'Look, I know I sent it in. It was even marked *Expedite*.'

'It's not in the log or in my computer.'

'I can't believe this! Of all the lab requests, you have to lose this one? I *need* those results.'

'We can't run a test without specimens,' said the tech with undeniable logic.

'Okay.' Kat sighed. 'Then give me the results from another case. Xenia Vargas. I sent that in April fourth. You *do* have that one?'

'It was logged in. Let me check . . .' There was a brief

silence, punctuated by the clicking of fingers on a keyboard. Then the tech said, 'It was shipped to an outside lab.'

'Why?'

'It says here, "Nonspecific opioids detected. Unable to identify using available techniques. Specimen referred to independent lab for further tests." That's all.'

'So I *will* get an ID? Eventually?'

'Eventually.'

'Thank you.' Kat hung up. Then it was something new. Something even the state lab couldn't identify.

But it was only one case. To prove a trend, she needed a second case, at the very least.

She rose and pulled on her lab coat. Then she walked down the hall to the morgue. One of the day attendants was tidying up the room. He glanced at her.

'Hey, Doc,' he said. 'What's up?'

'Hal, you remember those specimens I sent off on Monday? For Jane Doe? I put them in the out-box. Did you see the courier pick them up?'

'Don't tell me they went and lost something again?'

'They say they never got it.'

Hal rolled his eyes. 'Yeah, I heard them give Doc Clark the same story. So what do you want me to do? Run another set over?'

'If you're willing.' She glanced at her watch. 'It's

four. Take an hour of overtime. That'll cover the drive. And make sure they log it in.'

'Sure thing.'

Now there would be another long wait for results. Luckily, they'd retained several tubes of Jane Doe's blood and urine, for just this situation. While it was rare for specimens to be lost, it did happen.

Her head was starting to ache again, a reminder of last night's scuffle. She should go home early, put up her feet, and OD on the opiate of the masses – TV. But she'd accumulated too much paperwork.

Back at her desk, she shuffled through her in-box. There were dictations to sign, reports from ballistics, lab slips, pathology journals. She had just emptied her box when the mailroom clerk came in, whistling, and dumped another stack onto her desk.

'Forget this,' Kat muttered. 'I'm going home.'

Then she saw the envelope on the stack. *Dr. Novak* was scrawled on top. No address, no stamp; someone must have dropped it off at the front desk.

She opened the envelope and read the note.

Nicos Biagi results just back, MIT lab. Identified as new generation long-acting narcotic, levo-N-cyclobutylmethyl-6, 10 beta-dihydroxy class. Not FDA approved for use in humans. MIT says research patent application made six months ago. Trade name: Zestron-L. Applicant: Cygnus Corporation.

Sorry I'm cutting out on you, but I don't need the headache. Good luck, Novak. You'll need it.

Mike Dietz

The Cygnus Corporation. She stared at the name, stunned by the revelation. *Thanks, Dr. Dietz, you coward. You drop this can of worms on my desk, and then you turn and run.*

She grabbed the phone and called the state lab once again.

'About that tox screen, on Xenia Vargas,' she said to the technician. 'There's a specific drug I want you to test for. It's called Zestron-L.'

'You'll have to talk directly to the outside lab. They're handling it now.'

'Okay, I'll call them. Where did you send it to?'

'Cygnus Laboratories, in Albion. Do you want the number?'

Kat didn't answer. She kept staring at that note from Dietz, at the name: *Cygnus.* Pharmaceuticals. Diagnostic labs. How many tentacles did the corporation have?

'Dr. Novak?' asked the tech again. 'Do you want the Cygnus phone number?'

'No,' said Kat softly, and hung up.

It took her a few minutes to dredge up the courage

to make the next phone call. It had to be done; Adam Quantrell had to be confronted.

The phone rang once, twice. A male voice answered: 'Quantrell residence. Thomas speaking.'

'This is Dr. Novak.'

'Ah, yes, Dr. Novak. I hope the new automobile is working out.'

'It's fine. Is Mr. Quantrell in?'

'I'm afraid he just left for the evening. The mayor's benefit, you know. Shall I give him a message?'

And what message could she leave? she thought. *That I know the truth? It's your company, your drug, that's killing people?*

'Dr. Novak?' asked Thomas when she said nothing.

She folded Dietz's note and stuffed it in her purse. 'No message, Thomas. Thanks,' she said. 'I'll catch him at the benefit.'

Then she hung up and walked out of the office.

7

It took Kat an hour and a half to drive home, change her clothes, and fight her way back through midtown traffic. By that time, a major jam had built up along Dorchester Avenue, leading to the Four Seasons Hotel. All the red lights gave her time to shake her hair loose, dab on lipstick, brush on mascara while looking in the visor mirror. Even with a ton of face powder the bruises were still obvious, but at least she'd found a silk scarf to wrap around her neck and conceal the stitches. It actually looked rather dashing, that slash of red and purple silk trailing across the black dress. Too bad the whole effect required high heels; before the night was over, her feet would be killing her.

The ballroom of the Four Seasons was packed. There were probably enough furs and jewels in the room to fund the city budget for a year. A buffet table held platters of shrimp and smoked salmon, pastries and caviar, all of it served on real china, of course. A balalaika troupe was playing Russian music – a tribute to Albion's equally depressed sister city on the Volga. Kat handed her invitation to the official at the door and headed into the thick of things.

She was reminded at once of why she hated going to affairs like this, especially on her own. Bring an escort and you were an instant social circle; go alone and you're invisible. Sipping at the requisite glass of white wine, she wandered through the crowd and searched for a familiar face – any familiar face. Mostly she saw a lot of tuxedoes, a lot of mink, a lot of orthodontically perfect teeth bared in perfect smiles.

She heard her name called. Turning, she saw her ex-husband. 'And I thought you weren't going to vote for us,' he said as he approached.

'I didn't say I would. I just can't pass up a free invite.'

'Hey, I want to get a photo taken. You and the mayor together.' He glanced around and spotted Sampson off in a corner, surrounded by admirers. 'There he is. Come on.'

'I don't do photo ops.'

'Just this time.'

'I told you, I'm not here to endorse him. I'm here to partake of a few free drinks and—' She stopped, her gaze suddenly focusing across the room, on a man's fair hair. Adam Quantrell didn't see her; he was facing sideways, engaged in conversation with another man. Next to Adam stood Isabel, her equally blond hair done up in an elaborate weave of faux pearls. *The perfect couple*, she thought. A stunning pair in tuxedo and evening dress. The sort of couple you saw epitomized in *Cosmo* ads.

Adam must have sensed he was being watched. He glanced her way and froze when he saw her. To Kat's surprise, he abruptly broke off his conversation and began to move toward her, across the room. She caught a glimpse of Isabel's frown, of faces turning to look at Adam as his broad shoulders pushed past. And then all she could seem to focus on was *him*.

He was smiling at her, the relaxed greeting of an old friend. The bruise on his cheek was almost lost in the laugh lines around his eyes. 'Kat,' he said, 'I didn't know you were coming.' He reached out to her, and her hand felt lost in the warmth of his grip.

'*I* didn't know I was coming,' she said.

The sound of a throat being cleared caught her attention. She glanced sideways at Ed. 'I guess I should introduce you two,' she said. 'Ed, this is Adam Quantrell. Adam, this is Ed Novak. Our acting DA.'

'Novak?' said Adam as the two men automatically shook hands.

'I'm her ex-husband,' said Ed, grinning. 'We're still *very* close.'

'Speak for yourself,' said Kat.

'So you're both campaigning for Sampson?' asked Adam.

'Ed is,' said Kat. 'I'm not.'

Ed laughed. 'And I'm going to change her mind.'

'I came for the free meal,' said Kat. She took a sip of wine, then she looked directly at Adam, a cool, hard gaze that no one could mistake as flirtatious. 'And to see you.'

'Well,' said Ed. 'She always *did* favor the direct approach.'

'I'd like to say I'm flattered,' said Adam, frowning as he studied her face. 'But I get the feeling this isn't a social chat we're about to have.'

'It's not,' said Kat. 'It's about Nicos Biagi.'

'I see.' Suddenly he seemed stiff and guarded – as well he should be. 'Then perhaps we should talk in private. If you'll excuse us, Mr. Novak.' He placed a hand on Kat's shoulder.

'Adam!' called Isabel, moving swiftly toward them. 'I want you to meet someone. Oh, hello, Dr. Novak! Have you recovered from last night?'

Kat nodded. 'A few sore muscles, that's all.'

'You're amazingly resilient. I would have been terrified, having my life threatened that way.'

'Oh, I was terrified all right,' admitted Kat.

'And then to have your car stolen. How fortunate it was only a Subaru—'

'Will you excuse us?' said Adam, continuing to guide Kat toward the exit. 'I'll join you later, Isabel.'

'How much later?'

'Just later.' With a firm hand, he hustled Kat out to the lobby, where it was every bit as crowded. 'Let's go outside,' he suggested. 'At least we can get out of this madhouse.'

They found a spot near the hotel fountain, its trickling waters aglow in a rainbow of colored lights. The sounds of the gathering spilled out even here, in the darkness. From the ballroom came the faint strumming of balalaikas.

He turned to face her, his hair glittering in the reflected lights of the fountain. 'What's going on?' he asked.

'I could ask you the same question.'

'Are you angry at me for some reason?'

'Zestron-L,' she said, looking at him intently. 'You *have* heard of it, haven't you?'

She could see at once that he had. She caught a glimpse of shock in his eyes, and then his expression smoothed into unreadability. So he knew. All this time he knew which drug might be killing these people.

'Let me refresh your memory, in case you've forgotten,' she went on. 'Zestron-L is a long-acting narcotic, new generation, of the class levo-N-cyclobutyl—'

'I know what it is.'

'Then you also know Cygnus holds the patent.'

'Yes.'

'Did you also know your drug was out on the streets?'

'It's not possible. We're still in the research stage – primate trials. It hasn't gone to human trials yet.'

'I'm afraid human trials have already started. The lab is South Lexington. And the results aren't too encouraging. Bad side effects. Mainly, death.'

'But it hasn't been released yet!'

'Nicos Biagi got his hands on it.'

'How do you know?'

'The hospital couldn't ID it, so they sent the blood sample to a university lab. A lucky break, too. They were able to identify it.'

'There are two other victims—'

'Yes, and a funny thing happened to their blood samples. Jane Doe's got lost in transit. And as for Xenia Vargas, I won't trust any results I get back on hers. In fact, I half expect that *her* blood sample will get lost as well.'

'Don't you think you sound just the slightest bit paranoid?'

'Paranoid? No, I'm afraid I've never had much of an imagination. It's one of my faults.'

He moved closer to her, so threateningly close she had to fight the impulse to retreat a step. 'Whatever your faults, Dr. Novak, a lack of imagination isn't one of them.'

'Let me lay out the facts, disturbing but true. First, Jane Doe's specimens were lost. I know I labeled them properly, I filled out all the right forms, and put them in the right box.'

'The carrier could have lost it. Or it could've been stolen from his vehicle. There are dozens of possibilities.'

'Then there's the matter of Xenia Vargas. Her specimens *did* make it to the state lab, but they can't ID the drug. So they send it to an outside lab for further testing. Guess which lab?' She looked him in the eye. 'Cygnus.'

He didn't even flinch. Calmly he said, 'We routinely handle requests from the state. We're only thirty miles away and we're better equipped.'

'*Third*, there's the matter of Dr. Michael Dietz, Nicos Biagi's doctor. He identifies the drug as Zestron-L. Then he resigns from Hancock General and skips town. I think he was forced out by the hospital. Because Cygnus just *happens* to be a major donor to Hancock General.'

'Cygnus had nothing to do with Dietz's resignation. He was already on his way out.'

'How would you know that?'

'I'm on the hospital board. Three malpractice suits were more than we'd tolerate. Dietz was a disaster waiting to happen. His license was already in jeopardy.'

Kat paused. That *would* account for Dietz's reluctance to face the press. He didn't need the publicity.

'But Zestron-L *is* your drug. And someone's trying to keep its identity from the ME. Someone's protecting Cygnus.'

He began to pace back and forth by the fountain. 'This is bizarre,' he muttered. 'I don't see how that ID could be right.'

'You can't argue with a lab result.'

He stopped and looked at her, the gaudy lights from the fountain washing him in their watery glow. 'No,' he said at last. 'You're right. I can't.'

The absolute steadiness of his gaze made her want to believe that there were no lies between them, no hidden agendas, that his bewilderment was real. *I must be getting soft*, she thought. *A pair of blue-gray eyes, a tuxedo, a man too gorgeous for words, and my horse sense bites the dust. What is wrong with me?*

'Come with me,' he said, and held out his hand.

She didn't move, feeling shaken by the sudden temptation to take his hand, to feel her whole body swallowed in his warmth. This was what she'd fought against, from the first time they'd met, this quickening of desire.

He was still holding out his hand, still trapping her in a gaze she couldn't seem to escape. 'Come on, Kat,' he said.

'Where?'

'To Cygnus. The lab. Tonight, I'm going to root out the answers. And I want you there with me, as a witness.'

She shook her head. 'I'm not so sure that you'll like the answers.'

'You may be right. But it's clear to me that you're not going to let up. One way or another, you're going to dig up the truth. So I might as well work with you. Not against you.'

The logic of the devil. How could she argue with it?

She said, at last, 'All right. I'll go with you.'

'First let me smooth things over with Isabel.'

Back in the ballroom, she watched him approach Isabel, saw the hurried excuses, the apologetic head-shaking. Isabel glanced in Kat's direction with a poorly disguised look of annoyance.

Kat spotted Ed by the buffet table. She sidled up to him. 'Ed,' she said.

He grinned. 'Did the direct approach work?'

'Quantrell's taking me to his lab tonight.'

'Lucky you.'

'I want you to let Sykes and Ratchet know. Just in case.'

'In case what?'

Instantly she fell silent as Adam came towards her. 'Just keep it in mind,' she muttered to Ed. Then, with an automatic smile pasted in place, she followed Adam out the door.

They went into the hotel garage. 'We'll take your car,' he said. 'Isabel's going home in mine.'

'She didn't look too happy about it.'

'She hasn't much of a choice.'

Kat shook her head in disbelief. 'Are you always this thoughtful with your lady friends?'

'Isabel,' he sighed, 'is a lovely woman with a cozy inheritance. And a whole stable of suitors. She hardly needs me to keep her warm at night.'

'Do you?'

'Do you keep Ed Novak warm at night?'

'None of your business.'

He cocked his head. 'Ditto.'

They got into the rented Mercedes. The smell of leather upholstery mingled with the scent of his after-shave. It left her feeling a little light-headed.

Kat started the car, and they swung into evening traffic.

'How do you like the car?' he asked.

'It's okay.'

'Okay?' he said, obviously waiting for her to elaborate.

'Yeah. It's okay.'

He looked out the window. 'Next time, I'll have to choose something that'll *really* impress you.'

Kat put her foot on the gas pedal.

'A horse-drawn chariot,' Adam mused. 'Or maybe a team of sled-dogs.' He turned to her. 'How does that sound?'

'I'm allergic,' she replied, as they sailed onto the highway.

'To horses or dogs?'

'To chariots and sleds.'

'Ah.' He nodded solemnly. 'A unicycle it'll have to be, then.'

Kat felt a smile tug at the corner of her lips.

'There,' he said. 'Take the next turnoff. It's eight miles north.'

The road took them out of midtown Albion, into a district of industrial parks and corporate head-quarters. In the last ten years, many of the buildings had become vacant; dark windows and *For Lease* signs had sprung up everywhere. Albion, like the rest of the country, was struggling.

The Cygnus complex was one of the few that appeared to house a thriving corporation. Even at eight o'clock at night, some of the windows were still lit, and there were a dozen cars in the parking lot.

They drove past the security booth and pulled into a stall marked *Quantrell*.

'Your people work late,' said Kat, glancing at the parked cars.

'The evening shift,' said Adam. 'We run a twenty-four-hour diagnostic lab. Plus, some of our research people like to keep odd hours. You know how it is with eggheads. They have their own schedules.'

'A flexible company.'

'We have to be, if we want to keep good minds around.'

They walked to the front door, where Adam pressed a few numbers on a wall keypad and the lock snapped open. Inside, they headed down a brightly lit hallway. No smudged walls, no flickering fluorescent bulbs here; only the best for corporate America.

'Where are we going?' she asked.

'Diagnostics. I'm going to prove to you we're not engaged in a cover-up.'

'Just how are you going to do that?'

'I'm going to personally hand over to you Xenia Vargas's toxicology screen.'

The diagnostics lab was a vast chamber of space-age equipment, manned by a half-dozen technicians. The evening supervisor, a grandmotherly type in a lab coat, immediately came to greet them.

'Don't worry, Grace,' said Adam. 'This isn't a surprise inspection.'

'Thank God,' said Grace with a laugh. 'We just hid the beer keg and the dancing girls. So what can I do for you, Mr. Q.?'

'This is Dr. Novak, ME's office. She wants to check on a tox screen sent here from the state.'

'What's the name?'

'Xenia Vargas,' said Kat.

Grace sat down at a computer terminal and typed in the name. 'Here it is. Logged in just this afternoon. It's not checked priority, so we haven't run it yet.'

'Could you run it now?' asked Adam.

'It'll take some time.'

Adam glanced at Kat. She nodded. 'We'll wait,' he said.

Grace called to another tech: 'Val, can you check that box of requests from the state? We're going to run a STAT on Xenia Vargas.' She looked at Adam. 'Are you sure you want to hang around, Mr. Q.? This is going to be boring.'

'We'll be up in my office,' said Adam. 'Call us there.'

'Okay. But if I was dressed like *that*—' she nodded at their evening clothes, 'I'd be out dancing.'

Adam smiled. 'We'll keep it in mind.'

By the time they reached Adam's office, which was upstairs and down a long corridor, Kat's feet were staging a protest against her high heels and she was silently cursing every cobbler in Italy. The minute she hobbled through the office door, she pulled off her shoes, and her stockinged feet sank into velvety carpet. *Nice. Plush.* Slowly she gazed around the room, impressed by her surroundings. It wasn't just an office; it was more like a second home, with a couch and chairs, bookshelves, a small refrigerator.

'I was wondering how long you'd last in those shoes,' Adam said with a laugh.

'When Grace mentioned dancing, I felt like crying.' She sat down gratefully on the couch. 'I confess, I'm the socks and sneakers type.'

'What a shame. You look good in heels.'

'My feet would beg to differ.' Groaning, she reached down and began to massage her instep.

'What your feet need,' he said, 'is a little pampering.' He sat down beside her on the couch and patted his lap in invitation. 'Allow me.'

'Allow you to what?'

'Make up for that long walk down that long hallway.'

Laughing, she rose from the couch. 'It won't work, Quantrell. It takes more than a foot rub to soften up my brain.'

He gave a sigh of disappointment. 'She doesn't trust me.'

'Don't take it personally. When it comes to men, I'm just an old skeptic.'

'Ah. Deep-rooted fears. An unreliable father?'

'I didn't have a father.' She wandered over to the bookcase, made a slow survey of the spines. An eclectic collection, she noted, arranged in no particular order. Philosophy and physics. Fiction and pharmacology. Over the bookcase hung several framed diplomas, strictly Ivy League.

'So what happened to your father?' he asked.

'I wouldn't know.' She turned and looked at him. 'I don't even know his last name.'

Adam's eyebrow twitched up in surprise. That was his only reaction, but it was a telling one.

'I know he had light brown hair. Green eyes,' said Kat. 'I know he drove a nice car. And he had money, which was what my mother desperately needed at the time. So . . .' She smiled. 'Here I am. Green eyes and all.'

She expected to see shock, perhaps pity in his gaze, but there was neither. The look he gave her was one of utter neutrality.

'So you see,' she said, 'I'm not exactly to the manner born. Though my mother used to claim she had noble Spanish blood. But then, Mama said a lot of crazy things toward the end.'

'Then she's . . .' He paused delicately.

'Dead. Seven years.'

He tilted up his head, the next question plain in his eyes.

'Mama would say these really bizarre things,'

139

explained Kat. 'And she'd get headaches every morning. I was in my last year of medical school. I was the one who diagnosed the brain tumor.'

Adam shook his head. 'That must have been terrible.'

'It wasn't the diagnosis that was so wrenching. It was the part afterwards. Waiting for the end. I spent a lot of time at Hancock General. Learned to royally despise the place. Found out I couldn't stand being around sick people.' She shook her head and laughed. 'Imagine that.'

'So you chose the morgue.'

'It's quiet. It's contained.'

'A hiding place.'

Anger darted through her, but she suppressed it. After all, what he'd said was true. The morgue *was* a hiding place, from all those painfully sloppy emotions one found in a hospital ward.

She said, simply, 'It suits me,' and turned away. Her gaze settled on the refrigerator. 'You wouldn't happen to have anything edible in there, would you?' she asked. 'The wine's going straight to my head.'

He rose from the couch and went to the refrigerator. 'I usually stock a sandwich or two, for those impromptu lunch meetings. Here we are.' He produced two plastic-wrapped luncheon plates. 'Let's see. Roast beef or . . . roast beef. What a choice.' Apologetically he handed her a plate. 'Afraid it's not quite the mayor's benefit dinner.'

'That's all right. I didn't pay for my ticket anyway.'

He smiled. 'Neither did I.'

'Oh?'

'It was Isabel's ticket. She's a big fan of Mayor Sampson.'

'I can't imagine why.' Kat unwrapped the sandwich and took a bite. 'I think he's Albion's *Titanic*.'

'How so?'

'Just look at South Lexington. Sampson would like to pretend it doesn't exist. He caters entirely to the more suburban areas. Bellemeade and beyond. The inner city? Forget it. He doesn't want to hear about the Jane Does and Nicos Biagis.' She went back to the couch and sat down, tucking her stockinged feet beneath her.

He sat down as well. Not too close, she noted with a mingling of both relief and disappointment, but sedately apart, like any courteous host.

'To be honest,' he admitted, 'I'm not a fan of Sampson's either. But Isabel needed an escort.'

'And you didn't have any better offers for the evening?'

'No.' He picked up a slice of beef, and his straight white teeth bit neatly into the pink meat. 'Not until you turned up.'

Kat set the plate down on the coffee table and

141

slowly wiped her fingers on the napkin. 'You can flatter me all you want,' she said. 'It's not going to change things. I still have a job to do. Questions to be answered.'

'And suspects to be suspicious of.'

'Yes.'

'It doesn't bother me, being a suspect. Because I'm not guilty of anything. Neither is my company.'

'Still, the name Cygnus does keep popping up in all sorts of places.'

'What do you want me to say? Confess that I'm manufacturing some secret drug in the basement? Selling it on the streets for a profit? Or maybe we can come up with a truly diabolical scheme, say, I'm single-handedly trying to solve Albion's crime problem by killing off the junkies. The ultimate drug rehab! And *that's* why I was at the mayor's benefit. Because Sampson's in on it too!' He leaned forward and smiled. 'Come now, Kat,' he said. 'Doesn't that sound the slightest bit ridiculous?'

He did make it sound ridiculous, but she refused to back down. 'I don't discount any possibilities,' she said.

'Even wild and crazy ones?'

'Is it so wild and crazy?'

He was moving closer, but she was too stubborn to give up an inch of territory on the couch. She sat perfectly still, even as his hand reached up to touch her face, even as he stroked her cheek. Even as he leaned forward and pressed his lips against hers.

'Don't,' she said, as the sudden heat of desire flooded her face and roared through her veins. She said again, louder, '*Don't*,' and pressed her hands against his chest.

He pulled away, his gaze searching her face. 'What's wrong?'

'You. Me.' She pushed off the couch and rose to her feet. 'This won't work, Adam.'

'I thought it was working just fine.'

'*You* thought. Did you ask me how I feel about it? Do you even care?'

He gave a sheepish laugh. 'Man, I guess I misjudged *that*.'

'Why are you doing this?'

'I need an excuse for kissing an attractive woman?'

'You're trying to distract me with flattery, aren't you?'

'If you knew me, you wouldn't ask these questions.'

'That's just it. I *don't* know you. Except as a phone number in the hand of a corpse, and that doesn't exactly inspire confidence.'

The phone rang. Reluctantly he broke off eye contact and rose to pick up the receiver. 'Hello, Grace,' he said. A pause, then: 'We're on our way.' He turned to Kat. 'The results are back.'

They found Grace sitting in front of the computer terminal. A readout was just rolling out of the printer. She tore off the page and handed it to Adam. 'There you have it, Mr. Q. A little booze. Traces of decongestant. And that.' She pointed to a band on the chromatographic printout.

'Did you analyze this band?' asked Adam.

'I ran it against mass and UV spectrophotometry. I'm not a hundred percent sure of its structure. It'll take some more noodling around. But I can tell you it's a morphine analogue. Something new. Levo-N-cyclobutylmethyl-6, 10 beta-dihydroxy class.'

Kat looked sharply at Adam. He was staring at the printout in shock.

'Zestron-L,' said Kat.

Grace glanced at her in puzzlement. 'Zestron-L? What's that?'

'Check with the research wing,' said Kat. 'They'll help you run the immunoassay. That should identify it once and for all.'

'You mean *our* research wing?' Grace looked at Adam. 'Then it's . . .'

Adam nodded. 'The drug is one of ours.'

8

Lou Sykes looked blearily across his desk at Kat. He hadn't slept much last night – domestic homicide at 2:00 A.M. – and his normally smooth face was sprouting the bristly beginnings of a new beard.

'It's gone beyond a simple trio of ODs, Lou,' Kat said. 'We're talking corporate theft. An untested drug, out on the streets. And maybe more deaths on the way.'

Ratchet shuffled in, looking just as shaggy as Sykes. He carried with him the definite odor of McDonald's – a sausage and biscuit, which he eagerly unwrapped as he sat down at his desk.

'Hey, Vince,' said Sykes. 'Hear the latest? You'll be just *thrilled*.'

Ratchet took a bite of his breakfast. 'What's new?'

'Novak's got a tox ID on two of our overdoses.'

'So what is it?' asked Ratchet, obviously more interested in his sausage.

'Something called Zestron-L.'

'Never heard of it.'

'Of course you haven't. It's something new they're cooking up at Cygnus. Shouldn't be on the street at all.'

'Somehow,' said Kat, 'it got out of Cygnus. Which means they've had a theft.'

Ratchet shrugged. 'We're Homicide.'

'This *is* homicide. Three dead people, Vince. Now, you don't really want any more bodies, do you? Or are you that desperate for overtime?'

Ratchet looked balefully at Sykes. 'Are we chasing this?'

Sykes leaned back and groaned. 'If only it was nice and neat, you know? A bullet hole, a stab wound.'

'That's neat?'

'At least it's cut and dried. Homicide with a capital H. But this is spinning our wheels. Folks who OD, it's a risk they take, sticking a needle in their veins. I don't really care where they get the stuff.'

'Would you care if it was strychnine they were shooting up?'

'That's different.'

'No, it isn't. In large doses, Zestron-L is every bit as deadly. How do you know we haven't got some right-wing fanatic out there, some nut trying to clear the junkies off the streets? And by the way, he's doing a good job.'

Sykes sighed. 'I hate that about you, Novak.'

'What?'

'Your unassailable logic. It isn't feminine.' He hauled himself out of his chair. 'Okay. Let me arrange for us to duck out a couple of hours. We'll head over to Cygnus.'

'Man, oh, man,' grumbled Ratchet, after Sykes had left the room. 'I should've stayed home in bed.'

The smell of Ratchet's sandwich was making Kat's stomach turn. She shifted in her chair and glanced down at Sykes' desk. A reed-thin black woman and two kids smiled at her from a framed photo. Lou's family? She forgot sometimes that cops *had* families and homes and mortgage payments. Another photo stood beside it: Sykes and another man, grinning like two hucksters on the steps of the Albion PD.

'Was this Lou's partner?' asked Kat. 'The one who got hit in South Lexington?'

Ratchet nodded. 'Sitting in a marked car, can you believe it? Some guy drives by and just starts shooting. From what I hear, he and Lou, they were like *this*.' He pressed two fingers together. 'We lost two down there, the same corner. Bad luck spot. Got a lot of bad luck spots in this town. Bolton and Swarthmore, that's another one. That's where my partner went down. Drug bust went sour, and he got boxed in a blind alley.' He put the sandwich down, as though he'd suddenly lost his appetite. 'And we lost one down on Dorchester, just last month. One of our girls, a five-year vet. Perp got hold of her gun, turned it on her . . .' He shook his head mournfully and began to gather up all the sandwich wrappings.

That must be how every cop sees this town, Kat realized. An Albion policeman looks at a map of the city and he sees more than just street names and addresses. He sees the corner where a partner got shot, the alley where a drug deal went bad, the street where an ambulance crew knelt in the rain trying to save a child. For a cop, a city map is a grid of bad memories.

Sykes came back into the room. 'Okay, Vince,' he said. 'Things are quiet for the moment. Might as well do it now.'

Kat rose. 'I'll meet you there.'

Ratchet fished his cell phone out of the drawer and clipped it to his belt. 'We going to Cygnus?' he asked.

'No choice,' said Sykes. 'Seeing as Novak here isn't going to let it drop.'

'I'm just asking you to do your job, Lou,' she said.

'Job, hell. I'm doing you a favor.'

'You're doing the city a favor.'

'Albion?' Sykes laughed and pulled on his jacket. 'The junkies are killing themselves off. Far as I'm concerned, the biggest favor I could do Albion is to look the other way.'

*   *   *

'It's a secured area,' said Adam. 'Only our cleared personnel are allowed in this wing.' He punched a keypad by the door, and the words *passcode accepted* flashed onto the screen. Adam swung the door open and motioned for his visitors to enter.

Ratchet and Sykes went in first, then Kat. As she passed Adam, he reached out and gave her arm a squeeze. The unexpected intimacy of that contact and the whiff of his after-shave made her stomach dance a jig of excitement. He had seemed all business when he'd greeted them, so sober in his gray suit. Now, seeing that look in his eye, she knew the spell was still alive between them.

'I'm glad you came,' he murmured. 'How did you manage?'

'Wheelock's covering for me. I took the day off. Told him I had to buy a new car.'

'Why not the truth?'

'He'd prefer I dropped this case. So would they.' She nodded toward Sykes and Ratchet, who were peering curiously at a blinking computer screen. 'I think I'm being conscientious. They think I'm a pain in the ass.'

They all moved to a door marked *Area 8*.

'This is where Zestron-L's being developed,' said Adam, leading them inside.

Kat's first impression was that she'd stepped through a time portal into a future world of black and white and chrome. Even the man who hurried to greet them did not violate that color scheme. His coat was a pristine white, his hair jet black. 'Dr. Herbert Esterhaus, project supervisor,' he said, reaching out to shake their hands. 'I'm in charge of Zestron-L development.'

'And this is the area you manage?' asked Sykes, glancing about the lab where half a dozen workers manned the various stations.

'Yes. The project's confined to this section – the room you see here and the adjoining three rooms. The only access is through that door you entered, plus an emergency exit, through the animal lab. And that's wired to an alarm.'

'Only authorized personnel are allowed in?'

'That's right. Just our staff. I really don't see how any Zestron could have gotten out.'

'Obviously it walked out,' said Sykes. 'In some-one's pocket.'

Dr. Esterhaus glanced at Adam. There was a lot said in that glance, Kat thought. An unspoken question. Only now did she realize how skittery Esterhaus seemed, his bony fingers rubbing together, his rodent eyes noting Sykes' and Ratchet's every move.

'How well do you people screen your personnel?' asked Ratchet.

'When we hire someone,' said Adam, 'we're

interested in scientific credentials. And talent. We don't do polygraphs or credit checks. We like to assume our people are honest.'

'Maybe you assumed wrong,' said Sykes.

'Everyone in this project is a long-term employee,' said Adam. 'Isn't that right, Herb?'

Esterhaus nodded. 'I've been here six years. Most of the employees' – he gestured to the workers in white coats – 'have been with Cygnus even longer.'

'Any exceptions?' asked Ratchet.

Esterhaus paused and glanced at Adam. Again, that nervous look, that silent question.

'There was my stepdaughter, Maeve,' Adam finished for him.

Sykes and Ratchet exchanged looks. 'She worked in *this* department?' asked Sykes.

'Just cleanup,' said Esterhaus quickly. 'I mean, Maeve wasn't really qualified to do anything else. But she did an acceptable job.'

'Why did she leave?'

'We had some . . . disagreements,' said Esterhaus.

'What disagreements?' pressed Sykes.

'She . . . started coming in late. And she didn't always dress appropriately. I mean, I didn't mind the green hair and all, but all the dangly jewelry, it's not really safe around this equipment.'

Kat looked around at the two-tone room and tried to imagine what a splash of color Maeve Quantrell would have made. All these white-coated scientists must have thought her some wild and exotic creature, to be tolerated only because she was the boss's daughter.

'So what?' said Sykes. 'You fired her?'

'Yes,' said Esterhaus, looking very unhappy. 'I discussed it with Mr. Quantrell and he agreed that I should do whatever was necessary.'

'Why was she coming in late?' asked Kat.

They all looked at her in puzzlement. 'What?' asked Esterhaus.

'That bothers me. The *why*. She was doing her job, and then she wasn't. When did it start?'

'Six months ago,' said Esterhaus.

'So six months ago, she starts coming in late, or not at all. What changed?' She looked at Adam.

He shook his head. 'She was living on her own. I don't know what was going on with her.'

'Strung out?' asked Sykes.

'Not that I was aware of,' said Esterhaus.

'She was angry, that's what it was,' said a voice. It was one of the researchers, a woman sitting at a nearby computer terminal. 'I was here the day you two had that fight, remember, Herb? Maeve was angry. Furious, really. Said she wasn't going to take your . . . bullshit any longer, and then she stomped out.' The woman shook her head. 'No control, that girl. Very impulsive.'

'Thank you, Rose, for the information,' Esterhaus

said tightly. He motioned them towards the next room. 'I'll show you the rest of the lab.'

The tour continued, into the animal lab with its cages of barking dogs. The emergency exit was at the rear, and on the door was the sign: *Alarm will sound if opened.*

'So you see,' said Esterhaus, 'there's no way someone can just walk in and steal anything.'

'But somehow the drug got out,' said Sykes.

'There's one other possibility,' said Esterhaus. 'There could have been simultaneous development. Another lab somewhere, working on the same thing. For someone to steal *our* drug, they'd have to break into Cygnus, through a secured door. They'd have to know our access codes.'

'Which all your employees know,' said Sykes.

'Well, yes.'

'One question,' said Ratchet, who'd been jotting things in his notebook. 'Have you changed the access code lately?'

'Not in the last year.'

'So anyone employed here during the last year – say, Maeve, for instance – would know the code,' said Sykes.

Esterhaus shook his head. 'She wouldn't do it! She was difficult, yes, and maybe a little out of control. But she wasn't a thief. For heaven's sake, it's her father's company!'

'It was only an example,' said Sykes calmly.

Again, Esterhaus glanced at Adam. Suddenly Kat understood the looks that had flown between the two. They were both trying to cover for Maeve.

'Come on,' said Adam, smoothly redirecting their attention. 'We'll show you where the drug's stored.'

Esterhaus led them into a side room. One wall was taken up by a refrigeration unit. 'It's not really necessary to store it in here,' he said, opening the refrigerator door. 'The crystals are stable at room temperature. But we keep it in here as a precaution.' He pulled out a tray; glass vials tinkled together like crystal. Gingerly he removed a vial and handed it to Kat. 'That's it,' he said. 'Zestron-L.'

She raised the vial and studied it in wonder. Rose-pink crystals sparkled like tiny gemstones in the light. She turned the vial on its side and watched the contents tumble about, glittering. 'It's beautiful,' she murmured.

'That's just the crystalline form, of course, for storage,' said Esterhaus. 'What you're looking at is almost pure. It's injected in solution form. The crystals are dissolved in an alcohol and water solvent over heat. A little goes a long way.'

'How far *does* it go?'

'One of those crystals, just one, is enough to make, say, fifty therapeutic doses.'

'*Fifty?*' said Sykes.

'That's right. One crystal diluted in 50cc of solvent will make fifty doses.'

Ratchet was busy studying the catch on the re-frigerator door. 'This thing isn't locked,' he said.

'No. Nothing here's locked. I told you, we trust our employees.'

'What about inventory control?' said Sykes. 'You keep track of all those vials?'

'They're numbered, see? So we'd know if any vials were missing.'

'But is there some way the drug could still get out? Without you knowing?'

Esterhaus paused. 'I suppose, if someone were smart about it . . .'

'Yeah?' prompted Sykes.

'One could take a crystal or two. From each vial. And we might not notice the difference.'

There was a pause as they all considered the impli-cations. In that silence, the sudden ringing of a cell phone seemed all the more startling. Both cops auto-matically glanced down at their belts.

'It's mine. Excuse me,' said Sykes, and he retreated a few paces away to take the call.

'Well,' said Ratchet. 'I'm not sure there's much more we can do here. I mean, if two different labs can come up with the same stuff . . .'

'The odds are against simultaneous development,' said Adam. 'Zestron-L isn't something you just cook

155

up in your basement. It took us years to get this far, and it's still not ready for the market.'

'But Dr. Esterhaus says another lab *could* do it.'

'Cygnus is the only lab around here with the facilities.'

'You'd be surprised,' said Ratchet, 'what the mob can finance.' He closed his notebook. 'Let me be honest. We're not gonna have much luck here.'

'You could polygraph the staff,' said Kat. 'That would be a start.'

'It would also be an insult,' said Esterhaus. 'To every single one of them.'

'I don't see that you have a choice,' said Kat.

Adam shook his head. 'I hate to do it.'

'It'd probably be inconclusive, anyway,' said Ratchet. 'They'll all be nervous, upset. Chances are, you won't be able to pinpoint a leak, not this late in the game.'

'What about South Lexington?' said Kat. 'Check out the receiving end, Vince. Find out who's distributing it on the outside. Question the victims' families and friends. They might know the source.'

'Yeah. We could do that.' He turned as Sykes came back.

'Let's go, Vince,' said Sykes. 'We're done here.'

'Aren't you going to question anyone?' asked Kat.

'Later.' Sykes shook hands with Adam and Esterhaus, then he and Ratchet headed for the exit.

'Something's going on,' muttered Kat, watching them leave. 'Excuse me.'

She followed the two cops outside, into the parking lot. 'Hey! Lou!' she called.

Sykes turned to her with a look of weariness. 'What, Novak?'

'Why the abrupt exit?'

'Because I've got my ass to protect, okay? I also got a chief who's bitching about my wasting departmental time on this case.'

'That was a call from your chief?'

'Yeah. He wanted to know why I'm out saving the world's junkies when we've got murderers cruising the suburbs. And you know what? I couldn't think of a single good answer.' Sykes yanked open his car door. 'Let's go, Vince.'

'Wait. Who told the chief about it?'

'I didn't ask,' he snapped.

'But *someone* must have told him.'

Sykes got into the car and slammed the door. 'All I know is, I got orders from above. And we're out of here.' He looked at Ratchet and barked, '*Drive*.'

The car took off, leaving Kat standing alone in the parking lot.

I got orders. Whose orders? she wondered. Who had called the chief and told him to pull Sykes and Ratchet away? The mayor's office? Ed?

Suddenly she turned and gazed up at the letters

157

CYGNUS mounted on the building. It was a possibility she didn't want to consider, but it was staring her in the face.

If anyone had a reason to halt the investigation, it was him. The man whose company would suffer. The man whose name would be dragged through the mud. The man she'd seen dining and shmoozing at the mayor's benefit.

Where on earth did you park your brains, Novak?

She turned from the building and headed to her car.

It was hard for Kat to give up the Mercedes, but she had her principles to uphold. She didn't want to owe Adam Quantrell a thing, not a single damn thing.

She turned in the Mercedes at Regis Rentals and paid the bill herself. Then she walked around the corner to Lester's Used Cars.

She drove out in a Ford – five years old, with a few rust spots on the fender. It smelled a little stale, and there was a rip in the back seat, but the engine ran fine and the price was right.

And she didn't feel guilty driving it.

From there, she headed straight to City Hall.

She tried getting in to see Mayor Sampson, but there was no chance they'd let her in – not after that scene in his office a day earlier. So she went instead to the DA's office. She found her ex-husband at his desk. He kept his workspace neat, every paper in its place, every pen and paper clip relegated to the proper slot. Ed himself looked immaculate as always, not a crease in his hundred-percent-cotton shirt. She wondered how she'd stood being married to the man for two years.

He looked up in surprise as she came in. 'Kat! Is this a social visit?'

'Who whispered in the police chief's ear?' she asked.

'Ah. Not a social visit.'

'Was it Sampson?'

'What are you referring to?'

'You know *what*.' She leaned across his desk. 'Lieutenant Sykes was told to lay off Cygnus. Who gave the order? Sampson? You?'

He sat back and smiled innocently. 'Wasn't me. Cross my heart.'

'Sampson?'

'No comment. But you know the pressure he's under. The police start digging around, it turns into a media event. We don't need that kind of publicity, not now.'

'Did Quantrell have anything to do with it?'

'What?'

'Did he ask Sampson to call off the cops?'

Ed looked perplexed. 'Why would he? Look, I don't know why you're getting worked up about this. Or are you back with the old underdog crusade?'

'I was never on any crusade.'

'Sure you were. Hell, you think it was easy for me, living with you? Putting up with that attitude of yours? I don't recall taking a vow of poverty when I married you. But I'd buy a BMW or . . . or join a racquetball club, and you'd wince.'

She looked at him in mock horror. 'I *didn't*.'

'You did. And here you are, still at it. Kat, no one *gives* a damn about junkies. We have *tourists* getting mugged out there! Nice tourists, from nice places. *Those* are the people we should be protecting. Not the trash out on South Lexington.'

'Oh, Ed.' She shook her head and laughed. 'Ed, I have to say that, until this very minute, I *never* realized.'

'What didn't you realize?'

'What a kind and sensitive bastard you are.'

'There's that attitude problem again.'

'Not an attitude, Ed. A principle.' She turned for the door. 'Maybe you'd recognize it. If you had one of your own.'

Seconds after his ex-wife left the room, Ed Novak picked up the telephone and dialed the mayor's office. 'She was just here,' he said. 'And I don't think she's too happy.'

'You don't think she'll go to the newspapers, do you?' asked Sampson.

'If she does, we'll just have to stonewall them with *no comments*. Or deny there's a crisis.'

'That's the strategy we take. Make her look like a loose cannon. In the meantime, *do* something about her, will you? She's getting to be a pain in the ass.'

'I'll be honest, Mayor,' said Ed with a tired sigh. 'She always was.'

All afternoon, Adam waited for Kat to call. A nice meal to hash things out between them – that's what they needed. He was optimistic enough to make dinner reservations for two at Yen King. There he could make it clear that he was on her side, and that he intended to see more of her. But as the day wore on toward five o'clock, there was still no phone call.

When finally a call *did* come in, it wasn't from Kat. It was from his butler, Thomas.

'Dr. Novak returned the Mercedes,' said Thomas. 'I've just spoken with Regis Motors.'

'Yes, she said she was going to buy a car today.'

'The reason I'm calling, Mr. Q., is to tell you she paid for the Mercedes rental. The entire bill.'

'But the bill was supposed to be sent to me.'

'Precisely. And they explained it to her. But she insisted on paying it herself.'

'They should have refused her payment.'

'The staff at Regis tell me it was quite impossible to change her mind.'

161

What was going on with that woman? Adam wondered as he hung up. Just last night, she'd seemed pleased about the car. There had been no question that the rental was his gift. Why her sudden insistence on paying the bill?

At five-thirty, he left Cygnus and drove north. The Bellemeade turnoff was right on his way home; he decided to pass by Kat's house, on the off-chance he could catch her.

There was no car in the driveway, no answer to his knock on the door. He got back into his car and decided to wait.

Twenty minutes later he was about to give up and go home when he spotted a gray Ford coming around the corner. Kat was behind the wheel. She pulled into the driveway.

At once he was out of his car and moving toward her. She stepped out, holding a bag with *Hop Sing Take-out* printed on the side.

'Kat!' he said. 'I tried calling you—'

'I've been out all day.' Her tone was matter-of-fact and none too warm. She started toward her front door with Adam right behind her.

'Why don't we go out for some *good* Chinese food?'

'I happen to *like* Hop Sing,' she snapped, stepping through the door.

Determined not to be shut out, he followed her

inside, into the kitchen. 'I don't understand what's happened—'

'I understand perfectly, Adam. If Cygnus were my company, I'd block the investigation, too.'

He shook his head. 'I didn't block any investigation.'

'I mean, think of the PR disaster. The headlines. *Cygnus manufactures killer drug.*'

'You think I'd go that far to protect Cygnus?'

'Haven't you?' She set the take-out bag on the counter and began to unload the contents. 'Look, I'm starving. I'd like to eat this before it gets – oh, *damn.*'

'What?'

'I left the fried rice in the car.' She spun around and headed back out the front door.

He was right on her heels, following her across the lawn. 'Come on, let's go out.'

'No, thanks.' She reached into the car and retrieved the second take-out bag. 'Tonight, I'm a solo act. Dinner. A hot bath. And absolutely *no* excitement of any kind.' She turned away from the car.

A deafening blast shook the house. She felt the sting of flying glass as she was hurled backward by the violent pulse of the explosion. She landed on her back, in the grass. Chunks of wood, flakes of asphalt tile rained down on her.

Then, like a gentle snowfall, a cloud of dust settled slowly from the sky.

9

Kat was too stunned to make sense of what had happened; she could only lie on her back in the grass and stare dazedly at the sky. Then, gradually, she became aware that someone was calling her name, that someone was brushing the hair from her eyes, stroking her face.

'Kat. Look at me. I'm right here. *Look at me.*'

Slowly, she focused on Adam. He was gazing down at her, undisguised panic in his eyes. He was afraid, she thought in wonder. Why?

'Kat!' he yelled. 'Come on, *say something.*'

She tried to speak and found all she could manage was a whisper. 'Adam?'

Through her confusion, she heard the sounds of running footsteps, shouting voices, calls of 'Is she okay?'

'What happened?' she asked.

'Don't move. There's an ambulance coming—'

'*What happened?*' She struggled to sit up. The sudden movement made the world lurch around her. She caught a spinning view of bystanders' faces, of debris littering the lawn. Then she saw what was left of her house. With that glimpse, everything froze into terrible focus.

The front wall had been ripped away entirely, and the inner walls stood exposed, like an open dollhouse. Shreds of fabric, couch batting, splintered furniture had been tossed as far as the driveway. Just overhead, an empty picture frame swung forlornly from a tree branch.

'Jesus, lady,' murmured someone in the crowd. 'Did you leave your gas on or something?'

'My house,' whispered Kat. In rising fury she staggered to her feet. 'What did they do to *my house?*'

Then, as if there hadn't been enough destruction, the first flicker of fire appeared. Flames were spreading from what used to be the kitchen.

'Back!' shouted Adam. 'Everyone back!'

'*No!*' Kat struggled forward. If she could turn on the garden hose, if the pipes were still intact, she could save what little she had left. 'Let me go!' she yelled, shoving at Adam. 'It's going to burn!'

She managed only two steps before he grabbed her and hauled her back. Enraged, she struggled against him, but he trapped her arms and swung her up and away from the house.

'It's going to burn!' she cried.

'You can't save it, Kat! There's a gas leak!'

The flames suddenly shot higher, licking at the collapsing roof. Already the fire had spread to the living room, had ignited the remains of her furniture. Smoke swirled, thick and black, driving the crowd back across the street.

'My house,' Kat sobbed, swaying against Adam.

He pulled her against him and wrapped his arms tightly around her as though to shield her from the sight and sounds of destruction. As the first fire trucks pulled up with sirens screaming, she was still clinging to him, her face pressed against his shirt. The roar of the flames, the shouts of firemen, seemed to recede into some other, distant dimension. Her reality, the only one that mattered, was the steady thump of Adam's heart.

Only when he gently released her and murmured something in her ear was she wrenched unwillingly back into the real world. She found two uniformed men gazing at her. One was a cop, the other had an Albion Fire Department patch on his jacket.

'What happened?' asked the cop.

She shook her head. 'I don't know.'

'She'd just gotten home,' said Adam. 'We went inside, came back out again for a minute. That's when the house blew up. She caught the worst of it. I was standing behind her—'

'Did you smell gas?'

'No.' Adam shook his head firmly. 'No gas.'

'You're sure?'

'Absolutely. The fire started after the explosion.'

The cop and fireman looked at each other, a glance that Kat found terrifying in its significance.

She said, 'It was a bomb. Wasn't it?'

They didn't say a word. They didn't have to. Their silence was answer enough.

It was after midnight when they finally pulled into Adam's driveway. They'd spent two hours in the ER getting their cuts and bruises tended to, two more hours in the Bellemeade police station, answering questions. Now they were both on the far side of exhausted. They barely managed to stumble out of the car and up the front steps.

Thomas was waiting at the door to greet them. 'Mr. Q.!' he gasped, staring in horror at Adam's torn suit. 'Not *another* brawl?'

'No. Just a bomb this time.' He raised his hand to cut off Thomas's questions. 'I'll tell you all about it in the morning. In the meantime, let's get Dr. Novak to bed. She's staying the night.'

Thomas nodded, utterly unruffled. 'I'll prepare the guest room,' he said, and went up ahead of them.

Slowly Adam guided Kat up the stairs. Her body felt so small, so fragile, as he helped her up the last step, and down the corridor. By the time they reached the south guest room, Thomas had already turned down the covers, placed fresh towels on the dresser, and closed the drapes. 'I'll see to your room now, Mr. Q.,' he said, and discreetly withdrew.

'Come. Into bed with you,' said Adam. He sat her on the covers, knelt down to take off her shoes.

'I'm such a mess,' she murmured, staring down at her clothes.

'We'll clean these in the morning. Right now, you need some sleep. Can I help you off with your clothes?'

She looked up at him with a faint expression of amusement.

He smiled. 'Believe me, my intentions are purely honorable.'

'Nevertheless,' she said, 'I think I'll manage on my own.'

Adam sat down beside her on the bed. 'It's gone too far,' he said. 'Doing your job is one thing, Kat. And I admire your persistence, I really do. But now it's turned ugly. This time you were fortunate. But next time . . .' He stopped, unwilling to finish the thought.

But it didn't matter. Kat had already fallen asleep.

* * *

She was still asleep when Adam looked in the next morning.

Quietly he sat down in the chair beside her. Sunlight winked through the curtains, the beams dancing around the walls and the polished furniture. He'd forgotten how charming this guest room could be, how lovely it looked in the morning light. Or perhaps it never *had* been this lovely before; perhaps, with this woman sleeping beside him, he was seeing the room's charm for the very first time.

There was a knock on the door. He turned to see Thomas poke his head in.

'I thought perhaps she would like some breakfast,' whispered Thomas, nodding at the tray of food he was carrying.

'I think what she'd really like,' said Adam, rising to his feet, 'is to be allowed to sleep.' He followed Thomas into the hall and softly closed the door behind him. 'Did you collect her clothes?'

'I'm afraid they're quite beyond repair,' Thomas said with a sigh.

'Then would you arrange to have some things sent up to the house? She'll probably need her entire wardrobe replaced. I doubt anything survived the fire.'

Thomas nodded. 'I'll put a call in to Neiman-Marcus. A size six, don't you think?'

With sudden clarity, Adam remembered how

slender she'd felt against him last night, climbing the steps to the guest room. 'Yes,' he said. 'A six sounds about right.'

Downstairs, Adam lounged about the dining room, sipping coffee, picking at his breakfast without much appetite. He listened with amusement as Thomas made phone calls in the next room. A complete wardrobe, Thomas said. Yes, undergarments as well. What cup size? Well, how should *he* know? Thomas hung up, and came into the dining room, looking distressed. 'I'm having a problem with, er . . . dimensions.'

Adam laughed. 'I think we're both out of our depth, Thomas. Why don't we wait until Dr. Novak wakes up?'

Thomas looked relieved. 'An excellent idea.'

They heard the sound of tires rolling over gravel. Adam glanced through the window and saw a blue Chevy pull up in the driveway. 'Must be Lieutenant Sykes,' he said. 'I'll let him in.'

He was surprised to find both Sykes and Ratchet waiting at the front door. Apparently they came as a matched set, even on Saturdays. They were even similarly dressed in strictly nonregulation golf shirts and sneakers.

'Morning, Mr. Q.,' said Sykes, pulling off his sunglasses. He held up a briefcase. 'I got what you wanted.'

'Come in, please. There's coffee and breakfast, if you'd like.'

Ratchet grinned. 'Sounds great.'

The three men sat down at the dining table. Thomas brought out cups, saucers, a fresh pot of coffee. Ratchet tucked a napkin in his shirt and began to adorn a bagel with cream cheese. Not just a dab here and there, but giant slabs of it, topped with multiple layers of lox. Sykes took only coffee, heavily sugared – a favorite energy source, he said, from his patrolman days.

'So what do you have?' asked Adam.

Sykes took several files from the briefcase and laid them on the table. 'The files you asked for. Oh, and about the explosion last night—'

'Not a gas leak?'

'Definitely not a gas leak. Demolitions went over what was left of the house,' said Sykes. 'It appears there was a pull-friction fuse igniter, set off when the front door opened. The igniter gets pulled through a flash compound, lighting a sixty-second length of fuse. That in turn leads to a blasting cap. And a rather impressive amount of TNT.'

Adam frowned. 'A sixty-second fuse? Then that explains why it didn't go off right away.'

Sykes nodded. 'A delay detonator. Designed to blow up *after* the victim is in the house.'

'They aren't fooling around. Whoever they are,' Ratchet added, around a mouthful of bagel.

Adam sat back, stunned by this new information. Until now he'd hoped for some simple explanation. A faulty furnace, perhaps; a natural gas leak whose odor he hadn't detected. But here was incontrovertible evidence: Someone wanted Kat dead. And they were going to extraordinary lengths to achieve that goal.

He was so shocked by the revelation that he didn't realize Kat had come down into the dining room. Then he looked up and saw her. She seemed swallowed up in one of his old bathrobes, the flaps cinched together at the waist. She glanced around the table at Sykes and Ratchet.

'You heard what Lou said?' asked Adam.

She nodded. Then she took a deep breath. 'So I guess it's time to face the facts. Someone's really trying to kill me.'

After a silence, Adam said, 'It does appear that way.'

Hugging her arms to her chest, Kat began to move slowly around the room, thinking as she paced. She stopped by the window and gazed out at the sun-washed lawn and trees.

'Believe me, Kat,' said Sykes. 'Bellemeade Precinct's got all cylinders going on this. I've spoken with the detectives. They're checking all the possibilities—'

'Are they really?' she asked softly.

'There are a lot of angles to consider. Maybe it's someone you gave expert testimony against in court.

Or an ex-boyfriend. Hell, they're even questioning Ed.'

'Ed?' She laughed, a wild, desperate sound. 'Ed can't even program a VCR. Much less wire a bomb.'

'Okay, so it's probably not Ed. Not him personally, anyway. But he has been questioned.'

She turned to look at Sykes. 'Then everyone agrees. It's a bona fide murder attempt.'

'No doubt about it. It only takes one look at your house. Or what used to be your house.'

She looked out again, at the trees. 'It's because of them.'

'Who?'

'Nicos Biagi. Jane Doe. It's because of what's happening in the Projects.'

'You could have other enemies,' said Sykes. 'And you lost your purse, remember? One of those punks could've gotten into your house—'

'And set a sixty-second delay detonator?' She shook her head. 'I suppose they picked up a case of TNT at the corner grocery store. Lou, they were *kids*. I grew up with kids just like them! They wouldn't mess around with flash compounds or blasting caps. And what's their motive?'

'I don't know.' Sykes sighed in exasperation. 'They did rough you up—'

'But they didn't kill us! They had the chance, but they didn't.'

Adam looked at Sykes. 'She's right, Lieutenant. Those kids wouldn't know about fuse igniters. This bomb sounds like a sophisticated device. Built by someone who knew what he was doing.'

'A professional,' said Ratchet.

The word was enough to make Kat blanch. Adam saw her chin jerk up, saw the tightening of her lips. She was frightened, all right. She should be. In silence she moved to the table and sat down across from him. The bathrobe gaped open a little; only then did he realize she was naked beneath that terrycloth. How defenseless she looked, he thought. Stripped of everything. Even her clothes.

And at that moment, defenseless was exactly how Kat felt.

She sat hugging the robe to her breasts, her gaze fixed on the tabletop. She heard Sykes and Ratchet rise to leave; dimly she registered their goodbyes, their departing footsteps. Then there came the thud of the front door closing behind them. Closed doors. That's what she saw when she tried to look into the future. Closed doors, hidden dangers.

Once, life had seemed comfortably predictable. Drive to work every morning, drive home every night. A vacation twice a year, a date once in a blue moon. A steady move up the ranks until she'd assume Davis Wheelock's title of Chief ME. A sure thing, he'd told her once.

Now she was reminded that there were no sure things. Not her future. Not even her life.

'You're not alone, Kat,' said Adam.

She looked up and met his gaze across the tabletop.

'Anything you need,' he said. 'Anything at all—'

'Thanks,' she said with a smile. 'But I'm not big on accepting charity.'

'That's not what I meant. I don't think of you as some charity case.'

'But that's exactly what I am at the moment.' She rose and began to pace. 'Some sort of – of homeless person! Camping out in your guest bedroom.'

To her surprise, he suddenly laughed. 'To be perfectly honest,' he admitted, 'you *do* look a little threadbare this morning. Where did you find that bathrobe, by the way?'

She glanced down at the frayed terrycloth and suddenly she had to laugh as well. 'Your linen closet. I had to wear something, and I figured it was either this or a towel. Where are my clothes, by the way?'

'A lost cause. Thomas had to throw them out.'

'He threw out my clothes?'

'Some new things are being delivered.'

She caught his amused downward glance, and realized the robe had sagged open again. Irritably she yanked the edges back together.

She sat down and noticed the stack of papers on the table. 'What's all this?'

'Lieutenant Sykes dropped it off. They're police files. Or, rather, photocopies of files.'

'He *gave* them to you? That's highly irregular.'

'It's also just between us. He and I have what you might call a mutual back-scratching arrangement.'

'Oh. So what's in the files?'

Adam picked up the top folder. 'I have here Nicos Biagi. And Xenia Vargas. And Jane Doe.' He looked up at her, almost apologetically. 'I'll be honest with you, Kat. I didn't ask for these files on your behalf, but on mine. For Cygnus. I can't argue away the facts. That *is* my drug out there, killing people. I want to know how they got it.'

She focused on the top file. 'Let's see what's in there.'

He opened Nicos Biagi's folder. 'Names and addresses. His family might know where he bought the drug.'

'They won't talk. Even Sykes couldn't get it out of them.'

'Does that surprise you? They probably smelled *cop* a mile away. So I'm going to ask them.'

'I wonder what odor they'll pin on *you*.'

'The smell of money? It's very persuasive.'

'Adam, you can't walk into the Projects with a bulging wallet!'

'Can you think of a better incentive?'

'You go in there without protection, and they'll have you for an appetizer.'

'Then how am I supposed to *reach* these people?' he asked, pointing to the folders. 'I went through a half-dozen private detectives, trying to trace Maeve. So I don't have a lot of confidence in so-called professionals. I know that some friend of Nicos, or of Xenia Vargas, has to know the answers. You're the one who said it, Kat. If we can't pinpoint how the drug's getting out of Cygnus, perhaps we can figure out whom it's going to. And how he's getting it.'

'Are you sure you really want to find out?' she asked. 'What if the answer turns out to be a nasty surprise?'

'You're referring to Maeve?'

'Her name did cross my mind.'

He sighed. 'It's something I'll . . . have to face.'

'That's why you're doing this yourself, isn't it? Why you don't just hire a PI to do the legwork. You're afraid of what some outsider will find out about your daughter.'

He looked away. 'You know, I used to think I could protect her. Pull her off the streets and put her in some sort of program. But it's not going to happen. She refuses to be helped. And in the meantime, people are dying, and I don't know if she's the one responsible . . .'

'You can't protect her, Adam. One of these days, she'll have to face the music.'

'Don't you think I know that?' He shook his head in frustration. 'All these years, that's exactly what I've been doing! Protecting her, bailing her out. Paying her bills when she bounced her checks. Booking her appointments with therapists. I kept thinking, if she just had enough attention, if I could just do the right thing – whatever that was – that somehow she'd pull out of it. She wouldn't end up like Georgina.'

Georgina. She thought of the name she'd seen, inscribed on the plaque in Hancock General. *The Georgina Quantrell Wing.*

She asked, gently, 'How did your wife die?'

He was silent for so long, she thought perhaps he hadn't heard the question. 'She died of a lot of things,' he said at last. 'The official diagnosis was liver cirrhosis. But the illness really went back to her childhood. A father addicted to martinis and work. A mother addicted to pills and cigarettes. Georgina looked for comfort wherever she could find it. By the time we met, she'd already been through two husbands and Lord knows how many bottles of gin. I was twenty-four at the time. All I saw was this – this absolutely stunning woman with an adorable daughter. Georgina was adept at covering up. If she had to, she could go off the bottle for weeks at a time, and that's what she did before the wedding. But after we got back from the honeymoon, I noticed she was having a few too many highballs, a few too many glasses of wine. Then Thomas found the stash of bottles in the closet. And that's when I realized how far it had gone . . .' He shook his head and sighed. 'Fourteen years later, she was dead. And I'm still trying to deal with the aftermath. Namely, Maeve.'

'You stayed married to her through all that?'

'I felt I didn't have a choice. But then, neither did she. Self-destruction was in her genes, and she didn't have the will to fight. She just wasn't strong enough.' He paused, and added quietly, 'Unlike you.'

He looked at her then, and she found her gaze trapped in the blue-gray spell of his eyes. They reached out to each other across the table and their fingers touched, twined together. They held on, even through the ringing of the doorbell and the sound of Thomas's footsteps crossing the foyer to answer it.

Only the polite clearing of a throat made them finally look up. Thomas was standing in the doorway. 'Mr. Q.?' he said. 'The wardrobe consultant is here from Neiman-Marcus. I thought perhaps Dr. Novak would like to look over the selections.'

'*Wardrobe* consultant?' said Kat in surprise. 'But all I really need right now is a pair of jeans and a change of underwear.'

'You needn't take the consultant's advice,' said Thomas. 'Although . . .' He glanced at her bathrobe.

'I'm certain she'll have a number of, er, *helpful* suggestions.'

Kat laughed and pushed back from the table. 'Bring her on, then. I guess I need to wear something.'

'When you've made your selections, Dr. Novak,' said Thomas, 'just leave the bathrobe with me. I'll see that it's properly taken care of.'

'Whatever you say,' said Kat.

'Very good,' said Thomas and he turned to leave. As he walked out of the room, he muttered with undisguised glee, 'Because I'm going to burn it.'

Protection was what they needed in South Lexington. And when it came to hostile territory, Kat decided, the best to be had was from the natives. So it was to Papa Earl's apartment they went first, to have a talk with his grandson, Anthony. The boy might not hold any real power in the Projects, but he'd know how to reach those who did.

They found him slouched in his undershirt, watching *Days of Our Lives* in the living room.

'Anthony,' said Papa Earl. 'Katrina wants to talk to you.'

Anthony raised the remote control and changed the channel to *Jeopardy*.

'You listening, boy?' barked Papa Earl.

'*What?*'

'Katrina and her friend, they come to see *you*.'

Kat moved in front of the TV, deliberately blocking Anthony's view. He looked up at her with sullen dark eyes. It was heartbreaking to see how little was left of the child she used to babysit. In his place was a tinderbox of rage.

'We want to ask the big man a favor,' said Kat.

'What big man you talking about?'

'We're willing to pay up front. Safe passage, that's all we ask. And maybe a friend or two to watch our backs. No cops involved, we swear it.'

'What you want safe passage for?'

'Just to talk to some people. About Nicos and Xenia.' She paused and added, 'And you can tell Maeve we're not after her.'

Anthony twitched and looked away. So he was the one who had warned her, she decided. 'How much?' he asked.

'A hundred.'

'And how much does the big man get?'

The kid was sharp. 'Another hundred.'

Anthony thought about it a moment. Then he said, 'Move outta the way.' Kat stepped aside. He pointed the remote control and switched off the TV. 'Wait here,' he said. He stood up and walked out of the apartment.

'What do you think?' asked Adam.

'He's either going to come back with our body-guards,' said Kat, 'or a hit squad.'

'Don't know what I'm gonna do 'bout that boy,' said Papa Earl. 'I just don't know.'

Ten minutes passed. They all sat in the kitchen, where Bella banged pots and pans on the stove. The smell of old cooking grease, of frying sausages and simmering pinto beans, was almost enough to drive them out. Those smells brought back too many memories for Kat, of stifling summer evenings when the smells from her mother's stove would kill whatever appetite she had, when the heat from the kitchen seemed to suck the air out of every room. Now, as she watched young Bella, she saw the ghost of her own mother, squinting into the haze of hot oil.

A door banged shut. Adam and Kat turned to see Anthony come into the kitchen. With him were two other boys, both about sixteen, both with the cold, flat expressions of foot soldiers.

'You got it,' said Anthony. 'Just this one day. You want to come back again, you pay again. They'll watch your backs.' He collected his two hundred dollars from Adam. 'So where do you want to go first?'

'The Biagi flat,' said Kat.

Anthony looked at the boys. 'Okay. Take 'em there.'

10

Nicos was a good boy, insisted Mr. and Mrs. Biagi. It seemed to be a universal mantra of parents in South Lexington – *he was a good boy*. A kid could pick up a gun and commit mass murder, and that refrain would still pop out of his parents' mouths.

The Biagis had no idea what Nicos had been doing with that needle and tourniquet. He had not been a drug addict. He had been a student at Louis French Junior College and had worked nights as a stockboy in the Big E supermarket in Bellemeade. He had bought a new car, paid for his own clothes.

And his own drugs, Kat thought.

After an hour, she and Adam gave up trying to break through that wall of parental denial. Yes, Nicos must truly have been a saint, they agreed, and left the apartment.

Their two bodyguards were lolling on the front steps, watching a little girl skip rope.

'. . . Mama called the doctor and the doctor said,
Feel the rhythm of the heart, ding dong,
Feel the rhythm of the heart . . .'

As Kat and Adam came outside, the girl stopped her chant and looked up at them.

'We're through here,' said Kat. 'Didn't learn a damn thing.'

The two boys glanced at each other with a wry look of *We could've told you that*.

The girl was still staring at them.

'Okay, let's try Xenia Vargas,' said Adam. 'Do you know where she lived?'

'Two blocks over,' piped up the girl with the jump rope. 'But she's dead.'

For the first time, Kat focused on the child. She was about eight years old, small and wiry, with a tangled bird's nest of hair. Her smock dress had been patched so many times it was hard to make out the pattern of the original fabric.

'Get outta here, Celeste,' said one of the boys. 'Your mama's callin' you.'

'I don't hear nothing.'

'Well, she's callin'.'

'Can't be. She's workin' till seven. So there.'

Kat crouched down beside the girl. 'Did you know Xenia?' she asked.

The girl swiped at her runny nose and looked at her. 'Sure. I seen her around all the time.'

'Where?'

'All over. She'd hang out at the laundromat.'

'Anyone else hang out with her?'

'Sometimes. The boys, they liked talkin' to Xenia.'

'Ain't all they liked doin' to Xenia,' one of the bodyguards said with a snicker.

Celeste fixed him with a dirty look. 'Yeah, I seen those boys 'round *your* sister too, Leland.'

Leland's snicker died. He gave Celeste an equally dirty look. The girl smiled back.

'She ever hang out with Nicos Biagi?' asked Adam.

'Sometimes.'

'What about this lady?' Kat asked. She took out the morgue photo of Jane Doe. For a second, she hesitated to show it to the child, then decided she had to.

Celeste glanced at the picture with a clinical eye. 'Dead, huh?' Kat nodded. 'Yeah,' said Celeste. 'I don't know her name, 'xactly, but I seen her with Xenia. She's not a regular.'

'A regular?' inquired Adam.

'She doesn't live here. She just visits.'

'Oh. A tourist.'

'Yeah, like you.'

'Celeste,' said Leland. '*Scram.*'

The girl didn't move.

They started up the street. A block away, Kat

glanced back and saw the little figure still watching them, the jump rope trailing from her hand.

'She's all by herself,' said Kat. 'Doesn't anyone look after her?'

'Everyone here knows her,' said Leland. 'Hell, they can't get *rid* of the brat.'

Celeste was skipping rope again, her quick steps bringing her along the sidewalk in undisguised pursuit.

They ignored her and walked two blocks to Building Three. Leland directed them to the sixth floor. Kat knocked at the door.

A woman answered – a girl, really – with makeup thick as putty and plucked eyebrows reduced to two unevenly drawn black slashes. Heavy earrings jangled as she looked first at Kat, then – much longer – at Adam. 'Yeah?'

'I'm from the medical examiner's office,' explained Kat. 'We think your roommate—'

'I'm not talkin' to no one from the Health Department.'

'I'm not from the Health Department. I'm from—'

'I went in for my shots. I'm cured, okay? So leave me alone.' She started to close the door, but Leland stuck his hand out to block it.

'They wanna know 'bout Xenia. I brought 'em here.'

'Why?'

''Cause this where she lived.'

'No, stupid. Why they askin'?'

'She died of a drug OD,' said Kat. 'Did you know that?'

The girl glanced nervously at Leland. 'Yeah. Maybe I did.'

'Were you aware she was shooting up?'

A cautious shrug. 'Maybe.'

Adam moved forward to interject himself into the dialogue. 'Could we, perhaps, come inside for a moment?' he asked. 'Just to talk?' He smiled at her, a brilliant smile that showed off all those perfect white teeth of his. A smile, Kat suspected, that few females could resist.

The girl seemed suitably impressed. Her gaze took in his clothes – shirt without a tie, casual slacks, all of it displayed on a superb frame.

'You from the Health Department too?' she asked.

'Not exactly . . .'

'You a cop?'

'No.'

That seemed good enough for her. With a coquettish jangle of earrings, she indicated they could come in.

The place was like a Bedouin tent. Heavy drapes hung over the windows, casting the room in a purple gloom. Instead of chairs there were cushions on the floor and a single low-slung couch, its pillows embroidered with silk elephants and mirror chips. A familiar odor permeated the room – *pot*, thought Kat, with maybe the side-scent of patchouli. She settled on the couch next to Adam. Leland and his buddy stood off to the side, as though trying to blend into the Oriental wall hanging.

The girl – she told them her name was Fran – plopped down on a cushion and said, 'Xenia and I, we didn't talk a lot, you know? So don't go thinking I can answer a whole lot of questions.'

'Did you know she was a junkie?' asked Kat.

'She liked her stuff, I guess.'

'Where'd she get it from?'

'Lots of places.' Fran's gaze flicked sideways, toward Leland. She licked her lips. 'Mostly out of the neighborhood.'

'Where?'

'I don't know. I guess she had people she'd go to, uptown. I'd have nothin' to do with it, see. I'm into *natural* stuff. Stuff you get off plants.'

'Did she know Nicos Biagi?'

Fran laughed. 'Hell. Nicos was *everybody's* friend.'

Kat took out the morgue photo of Jane Doe. 'What about this girl? Recognize her?'

Fran paled as she realized it was a corpse she was looking at. She swallowed. 'Yeah. That's one of Nicos's friends. Eliza.'

'She's dead, too,' said Kat. 'Shot up the same stuff as Nicos and Xenia. Killed all three of them.'

Fran handed back the photo and looked away.

'She was your roommate, Fran,' said Adam. 'She must have told you something.'

'Look, she just lived here, okay? We weren't like best friends or somethin'. She had her room, I had mine.'

'What about her room? Are her things still there?'

'Naw, they already come and searched it.'

'Who did?'

'Cops, who else?'

Kat frowned at her. 'What?'

'You know, those creeps with the badges and billy clubs? They come and picked it all apart for evidence.'

'Did you get a name? A precinct?'

'You think I'm gonna argue when some guy's shovin' his badge in my face?'

Kat glanced at Adam, saw his look of puzzlement. Why had the police shown up, and what had they been searching for?

That question troubled her all the way back down the six flights of stairs. She and Adam stepped out into the pale sunshine and blinked up at the Project towers. *Those prison towers again*, she thought. A constant reminder that this was a world not easily escaped.

Or easily penetrated. They'd spent half the day in South Lexington, and had no information to show for it, except the knowledge that the three victims had indeed been acquainted.

Perhaps that was the best they could hope for.

They sent Leland and his buddy off with twenty bucks apiece extra, and walked back to Adam's car. It was still there, courtesy of Anthony's hired guards – an additional service, they were informed, requiring an additional fee. Once they had dispensed with those boys they got into the car and sat there, silently regarding the barren strip of South Lexington.

Adam let out a breath, heavy with disappointment. 'That wasn't very productive. Expensive, yes. But not productive.'

'Well, it's clear they all knew each other. Which means any one of them could've been the source, passed the drug on to the others. I'd bet on Nicos.'

'Why Nicos?'

'You heard what his parents said. He worked evenings at the Big E. Think about it. Since when can a part-time stockboy afford a new car?' She shook her head. 'He was dealing on the side. I'm sure of it. And somehow, he managed to get his hands on a supply of Zestron-L.'

They were quiet for a moment. Then Adam said, 'It could still be Maeve.'

She looked at him. He was staring ahead, his eyes focused on some faraway point. 'What if she *is* the source, Adam? What then?'

'I don't know.' He shook his head. 'I suppose there's no way around it. She'll have to be charged.

Sale of a dangerous drug. Theft. Whatever the law requires. It's not in my hands any longer. Not with three people dead.'

Again, they fell silent. *He knows it now*, she thought. *Maeve is beyond salvation*. The time to set her right had long passed. All those missed opportunities, the months, the years when he might have made a difference, would haunt him, as they did every parent of a wayward child.

The sound of skipping feet and rope snapping rhythmically against the pavement penetrated the silence of the car. Kat looked out and saw Celeste jumping rope, her bird's-nest hair bouncing with each skip. The girl drew even with the car window and she jumped in place, all the time nonchalantly ignoring the occupants of the car.

'Hello there,' called Kat.

The girl glanced sideways. 'Hi.'

'You seem to be everywhere today.'

'Gotta keep myself busy.' The girl panted. 'That's what my mama tells me.' She stopped jumping and sidled up to Kat's window. Curiously she peered inside. 'Like your car.'

'Thank you.'

'Didn't tell ya nothin', did she?'

Kat frowned at her. 'What do you mean?'

'No way Fran's gonna talk, y'know. Not with that Leland hangin' around.'

'Is she afraid of Leland?'

'Everyone is. He's Jonah's man.'

'Jonah?'

'You know. The main man. Can't take a step round here, 'less Jonah lets you.'

'We asked for Jonah's help. He sent us Leland.'

''Course he sent Leland. Wasn't gonna let you talk to no one without a set of his ears around.' Celeste suddenly glanced over her shoulder and spotted a boy watching her from a doorway. At once she began to skip rope again, moving away up the sidewalk. Kat thought the girl would continue on her way, but when Celeste reached the front of the car, she circled left, onto the street, and back along the other side of the car, toward Adam's window.

'Jonah, he's worried, you know,' said Celeste, all the time skipping lightly on the blacktop.

'Why?' asked Adam.

'He thinks you're one of them. But that's stupid. I can tell you aren't. 'Cause you're too *obvious*.'

'What do you mean by—' Adam didn't finish the question, as Celeste was already skipping away, toward the rear of the car. He and Kat glanced at each other. 'This kid ought to be on police payroll,' he muttered.

Celeste had rounded the rear bumper and was moving on the sidewalk again, coming alongside Kat's window.

'Who's he afraid of?' Kat asked the bouncing child.

'The folks who killed Nicos.'

'And Xenia?'

'Same ones.'

'Who are you talking about, Celeste? *Which* people?'

The girl stopped jumping and looked at them as if they were idiots. 'The police, of course!' she said. Then, with a snap of the rope, she was off and bouncing again.

Adam and Kat stared at the girl. 'That's crazy,' muttered Adam. 'It's just the mentality around here. People are afraid of authority. Naturally they'd blame the police for everything.'

'Fran was clearly afraid of *something*,' said Kat.

'Of that fellow Jonah, no doubt.'

By now Celeste was moving up the sidewalk, to make her second circle of the car. When she came around to Adam's side, he was ready to pose the next question through his window.

'Why does Jonah think the police killed Nicos?' he asked.

'Gotta ask *him*.'

'How do I reach him?'

'Can't.' She skipped rope in place. 'He don't talk to outsiders.'

'Well,' sighed Adam. 'That's that.'

'Show her Maeve's picture,' said Kat. 'See if she knows her.'

Adam took out the photograph and flashed it at Celeste. 'Have you seen this woman?' he asked.

Celeste glanced at the photo and did a double take. She stopped jumping for a moment and bent forward for a closer look. 'Sure looks like her.'

'Like who?'

'Jonah's lady.' With that, Celeste bounced off, away from the window.

Adam looked at Kat in shock. 'Dear God, *Maeve?*'

'Ask her to take another look.'

They glanced back to see where Celeste was in her jump rope circuit around the car. To their dismay, the girl was halfway down the block, skipping swiftly away.

Instead of Celeste, it was Leland approaching their car. He bent to speak into Kat's window. 'Time you got movin',' he said. 'Like, right *now.*'

'I want to talk to Jonah,' said Kat.

'He don't talk to nobody.'

'Tell him I'm on his side. That I only want to—'

'You want I should give your car a shove or what?'

There was a silence, heavy with the threat of violence.

'We hear you,' Adam said, and started the engine. Swiftly he pulled into the street and made a U-turn. Leland was still glowering at them as they drove away.

'Not taking any chances, is he?' said Adam, glancing in the rearview mirror.

'Jonah's orders.'

Just ahead, Celeste was jumping rope along the sidewalk. As they drove past, she stopped and raised her hand in farewell. Then, aware that she too was being watched, she grabbed both ends of the rope and continued her bouncing progress along South Lexington.

For two days, Dr. Herbert Esterhaus had avoided going home. Instead, he'd holed up under an assumed name at the St. Francis Arms and ordered all his meals delivered. It was a no-frills establishment, the sort of place frequented by traveling salesmen on tight budgets. The sheets were slightly frayed, the carpet well worn, and the water spewing from the faucet had a distinctly rusty tinge, but the room served his purpose; it was a place to hide while he considered his next move.

Unfortunately, he had few options to choose from.

That he'd soon be arrested, he had no doubt. The investigation into the Zestron-L theft had just begun; soon they'd be running background checks and polygraphing everyone in the lab, and he would fail the test. Miserably. Because he was guilty.

He could run. He could change his name, his identity. The way he had before. After all, it was a vast country, with countless little towns in which to hide. But he was weary of hiding, of answering to an assumed name. It had taken him ten years to feel comfortable with 'Herbert Esterhaus.' He loved his job. His work was valued and respected at Cygnus, and most important, *he* was valued and respected. Even by Mr. Q. himself.

Would they respect him when they learned what he had done?

He went to the window and stared down at the street. It was a blustery day, and bits of paper tumbled in the wind. Downtown Albion. All right, so it wasn't the city of his dreams, but it was home to him now. He had a house, a good paycheck, a job that kept him on the cutting edge of research. On Saturday nights he had his folk dancing club, on Sunday nights his watercolor classes. He didn't have the woman he loved, but there was always the chance Maeve would come back to him. 'This is my home now,' he said to himself. The sound of his own voice speaking aloud was startling. 'I live here. And I'm not going to leave.'

Which led to his second option: confession.

It carried consequences, of course. He would probably lose his job. But once they understood the circumstances, understood he was forced into the act, they wouldn't be so hard. Not when he could name names, point fingers.

This time, by God, I'm not going to run.

He reached for the telephone and dialed Adam Quantrell's house. Confession was good for the soul, they said.

But Quantrell wasn't home, the man at the other end told him. Would he care to leave a message?

'Tell him – tell him I have to talk to him,' said Esterhaus. 'But I can't do it over the phone.'

'What is this concerning, may I ask?'

'It's . . . personal.'

'I'll let him know. Where can you be reached, Dr. Esterhaus?'

'I'll be . . .' He paused. This slightly seedy hotel? It would be proof he'd fled, proof of his guilty conscience. 'I'll be at home,' he said. He hung up, at once feeling better. Now that he had decided on a course of action, all the energy that had been sucked into the useless machinery of uncertainty could be redirected to pure motion. He packed the few things he'd brought – a toothbrush, a razor, a change of underwear. Then he checked out and drove home.

He parked in his carport and entered through the side door, into the kitchen. Familiar smells at once enveloped him, the scent of the Cloroxed sink, the fresh paint from the newly redone hallway. Here, in his house, he felt safe.

The phone rang in the living room. Quantrell? The thought set his heart pounding. Fully prepared to blurt out the truth, he picked up the receiver, only to hear a child's voice ask, 'Is Debbie there?' He didn't hear the footsteps on the porch, or the wriggling of the doorknob.

But he did hear the knock.

He hung up on the kid and went to open the front door. 'Oh,' he said. 'It's you—'

'Everything's fixed.'

'It is?'

'I told you it would be.' The visitor stepped inside, shut the door.

'Look, I can't deal with this! I never thought it'd go this far—'

'But Herb, I'm telling you, you don't have a thing to worry about.'

'Quantrell's going to find out! It's only a matter of—' Esterhaus paused, staring at his visitor. At the gun. He shook his head in disbelief.

The gun fired twice, two clean shots.

The impact of the bullets sent Esterhaus jerking backwards. He sprawled against the couch, his blood sliding in rivulets across the fabric. Through fading vision, he stared up at his murderer. 'Why?' he whispered.

'I told you, Herb. You don't have a thing to worry about. And now, neither do I.'

Thomas, as usual, was waiting at the front door to greet them. By now he seemed a built-in part of the house, as affixed to it as the mantelpiece or the wainscotting, and just as permanent. The difference was, Thomas actually *wanted* to be there. Kat saw it now, in his smile of welcome, in the fatherly affection with which he helped Adam remove his coat. It was apparent they went back a long way, these two; she could almost see them as they must have been thirty years ago, the young man reaching down to assist the boy struggling out of his winter coat.

Thomas hung their jackets in the closet. 'There were two calls while you were out, Mr. Q.,' he said.

'Anything important?'

'Miss Calderwood phoned to ask if you were still on for the afternoon with the Wyatts. And if so, where were you?'

Adam groaned. 'Good Lord, I forgot all about Isabel!' He reached for the hall telephone. 'She's going to be furious.'

'She did seem rather put out.'

Adam dialed Isabel's number and stood waiting while it rang. 'Who else called?'

'A Dr. Herbert Esterhaus. About two hours ago.'

'Esterhaus?' Adam glanced up sharply. 'Why?'

'He wouldn't say. Something about the laboratory, I assume. He did imply it was somewhat urgent.'

'Where is he?'

'That's his number there, on the notepad.'

Adam hung up and dialed the number Thomas had written down. It kept ringing.

'He said he'd be home all day,' said Thomas. 'Perhaps he stepped out for a moment.'

Adam glanced at Kat. It was a look, nothing more, but she saw in his eyes a flicker of apprehension. *Something's happened. He feels it too.*

Adam hung up. 'Let's drive by his house.'

'But you've only just arrived,' said Thomas.

'It doesn't feel right. Herb wouldn't call me at home unless it was important.'

Resignedly, Thomas reached back into the closet for their jackets. 'Really, Mr. Q. All this rushing around.'

Adam smiled and patted him on the shoulder. 'At least you won't have us underfoot, hm?'

Thomas merely sighed and walked them to the door.

Just as they climbed into Adam's car, a Mercedes pulled into the driveway, its tires spitting gravel. Isabel stuck her head out the window. 'Adam!' she called. 'Have you forgotten about the Wyatts?'

'Give them my regrets!'

'I thought we were on for this afternoon—'

'Something's come up. I can't make it. Look, I'll call you later, Isabel, all right?'

'But Adam, you—'

Her words were cut off by the roar of the Volvo as

Adam and Kat drove off. She was left behind in the driveway, staring in disbelief.

Adam glanced in his mirror at the receding Mercedes. 'Damn. How am I going to explain this away?'

'Just tell her what happened,' said Kat. 'She already knows what's going on, doesn't she?'

'Isabel?' He snorted. 'First, Isabel is not equipped to deal with unpleasantness of any sort. It's not in her sphere of knowledge. Second, she's not good at keeping secrets. By the time the gossip got down the street and back again, I'd be a major drug dealer and Maeve would have three heads and be practicing voodoo.'

'You mean . . . she doesn't know about Maeve?'

'She knows I have a stepdaughter. But she never asks about her. And I don't fill her in on the gory details.'

'Isn't a problem kid something you'd want to sort of *mention* to your girlfriend?'

'Girlfriend?' He laughed.

'Well, what *do* you call her then?'

'A social companion. Suitable for all occasions.'

'Oh.' She looked out the window. 'I guess that covers everything.'

To her surprise, he reached over and squeezed her thigh. 'Not quite everything.'

She frowned at his laughing eyes. 'What does it leave out?'

'Oh, street fights, exploding houses, the sort of occasions she wouldn't appreciate.'

'I'm not sure *I* appreciate them.'

He turned his gaze back to the road. 'I've never slept with her, you know,' he said.

That statement was so unexpected, Kat was struck silent for a moment. She stared at his unruffled profile. 'Why did you tell me that?'

'I thought you should know.'

'Well, thank you for satisfying my *burning* curiosity.'

'You're very welcome.'

'And what am I supposed to do with this knowledge?'

He winked. 'File it away in that amazing brain of yours.'

She shook her head and laughed. 'I don't know what to make of you, Quantrell. Sometimes I think you're flirting with me. Other times, I think it's all in my head.'

'Why wouldn't I? You know I'm attracted to you.'

'Why?'

He sighed. 'You're not supposed to say, "Why?" You're supposed to say, "And I'm attracted to *you*."'

'Nevertheless, *why*?'

He glanced at her in surprise. 'Is it so difficult to believe? That I'd find you attractive?'

'I think it's because I'm a novelty,' she said.

'Because I'm not like your other . . . companions.'
   'True.'
   'Which means it'd never work.'
   'Such a pessimist,' he sighed. He gave her thigh another squeeze, flashed her another grin, and looked back at the road.

Rockbrook was one of those anonymous suburbs that lie on the outskirts of any large city. It was a white-bread world of trim lawns, two cars in every garage, yards strewn with kids' bicycles. The house where Herbert Esterhaus lived had no bicycles in the yard, and only one vehicle in the carport, but in every other way it was typical of the neighborhood – a tract home, neatly kept, with a brick walkway in front and azaleas huddled on either side of the door.
   No one seemed to be home. They rang the bell, knocked, but there was no answer, and the front door was locked.
   'Now what?' said Kat. She glanced up the street. A block away, two boys tossed a basketball against their garage door. The buzz of a lawnmower echoed from some unseen backyard.
   They circled around to the carport. 'His car's here,' Adam noted. 'And that looks like today's paper on the front seat. So he's driven it today.'
   'Then where is he?' said Kat.
   Adam went to the side door of the house. It was

unlocked. He poked his head inside and called out: 'Herb? Are you home?'

There was no answer.

'Maybe we should check inside,' suggested Kat.

They stepped into the kitchen. Again, Adam called out: 'Herb?' A silence seemed to hang over the house. And the sense of dead air, as though no window, no door, had been opened for a very long time.

Kat spotted a set of keys on the kitchen counter. That struck her as odd, that a man would leave the house without his keys.

'Maybe you should call Thomas,' she said. 'Esterhaus might have left you another message.'

'It's a thought, but first let's check the living room.' He headed out of the kitchen.

Seconds later, Kat heard him say, 'Oh, God.'

'Adam?' she called. She left the kitchen and crossed the dining room. Through the living room doorway, she spotted Adam, standing by the couch. He seemed frozen in place, unable to move a muscle. 'Adam?'

Slowly he turned to look at her. 'It's . . . him.'

'What?' She moved across the living room. Only as she rounded the couch did she see the crimson stain soaking the carpet, like some psychiatrist's nightmare inkblot. Stretched across the blood was an arm, its hand white and clawed.

The hand of Herbert Esterhaus.

11

The flash of the photographer's strobe made Kat wince. He was a crime lab veteran, and he strode casually around the body, choosing his shots with an almost bored detachment. The repeated camera flashes, the babble of too many people talking at the same time, the whine of yet another siren closing in, left Kat feeling disoriented. She'd been to crime scenes before, had been part of other, equally chaotic gatherings, but this scene was different, this victim was different. He was someone she knew, someone who, just a few short days ago, had met her handshake with one of warm flesh. His death was far too close to her, and she felt herself withdrawing into some safe, numb place where she floated on a sea of fatigue.

Only when a familiar voice called to her did her brain snap back into focus. She saw Lieutenant Sykes moving toward them.

'What the hell happened?' he asked.

'It's Esterhaus,' said Adam. 'He phoned me this afternoon. Said he wanted to talk. We came by and . . .'

Sykes glanced at the dead body sprawled on the couch. 'When?'

'We got here around five.'

'He's been dead awhile,' murmured Kat. 'Probably early afternoon.'

'How do you know?' asked Sykes.

She looked away. 'Experience,' she muttered.

The Rockbrook detective approached and greeted Sykes. 'Sorry you got dragged over, Lou. I know this one's technically ours, but they insisted I call you.'

'So what've you got?'

'Two bullet wounds in the chest. Took him down fast. No signs of forced entry. No witnesses. ME'll have to do a look-see, give us an approximate time.'

'Dr. Novak says early afternoon.'

'Yeah, well . . .' The detective shifted uneasily. 'They're sending over Davis Wheelock.'

Because they're not about to trust me on this one, thought Kat. The Rockbrook detective was a cautious cop. He couldn't be sure of Kat's role in all this. Her status had changed from ME to . . . what? Witness? Suspect? She could see it in the way he watched her eyes, weighed her every statement.

Now Sykes began to ask questions, the same ones

they'd already answered. No, they hadn't touched anything except the phone. And, briefly, the body – to check vital signs. Events were dissected, over and over. By the time Sykes had finished, Kat was having trouble concentrating. Too many voices were talking in the room, and there were the sounds of the crowd outside, the neighbors, all pressing up against the yellow police line.

Esterhaus's body, cocooned in a zip-up bag, was wheeled through the front door and out of the house, into a night blazing with the flash of reporters' cameras.

Adam and Kat followed the EMTs out of the house. It was bedlam outside, cops shouting for everyone to stand back, radios crackling from a half-dozen patrol cars. Two TV vans were parked nearby, klieg lights glaring. A reporter thrust a microphone in front of Kat's face and asked, 'Were you the people who found the body?'

'Leave us alone,' said Adam, shoving the microphone away.

'Sir, can you tell us what condition—'

'I said, *leave us alone*.'

'Hey!' another reporter yelled. 'Aren't you Adam Quantrell? Mr. Quantrell?'

Suddenly, the lights were redirected into their eyes. Adam grabbed Kat's hand and pulled her along in a mad dash for the car.

The instant they were inside, they slammed and locked the doors. Hands knocked at the windows.

Adam started the engine. 'Let's get the hell out of here,' he growled, and hit the gas pedal.

Even as they roared away, they could hear the questions being shouted at them.

Kat collapsed back in exhaustion. 'I thought they were going to keep us there all night.'

He shot her a worried look. 'Are you all right?'

She shivered. 'Just cold. And scared. Mostly scared . . .' She looked at him. 'Why did they kill Esterhaus? What is going on, Adam?'

He stared ahead, his gaze locked on the road, his profile hard and white in the darkness. 'I wish to God I knew.'

They arrived home to find Thomas waiting for them.

'Mr. Q., the reporters have been calling—'

'Tell them to go to hell,' said Adam, guiding Kat toward the stairs.

'But—'

'You heard what I said.'

'Is that a . . . literal request?'

'Word for word.'

'Goodness,' said Thomas, sounding uncomfortable. 'I don't know . . .' He watched them climb up to the second floor landing. 'Is there anything you'll require, Mr. Q.?' he called.

'A bottle of brandy. And answer the phone, will you?'

Thomas glanced at the telephone, which had begun to ring again. Reluctantly he picked up the receiver. 'Quantrell residence.' He listened for a few seconds. Then, drawing himself to his full and dignified height, he said: 'Mr. Quantrell wishes to convey the following message: Go to hell.' He hung up, looking strangely satisfied.

'The brandy, Thomas!' called Adam.

'Right away,' said Thomas, and went off toward the library.

Adam turned Kat gently toward the bedroom. 'Come on,' he whispered. 'You look ready to collapse.'

He brought her into his room and sat her down on the bed. He took her hands in his. Her touch was like ice.

Thomas came into the room, bearing a tray with the brandy and two glasses.

'Leave it,' said Adam.

Thomas, ever discreet, nodded and withdrew.

Adam poured a glass and handed it to Kat. She looked blankly at it.

'Just brandy,' he said. 'A Quantrell family tradition.'

She took a sip. Closing her eyes tightly, she whispered, 'You Quantrells keep fine traditions.'

He reached up and gently brushed a lock of hair off her face. Her skin felt as cool as marble, but the woman beneath was alive and trembling and in need.

'If only I knew,' she said. 'If I just knew what I was fighting against. Then I wouldn't be so afraid.' She looked at him. 'That's what scares me. Not knowing. It makes the whole world seem evil.'

'Not the whole world. There's me. And I'll take care of you—'

'Don't make promises, Adam.'

'I'm not promising. I'm telling you. As long as you need me—'

She pressed her fingers to his lips. 'Don't. Please. You'll back yourself into a corner. And then you'll feel guilty when you can't keep your word.'

He grasped her hand, firmly, fiercely. 'Kat—'

'No promises.'

'All right. If that's what you want, no promises.'

'From either of us. It's more honest that way.'

'You'll stay here, though? As long as you need to. Unless . . . there's some other place you'd rather go?'

She shook her head.

He felt an intoxicating rush of happiness, of relief, that here was where she wanted to be. *With me.*

'There's no other place,' she said softly.

He had not planned to kiss her, but at that moment she looked so badly in need of a kiss that he drew her closer, and cupped her face in his hands.

It was only a brushing of lips, a taste of her brandied warmth. No passion, no lust, merely kindness.

And then, like a spark striking dry tinder, something else flared to instant brightness. He saw it in her eyes, and she in his. They stared at each other for a moment in shared wonder. And uncertainty. He wanted badly to kiss her again, but she was so vulnerable, and he knew that if he pressed her, she would yield. She might hate him in the morning, and she would have good reason. That, most of all, was what he didn't want.

He took a much-needed lungful of fortifying air and pulled away from her. 'You can stay here, in my room. It will feel safer.' He rose to leave. 'I'll sleep in yours.'

'Adam?'

'In the morning, we'll have to talk about what happens next. But tonight—'

'I want you to stay here,' she said. 'In this room. With me.'

The last two words came out in barely a whisper. Slowly he settled back down beside her and tried to look beyond the glaze of fear in her eyes. 'Are you sure?' he asked softly.

Her answer left no doubt. She reached out to him, wrapped her arms around his neck, and pulled him against her. Their lips met. Hers were desperate, seeking, and he responded instantly to that un-expected assault with a hunger just as fierce.

He reached out to bury his fingers in her hair. It felt like the mane of a wild animal, crackling and alive. Suddenly *she* came alive, and all of her fear and exhaustion broke before a swelling tide of desire. Her hair brushed his face, and he inhaled the warm and feral scent of a woman. Such delicious sounds she was making, little whimpers and sighs, as her mouth eagerly met his, again and again.

They tumbled back onto the bed and rolled across the covers. First she was on top, her hair spilling like sheets of silk over his face. Then he was on top, covering her body with his. No passive participant was she; already, he felt her pressing up against him, her back arching, her body starved for more intimate contact. Fear had made her desperate; he could sense it in her kisses.

He forced himself to pull back. 'Kat,' he said. 'Look at me.'

She opened her eyes. They had the brief, bright glow of tears.

He took her face in his hands, cradled her cheeks so she could not turn away from him. 'What's wrong?'

'I want you,' was all she said.

'But you're crying.'

'No, I just want you . . .'

'And you're afraid.'

There it was – the briefest of nods, as though she didn't want to say it. 'I'm afraid of everything,' she said. 'Everyone. The whole world.'

'Even me?'

She swallowed back another flash of tears. 'Especially you,' she whispered.

Long after he'd fallen asleep, Kat lay awake in his arms. They might both be exhausted, but only he was able to sleep untroubled and unafraid.

He wasn't the one falling in love.

She burrowed closer, wondering about the man who lay beside her. The man who had everything.

Now he has me, as well.

She felt helpless, trapped not only by her own heart, but by circumstances. Rule number one for the independent woman: Never let a man become indispensable. It was the rule she tried to live by, and already she'd violated it.

She looked at Adam and felt yet again that stirring of hunger. And something else, having nothing to do with desire. Tenderness. Joy. She felt pushed and pulled between wanting to believe in love and knowing better.

When she finally did sleep, it was like falling into some small, dreamless space. A prison without windows.

* * *

She was the first to awaken. Sunlight was shining through the curtains. Adam slept on, his golden hair tousled beyond help of any mere combing. She left him and went into the bathroom to shower. It was only when she came out again, bundled in his robe, that he stirred awake and gazed at her with amusement.

'Good morning,' he murmured. 'Are you an early riser or am I just lazy?'

She smiled. 'Since it's already eight-thirty, I guess that makes you lazy.'

'Come here.' He patted the bed. 'Sit down with me.'

Reluctantly she complied and was reminded yet again of how susceptible she was to his attractions. Already, those hormones were doing their work; she could feel them flooding her face with heat.

'I dreamt about you last night,' he said, his fingers lightly tracing the length of her spine.

'Adam,' she said. 'What happened last night—' She felt a shudder of pleasure as his hand moved upward, crept under the flap of the robe to graze her breast. At once she stood up and moved away from the bed. She shook her head. 'It's not going to work.'

He didn't say a thing. He just watched her, his gaze too searching for comfort.

She began to move around the room, anything to

avoid that look of his. 'I walk into your bathroom,' she said. 'And everything's marble and – and gold. The soap's French. And the towels all match.' She stopped and laughed. 'Adam, in all my life, I've *never* had towels that matched.'

'You're saying it won't work because of my towels?'

'No, I'm saying I can't see myself . . . fitting in here. I can't see your friends accepting me. Or *you* accepting me. Right now, maybe, I'm exciting for you—'

'Without a doubt.'

'But it doesn't last, the novelty of a girlfriend from South Lexington. Look, you're a nice guy. I know you don't mean to hurt me. Maybe you'll even feel guilty about it when it falls apart. But I'm not the kind of woman who gets hurt, okay? I *refuse* to be hurt. And that's why I'd much rather stay your friend.'

'Because you think our relationship is doomed?'

'Well, yes. I guess.'

For a moment he considered that statement without apparent emotion. Then he said, quite calmly, 'I suppose it *is* better for you. We both know how it is with these rich bastards. Love 'em and leave 'em – that's what you say, isn't it?'

'Oh, Adam.' She sighed. 'Please.'

He rose from the bed, snatching up his clothes. 'I'm insulted. I'm really insulted. We make love – what I *thought* was love – and then you hand me the script to the rest of the affair!'

'Because I've played this part before. With Ed. With other men—'

'Also rich bastards?'

The knock on the door startled them both.

'What is it?' snapped Adam.

Thomas entered, looking quite taken aback at his employer's tone of voice. 'I . . . thought perhaps you should know. The police are downstairs.'

'What?'

'Lieutenant Sykes and that chubby sergeant. Shall I set breakfast?'

Adam sighed. 'Go ahead. Lay on the bagels for Ratchet.'

'And some extra cream cheese,' Thomas added and withdrew.

Adam and Kat looked at each other. The tension was still there, crackling between them. So was the desire.

Push and pull. Attraction and fear. That was what she felt when she looked at him.

She picked up her clothes. 'I'll see you downstairs,' she said. Then she left to get dressed in the other room.

The two cops were sitting at the dining table, Sykes nursing a cup of black coffee, Ratchet wolfing down scrambled eggs and sausages. Both men seemed quiet, maybe a little cautious, this morning. As though they had to be careful about what they said.

Something has changed, thought Kat, studying them.

She and Adam sat across the table from them. Though Adam was right beside her, he didn't touch her, didn't glance at her. She felt the distance between them widen with every minute that passed.

Sykes said, 'It's about the Esterhaus murder. Rockwood Precinct's handed the case to us.'

'Why?' asked Adam.

'Because of what's come to light.' Sykes put a large envelope on the table and slid it across to Adam. 'I'm sorry to be the one to show these to you. But I need you to confirm the identity.'

Puzzled, Adam pulled out a dozen photographs. At his first glimpse of the woman in the pictures, he paled. They were nude shots, in grainy black and white, amateurish and obviously home-processed. In one, the woman was sprawled suggestively across a bed, her hair fanned out, her hands cupping her breasts. In another, she pouted seductively from a bar stool, a whiskey glass raised to the camera. More photos, some taken with an apparent effort at artistic shading, others blatantly prurient. Adam stared at the thin and girlish face gazing back at him from an array of poses. Then he looked away and dropped his head in his hands.

Sykes asked: 'Is it her?'

'Yes,' murmured Adam. 'It's Maeve.'

Sykes nodded. 'I thought so. I recognized her face from the photos you gave me earlier.'

Adam looked up. 'Where did you find these?'

'In Herbert Esterhaus's bedroom.'

'*What?*'

'They were in a bureau drawer. Along with a lot of other . . . interesting things.'

Adam stared at him, shocked by the revelation. 'Esterhaus and Maeve . . .'

'We're trying to find her, bring her in for questioning. But we can't seem to get near her. That's a tight group she hangs out with in South Lexington. It's only routine questions, of course. Ex-girlfriends are always on the list—'

'You don't think *Maeve* had anything to do with it?'

'As I said, it's routine. Just a drill we go through—'

Adam pointed to the photos. 'I'd say Maeve is the victim here, Lieutenant!' he shot back.

'I know exactly how you feel, Mr. Q.,' said Sykes. 'I've got a little girl of my own, and I'd want to wring the neck of any bastard who used her like this. But a man's been killed. And now we have to go through the paces.'

'I know Maeve! She wouldn't—'

'Did you know about her and Esterhaus?'

Adam paused. 'No,' he admitted at last. 'I didn't.'

Sykes shook his head. 'There's a lot you never know about people. Even your own family. I'm not saying you should get panicked or anything. You're probably right, she had nothing to do with it. With the evidence we found, I'm ninety-nine percent sure she didn't. Still—'

'What evidence?' asked Kat.

'Things we found. In the victim's house.'

'Aside from nude photos of ex-girlfriends?'

'Yes.' Sykes looked at Adam. 'What did you know about Esterhaus when you hired him?'

'Just what was in his résumé. As I recall, he came well-qualified. Excellent references. Had a research position somewhere out in California.'

'That should've tipped you off right there,' said Ratchet, spearing another sausage. 'Who in his right mind leaves sunny California and moves to Albion?'

'You mean his references were falsified?' asked Kat.

Sykes nodded. 'Courtesy of the U.S. government.'

'*What?*'

'See, the name Herbert Esterhaus was an alias. We found his old IDs in his house. His real name was Dr. Lawrence Hebron. Oh, he was a biochemist, all right, but he didn't work for a company in California. He worked in Miami. A designer drug lab owned by the mob. A real genius, so I hear. Then he got busted and turned state's evidence. They put him in the Witness

219

Protection Program, gave him a new name, a new résumé. And a new job, with Cygnus. Where, I take it, he was working out just fine.'

Adam nodded. 'He was one of our best.'

'And you think that's why he was killed?' asked Kat. 'Old mob connections?'

'There are folks in Miami who aren't happy with him. If they traced him to Albion, then he was a dead man.'

'We figure,' said Ratchet, wiping sausage grease from his mouth, 'Esterhaus is the key to it all. Maybe he needed some extra cash, so he rips off a few grains of Zestron-L from the lab, sells it on the street. A few junkies die as a result. Then his old buddies from Miami get wind of his whereabouts, come up, and perform a little thirty-eight caliber justice.'

There was a silence as Kat and Adam considered the theory. 'So we're supposed to believe that Miami boys drove up and did your job for you?' said Kat. She shook her head. 'Too neat. And who blew up my house?'

'Esterhaus was a biochemist,' said Ratchet. 'He could put together a respectable bomb.'

'Why? Just to shut me up?'

Sykes laughed. 'There are times, Novak, when I would *love* to shut you up. Consider what the man was faced with, if you kept pushing your investigation. Charges of theft. Manslaughter, for those junkies. Plus, you'd blow his cover identity, so his life was at stake as well.'

'And Maeve?' said Kat, glancing at the nude photos. 'How does she figure in?'

'We don't know,' said Sykes. 'We thought maybe Mr. Q. could shed some light.'

Adam shook his head, troubled by what he'd heard. 'Maeve never said a word to me about any of this.'

'You had no idea she was seeing Esterhaus?'

'She had her own life, her own apartment. I suspected there was a man, but I didn't know his name. And she wouldn't bother telling *me*.' In disgust, he swept up the photos and stuffed them back in the envelope. 'I'd strangle him myself, if he weren't already dead.'

Kat caught the glance that flew between Sykes and Ratchet. *Careful, Adam*, she thought. *They're looking for suspects. Don't provide them with one.*

She said, quickly, 'Do you think Maeve knew about his real identity? We know she and Esterhaus weren't getting along – those arguments at the lab, remember? Maybe it had nothing to do with the job. Maybe it was personal. Maybe she learned the truth about him. And she walked out. Not on the job, but on *him*.'

'She could have told me,' said Adam. 'But she didn't. Lord, what a disaster I've been as a father.'

Kat touched his arm. It wasn't enough to close the

gap yawning between them; perhaps nothing could close that gap. But it let him know she cared. 'Maybe she couldn't tell you. Maybe she was ashamed she had fallen for the guy in the first place. Or scared.'

'Of what?'

'The man she was sleeping with had a price on his head. And he was pushing poison on the street. That would scare a lot of people.'

'Then why didn't she come to *me*?' said Adam. 'I would have kicked him out of Cygnus so fast, he wouldn't know what hit him.'

'You may have answered your own question,' said Kat. 'If she had any feelings at all for Esterhaus, she wouldn't expose him. So she just walked away. Went some place he couldn't find her.'

'South Lexington?' Ratchet snorted. 'I can think of better neighborhoods to hide in.'

Sykes scooped up the envelope of photos and rose to leave. 'We'll keep trying to find her,' he said. 'But I'm afraid it's turned into a game of hide-and-seek. And Maeve's pretty damn good at it.' He glanced at Adam. 'As you already know.'

Adam shook his head, a weary gesture of acceptance. Defeat. 'You won't find her,' he said. 'No one will. Not unless she wants to be found.'

They spotted Celeste a block away, her curlicued hair bouncing up and down as she skipped rope. She didn't break stride as they drove closer and pulled up next to her. She was counting to herself in a soft, flat drone: 'One twenty-eight, one twenty-nine, one thirty . . .'

'Are you sure this is a good idea?' Adam whispered to Kat. 'Maybe we should try Anthony again.'

'And lose another two hundred dollars?' Kat shook her head. 'This kid knows her way around. Let's see if she'll help us out.'

'One thirty-eight, one thirty-nine . . .'

'Hello, Celeste,' Kat called through the open car window. 'Can we talk to you?'

'One forty-four, one forty-five.'

'We need a little help.'

'One forty-eight . . .' The rope suddenly fell limp, snagged by Celeste's shoe. She stamped her foot in annoyance. 'I was goin' for a record, too.' Resignedly she turned to Kat. 'So what do you need?'

'We want to talk to Jonah,' said Kat. 'The big man.'

'What for?'

'Just talk. About what's coming down.'

'Jonah doesn't talk to outsiders.'

'Maybe he'll talk to us. A new jump rope says he will.'

'I'd rather have a watch. Y'know, with all those fancy dials and things.'

'And you thought Anthony was steep,' muttered Adam.

'Okay,' said Kat. 'A watch. But only if he talks to us.'

Celeste grinned. 'Wait here,' she said, and trotted off down the street. She turned left, into an alley, and vanished.

'Is this going to work?' said Adam.

'We can't get to Maeve any other way. So we have to try going to the top. If she's Jonah's lady, that's where she'll be. With him.'

'Maeve won't talk to us. She won't let us anywhere near her.'

'But things have changed. Esterhaus is dead. She's a suspect. So she'd better talk to us. Before the police *make* her talk.' She looked at Adam. 'Besides, this is your chance to call off the feud, or whatever it is between you two. It's gone on long enough. Don't you think it's time for you and Maeve to be a family again?'

He gazed down the street, at the alley where Celeste had vanished. 'You're right,' he said softly. 'It's time . . .'

They waited. Ten minutes, fifteen.

Instead of Celeste, it was their old escort Leland who emerged from the alley. He sauntered over to their car and peered inside.

'You two again,' he said.

'We want to see Jonah,' said Kat.

'What for?' demanded Leland.

'This place is gonna be thick with cops. I thought the big man might want to know what's coming down.'

Leland looked skeptical. 'You doin' him a favor? Sure.'

'I got one to ask in return.'

An exchange of favors – that concept, Leland could grasp. He opened Kat's door. 'Okay, you're on. Just you, not the dude.'

'Now wait a minute,' said Adam, climbing out of the car as she did.

'It's the chick or nobody.'

'She's not going in there without me.'

'Then she ain't goin' in at all.'

'If those are the terms, then we're not—'

'Adam, can I speak to you?' Kat grabbed his arm and pulled him aside. 'Don't ruin it.'

'You don't know anything about this Jonah character!'

'And I never will, if I don't go in.'

Adam glanced at Leland, who was standing by the rear bumper. 'He's twice your size. No, he's twice *my* size. If he wanted to, he could—'

'Do you want to contact Maeve or not?'

'Not if it means sending you off with him.'

Her eyes narrowed. 'I'm not afraid of him, you know.'

'Which says something about your sanity.'

'There's a code of honor here, Adam. You may not

believe it, but people do play by the big man's rules. Jonah says I'm in, then I'm in. And no one touches me.'

'What if the rules have changed?'

'I'm gambling they haven't.'

'There's the word for it. Gambling.'

'Are you comin' or what?' said Leland.

'I'm coming,' said Kat, and turned to follow him.

Adam caught her arm. 'One question, Kat. Why are you doing this?'

'Because you need your daughter. And I think she needs you.' With that she pulled away and followed Leland up the street.

They turned left, into the alley, then right, up another alley. There Leland halted. He pulled out a bandanna and tossed it to her. 'Put it over your eyes,' he said.

'You boys got a secret hideout?'

'We wanna keep it that way.'

Stupid kid stuff, she thought as she wrapped the bandanna over her eyes and tied it at the back. The cloth stank of cheap after-shave. 'Okay. I'm blind as a bat. Now don't screw up and let me trip on anything.'

'You, lady, I'll be happy to throw out a window. Come on.' She felt his paw take hold of her arm – not gently, either.

They moved forward. She felt glass skitter away before her blindly shuffling feet. Leland's grip remained firm, her only link to the world. She tried counting paces, then gave up after awhile, knowing only that they'd traveled a long way – maybe in circles. She stumbled over a threshold, was dragged back to her feet. They were in a building, she realized, listening to their footsteps echo across the floor. Too many turns to keep track of now. Up some stairs, then back down. Cold air on her face – outside? A walkway, perhaps? Back inside – those echoing footsteps again.

The echoes elongated, bounced off widely spaced walls. There were others here; she could hear footsteps and a murmur of voices.

Leland halted.

'Where are we?' she asked.

'My castle,' said a voice – one she didn't recognize. It boomed forth, like an actor's from the stage.

'Are you Jonah?' asked Kat.

'Why don't you see for yourself?' said the man. 'Take off your blindfold.'

Kat hesitated. Then, slowly, she reached up and pulled off the bandanna.

12

She was standing in a dark room – a warehouse. On her right was a window, covered over by fabric. Only the faintest light managed to seep through the weave, offering her a dim view of scattered crates, sagging posts. *I have an audience*, she thought with a sudden flash of nervousness as she realized shadows were moving around her.

A light sprang on, a single bare lightbulb swaying from a wire.

She squinted against the glare, trying to make out the faces surrounding her. There were at least a dozen of them, all with eyes trained on her, watching her, waiting for signs of fear or vulnerability. She tried not to show either.

'So,' she said, 'which one of you is Jonah?'

'That depends,' someone said.

'On what?'

'On who *you* are.'

'The name's Kat Novak. And this used to be my neighborhood.'

'She's a cop,' said Leland. 'Goes around askin' questions like one, anyway.'

'Not a cop,' said Kat. 'I work for the medical examiner's office. People die, my job's to find out why. And you've had folks dying around here.'

'Hell,' someone said with a laugh. 'Folks dyin' all the time. Nothin' special.'

'Nicos Biagi wasn't special? Or Xenia? Or Eliza?'

There was a silence.

'So why do *you* care, Kat Novak?'

Even before she turned to face the speaker, she knew it was Jonah. The tone of command in his voice was unmistakable. She found herself gazing at a magnificent man, towering, with unnaturally pale eyes and a lion's mane of brown hair. The others remained silent, as he moved forward to confront her in the circle of light.

'Is it so hard to believe, Jonah, that I *would* care?' she asked.

'Yeah. Because no one else does.'

'You forget. This was my neighborhood. I used to hang out on the same streets you hang out on now. I knew your mothers. I grew up with them.'

'But *you* left.'

'No one ever really leaves this place. You can try all

your lives, but it stays with you. Follows you wherever you go.'

'Is that why you're here? To help the lost souls you left behind?'

'To do my job. To find out why people are dying.'

'To do your job? Is that all?'

'And—' She paused. 'To warn your lady, Maeve.'

Jonah stood stock-still. No one moved.

Then the steady click-click of boot heels across the floor cut through the silence. A shadow, sleek as a cat's, came out of the darkness. Casually the woman strolled into the circle of light where she stood with arms crossed, gazing speculatively at Kat. She was dressed all in black, but in various textures of black: leather skirt, knit turtleneck, a quilted jacket with patches of shimmery satin. Her hair looked like broomstraw – stiff and ragged, the blond strands tipped with a startling shade of purple. She was thin – too thin, her eyes dark hollows in a porcelain face.

The woman walked a slow, deliberate circle around Kat, studying her from the side, from behind. She came around to the front, and the two women stood face to face.

'I don't know you,' said Maeve. Then, with that declaration, she turned and started to walk away, back into the shadows.

'But I know your father,' said Kat.

'Congratulations,' said Maeve over her shoulder.

'And I knew Herb Esterhaus. Before he was shot to death.'

Maeve froze. She turned to face her.

'You're a suspect,' said Kat. 'The police'll be coming around, asking questions.'

'No, they won't.'

'Why not?'

'Because they already know the answers.'

Kat frowned. 'What do you mean?'

Maeve glanced at Jonah. 'This is between me and her.'

After a pause, Jonah nodded and snapped his fingers. 'Out,' he said.

Like magic, the circle of people melted into the shadows. Maeve waited for the last footsteps to fade away, then she reached for a crate and shoved it toward Kat. 'Sit,' she said.

'I'll stand, thank you,' said Kat, unwilling to yield the advantage of height.

Maeve, unruffled, propped one black boot on the crate and regarded her adversary with new interest. 'Where did you meet my father?'

'The city morgue.'

Maeve laughed. 'That's a new one.'

'He came in to look at a body. We thought it might be yours.'

'He must've been disappointed when it wasn't.'

'No, as a matter of fact, he was terrified by the

prospect. As it turned out, it was someone you probably knew.'

'Eliza?' Maeve shrugged. 'Everyone knew her. You couldn't avoid it. She'd empty your pockets one way or another.'

'And your last matchbook?'

'What?'

'She had a matchbook. L'Etoile Restaurant. Had your father's phone number written in it.'

Again, Maeve shrugged. 'She needed the matches. I didn't.'

'What about Nicos and Xenia? Did you know them too?'

'Look,' said Maeve. 'They were stupid, that's all. Took some bad medicine.'

'Who passed it to them?'

Maeve didn't answer.

'You know, don't you?'

'Look, it was a mistake—'

'On whose part?'

'Everyone's. Nicos's. Xenia's—'

'Yours?'

Maeve paused. 'I didn't know. The bastard never bothered to tell me. He just said he wanted to make a delivery, needed a runner out to Bellemeade.'

'And you told him Nicos was available.'

'I didn't know Nicos was dumb enough to snitch a sample for himself. Pass it to his girlfriends.'

'So you arranged it all,' said Kat, not bothering to keep the disgust out of her voice. 'You do this sort of thing all the time?'

'No! It was a favor, that's all! Old times' sake. I didn't know—'

'That it was poison?'

'He said it was a one-time thing! All he wanted was a delivery boy.'

'All *who* wanted?'

Maeve let out a breath and looked away. 'Herb. Esterhaus. He and I, we used to be . . .'

'I know, Maeve. We saw the photos.'

'Photos?'

'You know. All that X-rated posing you did for your good friend Herb.'

There was a flash of regret in Maeve's eyes. 'Dad saw them too?'

'Yes. He wasn't pleased. Would've strangled Esterhaus if the man wasn't already dead.'

Maeve snorted. 'I'd like to strangle him myself. For using me.'

'Did he use you often? For these deliveries?'

'I told you, it was just a one-time thing.' She shook her head. 'And I thought he was clean, you know? After he got busted last year, he was real careful to—'

'Wait. Esterhaus was arrested? When?'

'About a year ago. It was small time, a few pot

plants in his backyard. I don't know how he squirmed out of the charges, but he did. I figure, the feds stepped in and helped him out. They look after their witnesses.'

'You knew he was in the Witness Protection Program?'

'He told me about Miami. When he got busted, that really scared him. He didn't want Miami to find out. And he didn't want to lose his job. Hell, he *liked* being cooped up in that lab! Me, I hated it. After a while I couldn't take *him* either.'

'So you left him.'

'I wasn't mad at him or anything. I just got bored.'

'The police say you're a suspect in his murder.'

'They'd say anything.'

'You have a better suspect?'

Maeve moved away from the crate and began to pace, weaving in and out of the shadows. 'Herb was just your average guy, trying to make a living. And trying to stay clean.'

'Then why was he stealing Zestron-L? Moving it out onto the streets?'

'He was being squeezed.'

'By whom?'

Maeve turned to look at her. 'Try the people at the top. The ones who'd like to wipe South Lexington off the map.'

'Who, City Hall? The cops?'

'The list goes on and on. People at the top, they look down at us like we're rats, crawling around in the sewers. And what do people do with rats? They exterminate them.'

Kat shook her head. 'Wild accusations won't earn you any points, Maeve.'

'No. People like you never listen to people like us.'

'Hey, you're not exactly scraping bottom, okay? You're a *Quantrell*.'

'Don't remind me,' snapped Maeve. She turned and started to walk away.

'Your father's waiting out on the street,' Kat called after her. 'He wants to talk with you.'

Maeve turned around. 'Why? He never bothered to talk with me before. It was always *at* me, not with me. Ordering me around. Telling me to clean up my act, toss out my cigarettes. He's not even my real father.'

'He wanted to be.'

'But he isn't, okay?'

'So where *is* your real father? Tell me that.'

Maeve glared at her, but said nothing.

'He isn't here, is he?' said Kat.

'He's living in Italy.'

'Right. In Italy. But Adam's *here*.'

'He's *not* my father.'

'No, he just acts like one. And hurts like one.'

Maeve shoved away a crate and sent it toppling.

'Oh, great,' said Kat. 'Now we're going to have a tantrum.'

'You're a bitch.'

'Maybe. But you know what I'm not? Your mother. And I don't have to take this crap.' With that, Kat turned and walked away. She heard, off in the shadows, a scrambling of footsteps, then Maeve's command: 'Forget it. Let the bitch go.'

Kat managed to navigate her own way out of the building. It took her a few wrong turns, a half-dozen rickety flights of stairs, but she finally found her way outside. Looking back, she realized she'd been in the abandoned mill building. Boarded-up windows and graffiti-splashed brick was all one saw from the street. She wondered how many pairs of eyes were watching her from behind that wall.

She walked on, heading briskly back to South Lexington Avenue, back to Adam.

She saw him pacing by the car, his fair hair tumbled by the wind, his hands deep in his pockets. The instant he spotted her, he started toward her.

'I was about to call the police,' he said. 'What happened?'

'I'll tell you all about it.' She opened the car door and got inside. 'Let's get out of here.'

He slid in beside her. 'Did you see Jonah?'

'Yes.'

'And?'

'It was an unforgettable experience.'

He started the engine and muttered, 'So was waiting for you.'

They pulled onto South Lexington and headed north.

'I saw Maeve,' said Kat.

Adam almost slammed on the brakes. 'She was *there*?'

'Celeste got it right. She's Jonah's lady.' She glanced back at the line of cars honking behind them. 'Keep moving, you're holding up traffic.'

Adam, still rattled, turned his attention back to the road. 'Did she seem . . . happy?' he asked.

'To be honest?' Kat shook her head. 'I don't think that kid was ever happy.'

'Will she talk to me?'

Kat heard it in his voice and saw it in his face: a father's fear, a father's despair. All at once she wondered about her own father, that nameless man with the green eyes. She wondered where he was, if he knew or cared he had a daughter. *Of course he doesn't*, she thought. *Not the way this man does*.

She looked ahead, at the line of traffic. 'She isn't ready to see you,' she said.

'If I tried to—'

'It isn't the time, Adam.'

'When *will* it be the time?'

'When she grows up. If she ever does.'

He gripped the steering wheel, staring ahead in frustration. 'If I only knew what I did wrong . . .'

'Some kids are just born angry. In Maeve's case, my guess is she's angry at her real father. But he's not around to scream at, so she takes it out on you. Nothing you do is right. You exert a little control, and you're a tyrant. You try to set limits, she smashes them.' Kat reached over and touched his knee. 'You did the best you could.'

'It wasn't enough.'

'Adam,' she said gently, 'it never is.'

He drove in silence, his troubled gaze focused on the road. How quickly he accepted the blame, she thought. As if Maeve had no responsibility for her own life, her own mess.

'She did clear up a few things,' said Kat. 'In fact, she cleared up a lot. Esterhaus *was* the source. He stole the Zestron and passed the drug to Nicos for a delivery. Nicos must have kept some for his own use. That's how it got into the Projects.'

'A delivery? To whom?'

'Maeve didn't say. But you know who she says is behind it all?' Kat laughed. 'The city elite, un-specified. Meaning all the creeps in power. She figures they're distributing the drug in order to clean the trash off the streets.'

'I hate to admit it, but she's got the city elite pegged just about right.'

238

Kat glanced at him with a raised eyebrow. 'But systematically pushing poison? To clean the riffraff from Albion? That's a big leap.' She gazed out at the numbing landscape of abandoned buildings, shattered windows. 'Still, I admit the same thought did cross my mind a few days back. But that's paranoia for you. Conspiracies are seductive . . .' She paused. 'By the way. Did you know Esterhaus was arrested a year ago? Possession of marijuana plants.'

'No, I was never informed.'

'Somehow it stayed off his record, and he walked. Maybe the feds stepped in to protect their old witness. Had him released.'

There was silence. Quietly Adam said, 'What if it wasn't the feds?'

'Come again?'

'What if he made, say, other arrangements to avoid the charges?'

'You mean . . . bribery?'

'He had access to an inexhaustible supply of narcotics. At Cygnus. That's a pretty persuasive bribe.'

'So he cuts a deal. With a judge. Or . . .'

'The police,' Adam finished for her.

They were back on the old conspiracy kick, but it was hard to let it go. Esterhaus's death had been an apparent execution. She thought of what Maeve said – that Esterhaus was being pressured to steal the

Zestron and deliver it somewhere. The bombing of
her house had been a professional job. She thought
about all the doors that had slammed in her face
when she'd tried to publicize the overdose victims.
The powers that be in Albion had systematically
shrugged off the deaths of those three junkies in
South Lexington.

Shrugged off? Or covered up?

'Head downtown,' she suddenly said.

'Why?'

'We're going to City Hall. I want to see Ed.'

Adam turned onto the downtown exit. 'Why?'

'Force of habit – I like to torment him. Plus, he
might get us the information we need. Namely, which
cop arrested Esterhaus – and then let him go. And
what else the said cop has been involved in.'

'Would Ed know that?'

'He has a direct pipeline into Police Internal
Affairs. If there's a crooked cop involved, they might
have a file on him.'

'Unless they're all crooked.'

'Please,' she groaned. 'Don't even mention the
possibility.'

City Hall had been turned into a media circus.
Banners were everywhere: *Mayor Sampson Presents
the Albion Bicentennial, 200 Years of Vision, Albion:
looking toward the third century.* In the hall was

posted a map of Friday's two-mile parade route. Anyone who bothered to study that map would see that the parade didn't even go anywhere near Albion's center, but skirted around it, along the northern city limits, thereby avoiding the South Lexington district entirely.

Ed was in his office, barricaded by a fortress of papers. Campaign posters were plastered across the wall behind him. A picture of a kid serenely skipping rope caught Kat's eye: *Albion. Safe, and getting safer.* *For whom?* she felt like asking.

Ed, as usual, did not look happy to see her. 'I haven't got a lot of time, okay?' he grumbled as Kat and Adam settled into chairs. 'This bicentennial thing is turning into a disaster. The weatherman says rain. Three high school bands have dropped out because of sniper rumors. And now the cops say they can't guarantee crowd control.'

'Yep, that's our town,' said Kat sweetly. 'Safe, and getting safer.'

'What do you want?' snapped Ed.

'Some service for my tax dollars, Mr. DA.'

He sighed. 'This isn't about the drug ODs again, is it?'

'Peripherally. By now, you've heard about my exploding house. And the dead Cygnus researcher.'

'That was a paid hit, Miami mob. At least, that's what the cops tell me.'

'The cops also say Esterhaus stole the drug from Cygnus and bombed my house to stop me from asking too many questions.'

Ed laughed. 'I can think of a lot of reasons to bomb your house.'

'But that theory strikes us as too simple,' said Adam. 'Blame all those acts on a dead man. Esterhaus kept his nose clean for years. He had only one arrest – a year ago, for growing marijuana.'

'I didn't hear about that,' said Ed.

'He wasn't charged. It appears he was rather quickly released. We want to know who made the arrest.'

'Why?'

'Pot growing's an open-and-shut case,' said Kat. 'Find the plants, you've got your conviction. Now, why go to the trouble of arresting someone, and then let him walk without charges?'

'The decision could've been made on a number of levels.'

'We want to know the street level,' said Kat. 'The name of the cop.'

'Yeah? What else do you want?'

'We want to know if Esterhaus might have offered this cop a bribe. Whether this particular cop suddenly found some new . . . prosperity. Check with Internal Affairs, see if there's a file.'

'There may not be.'

'Then just the name, Ed. Get me that.'

Ed shook his head. 'You're just fishing, Kat. You've got nothing.'

'I've got an empty lot where my house used to be.'

'And I've got a dead researcher,' said Adam.

Ed leaned back. 'So you're *both* fishing, huh?'

'You should be too,' said Adam. 'It's part of your job, Mr. DA.'

'And he's a terrific one, too,' said a voice from the doorway. They turned to see Mayor Sampson, looking dapper in a three-piece suit. He strolled into the office and, like any good politician, reached out to pump Adam's hand. 'Mr. Quantrell, good to see you again. Coming to the bicentennial ball, aren't you?'

'I hadn't made plans.'

'But I thought Isabel reserved two inner-circle tickets.'

'She didn't mention them to me.'

Sampson glanced at Kat and she saw the look of dislike on his face, quickly smothered by a smile. 'Keeping busy, Dr. Novak?' he asked.

'Too busy,' grumbled Ed.

'Oh, Lord. Not those junkies again?' Sampson gave Kat an indulgent pat on the shoulder, the sort of gesture she resented. 'You are taking this case entirely too personally.'

'Yeah. It got *real* personal when my house blew up.'

'But Ed is right on top of things,' said Sampson. 'Aren't you?'

'Absolutely.'

'Now, isn't it time we got moving?' asked Sampson.

'Huh?' Ed glanced at his watch. 'Oh, yeah. Gotta go, Kat. Parade committee.'

They all walked out of the office together. In the hall, Ed raised an arm, a gesture that could've meant either goodbye or good riddance, and headed off with the mayor. Kat watched the two men disappear around the corner and then snorted in disgust. 'Our tax dollars, hard at work. I'll be glad when this damn bicentennial is over.'

They got into the elevator, joining a City Hall clerk, her arms loaded down with a pile of gaudy flyers. 'Take one!' she said in a cheery voice.

Kat snatched one up and read it: *Mayor Sampson's Bicentennial Ball. General Tickets: $500. Contributor: $2,500. Inner Circle: $10,000.*

'Do you think Ed will help us out?' asked Adam.

'I'll hound him to the grave if he doesn't.'

Adam laughed. 'I'd say that's a pretty potent threat, coming from you.'

They stepped off the elevator. 'Hardly,' said Kat, still gazing down at the flyer.

Inner circle tickets were $10,000 each and Isabel had two of them.

'I'm not a threat to anyone,' she muttered. Then she tossed the flyer into a trash can.

The cook had laid out a lovely dinner for them: Cornish hens glazed with raspberry sauce, wild rice, a bottle of wine chilling in the bucket. And candle-light, naturally. Everything, thought Adam, was perfect. Or *should* have been perfect.

But it wasn't.

Kat was chasing a sliver of carrot around her plate now. Where *was* her appetite? With a sigh, she put down her fork and looked at him.

'Thinking about Esterhaus again?' he asked.

'And . . . everything, I guess.'

'Including us?'

After a pause, she nodded.

He picked up his wineglass and took a sip. She watched him, waiting for him to say something. It was unlike her to hold back words. *Are we so uncomfortable with each other?* he wondered.

'It's not healthy for me,' she said. 'Staying here.'

He glanced at her scarcely touched meal. 'At least you'd eat properly.'

'I mean, emotionally. I'm not used to counting on a man. It makes me feel like I'm up on stilts, tottering around. Waiting to fall. I mean, *look* at this.' She waved at the elegant table setting, the flickering candles. 'It's just not *real* to me.'

'Am I?'

She looked directly at him. 'I don't know.'

He pinched his own arm and said with a smile, 'I seem real enough to myself.'

She didn't appreciate his humor. In fact, he couldn't get even the glimmer of a smile out of her. He leaned forward. 'Kat,' he said. 'If you always expect to be hurt, then that's what will happen.'

'No, it's the other way around. If you're ready for it, then you can't be hurt.'

Resignedly he sat back. 'Well, that pretty much wraps up the future.'

She laughed – a sad, hollow sound. 'See, Adam, I take one day at a time. Enjoy things while I can. I can enjoy this, being with you. But I'm going to ask you to promise something: When it's over, tell me. No BS, just the straight scoop. If I'm not what you want, if it's not working, tell me. I'm not crystal. I don't break.'

'Don't you?'

'No.' She picked up her wine and took a nonchalant sip. The truth was, he thought, that she had a heart as fragile as that wineglass, and she wouldn't let it show. It was beneath her dignity to be weak. To be human. She was convinced that one of these days he would hurt her.

And maybe she's right.

He pushed his chair back and rose to his feet. 'Come on,' he said.

'Where?'

'Upstairs. If this is a doomed affair, then we should make the most of it. While we can.'

She gave him a careless laugh and stood up. 'While the sun shines,' she said.

'And if it doesn't work—'

'We'll both be fine,' she finished for him.

They headed up the stairs, to his bedroom, and closed the door, shutting out the rest of the world. *One day at a time*, he thought as he watched her unbutton her clothes, watched the garments slide to the floor, *one moment at a time*.

And what comes after is for tomorrow to decide.

He took her in his arms, kissed her. He wanted to be gentle; she wanted to be fierce. As though, in making love, she was battling some inner demon, struggling against it and him, against even herself. Love and war, delight and despair, it was what he felt that night, making love to her.

When it was over, when she'd fallen asleep in pure exhaustion, he lay awake beside her. He gazed around his darkened bedroom, saw the gleam of antique furniture, the vaulted ceiling. *It comes between us*, he thought. *My wealth. My name. It scares her.*

Clark was back from vacation, sporting a red sunburn and even redder mosquito bites. While the mosquitoes had found the pickings good, Clark, it seemed, had not.

'One lousy fish,' he said. 'The poorest excuse for a trout I ever saw. I didn't know whether to cook it or put it in a bag of water for my kid's goldfish bowl. A whole damn week, and that's what I had to show for it. Lost three of my best lures, too. I tell you, the rivers up there are fished out. Totally fished out.'

'So how many did Beth catch?' asked Kat.

'Beth?'

'You know. Your wife.'

Clark coughed. 'Six,' he mumbled. 'Maybe seven.'

'Only seven?'

'Okay, maybe it was more like eight. A statistical fluke.'

'Yeah, she's good at those flukes, isn't she?'

Clark yanked his lab coat off the door hook and thrust his arms into the sleeves. 'So how's it been here? Anything exciting happen?'

'Not a thing.'

'Why do I bother asking?' Clark muttered. He went over to the in-box and fished out a pile of papers. 'Look at all this stuff.'

'All yours,' said Kat. 'We left 'em for you.'

'Gee, thanks.'

'And you've got two dozen files on your desk, waiting for signatures.'

'Okay, okay. It's enough to keep a guy from ever

going on vacation.' He sighed and headed down the hall to his office.

Kat sat at her desk, listening to the familiar squeak of his tennis shoes moving down the hall. It was back to business as usual, she thought. The same old routine she had had for years. So why was she so depressed?

She rose and poured another cup of coffee – her third this morning. She was turning into a caffeine junkie, a sugar junkie. A love junkie. Hopeless relationships – that was her specialty. She dropped back into her chair. If she could just stop thinking about Adam for a day, an hour, maybe she'd regain some control over her life. But he had become an obsession for her. Even now, she wondered what he was doing, whether he was sitting at *his* desk, missing *her*.

She grabbed a file from the stack on her desk, signed her name, and slapped the file shut again. She almost groaned when she heard those tennis shoes come squeaking back down the hall toward her office.

Clark reappeared in her doorway. 'Hey, Kat,' he said.

'What?'

'What the hell's this supposed to mean?' He read aloud from a lab slip. ' " Results of mass and UV spectrophotometry show following, nonquantitative:

Narcotic present, levo-N-cyclobutylmethyl-6, 10 beta-dihydroxy class. Full identification pending."'
He looked up at her. 'What's all this?'

'You must have one of my slips. The drug's Zestron-L.'

'Never heard of it.'

'Here, I'll take care of the report.'

'But it's got my name on it.'

A frightening thought suddenly occurred to Kat. 'Who's the subject?'

'Jane Doe.'

'Oh.' Kat sighed with relief. 'Then that's mine.'

'No, it's *my* Jane Doe.' He held the slip out to her. 'See? There's my name.'

Frowning, Kat took it. On the line next to *authorizing physician* was typed the name Bernard Clark, M.D. She scanned the Subject ID data. Name: unknown. Sex: female. Race: White. ID #: 372-3-27-B. Processing date: 3/27.

A full week before *her* Jane Doe had rolled in the morgue doors.

'Get me this file,' she said.

'Huh?'

'*Get me the file.*'

'Whatever you say, mein Führer.' Clark stalked away and returned a moment later to slap a folder on her desk. 'There it is.'

Kat opened the file. It was, indeed, one of Clark's

cases. She had seen this file before; she remembered it now. This was the Jane Doe of the glorious red hair, the marble skin. The page from the central ID lab was clipped to the inside front flap, with a notice of a fingerprint match. As Kat now remembered, the corpse's name was Mandy Barnett. She had a police record: shoplifting, prostitution, public drunkenness. She was twenty-three years old.

'Do we still have the body?' asked Kat.

'No. There's the release authorization.'

Kat glanced at the form. It was signed by Wheelock the day before, releasing the body to Greenwood Mortuary.

'I called it a probable barbiturate OD,' said Clark. 'I mean, it seemed reasonable. There was a bottle of Fiorinal next to her.'

'Were barbs found in her tox screen?'

'Just a trace.'

'No needles found on site? No tourniquet?'

'Just the pills, according to the police report. That's why I assumed it was barbs. I guess I was wrong.'

'So was I,' she said quietly.

'What?'

She reached for the telephone and dialed the police. It rang five times, then a voice answered, 'Sykes, Homicide.'

'Lou? Kat Novak. We've got another one here.'

'Another what?'

'Zestron OD. But this one's different.'

She heard Sykes sigh. Or was that a yawn? 'I'm *real* interested.'

'The victim's name is Mandy Barnett. She was found in Bellemeade – a week before the others. And get this – she was set up to look like a barbiturate OD.'

'Are you going to tell me what is going *on*?' whined Clark.

Kat ignored him. 'Lou,' she said. 'I'm going to stick my neck out on this one.' She paused. 'I'm calling it murder.'

13

Sykes tossed the police file down on his desk and looked across at Kat. 'Dead end, Novak. No motive. No witnesses. No signs of violence. Mandy Barnett was a loner. We can't locate even a single relative or friend.'

'Someone must have known her.'

'No one who'll come forward.' Sykes leaned back in his chair. 'We're stuck. If it's murder, then someone's committed the perfect crime.'

'And chosen the perfect victim,' said Kat. She looked at Ratchet, who was hunched at his desk, making a ham sandwich disappear. 'Vince? You talk to Greenwood Mortuary?'

'They've had no calls, and the burial's tomorrow. But someone *did* pay the expenses.'

'Who?'

'Anonymous. Envelope stuffed with cash.'

Kat shook her head in disbelief. 'And you guys aren't chasing that?'

'Why? Not a crime to pay for a woman's burial.'

'It shows that *someone* knew her. And cared about her. Don't you guys have anything?'

'We know she lived out in Bellemeade,' said Sykes. 'Had an apartment on Flashner and Grove. We asked around the building, and you know what? No one even knew her name. They'd seen her come and go, but that was it. So much for witnesses.'

'How did she get the drug?'

Sykes shrugged. 'Maybe she bought it off Esterhaus. Or got a free sample in exchange for, uh, services.'

'Prostitution?'

'She'd been busted for it before. It's hard to teach an old dog new tricks, pardon the double entendre.'

'So we're back to blaming Herb Esterhaus?'

'I don't know who else to blame. It's a dead end for us.'

For Mandy Barnett as well, thought Kat. She remembered the woman's flame-colored hair, her porcelain beauty, shrouded in the cold mist of the morgue drawer. Not the sort of looks that went unnoticed in this world. Surely there'd been friends, lovers? Men who'd known the pleasures of her company, if only for a night. Where were they now?

A woman dies, and no one seems to notice. She

thought about this as she walked through the police station. She thought about herself, wondered how many would notice *her* death, would come to *her* funeral. Clark, of course. Wheelock, out of duty. But there'd be no husband, no family, no giant mounds of flowers on the grave. *We're alike, Mandy and I. Whether by choice or by circumstance, we've made our way alone through life.*

She stopped at the elevators and punched the Down button. Just as the floor bell rang, she heard a voice say behind her, 'Well, speak of the devil.'

Turning, she saw her ex-husband emerge from the chief's office. *You wouldn't come to my funeral, either*, she thought with a sudden dart of hostility.

'My, what a nice scowl you're wearing today,' said Ed.

They both stepped into the elevator and the doors slapped shut. He was looking dapper as usual, not a scuff on his shiny Italian shoes. What had she ever seen in him? she wondered. Then she thought morosely, what had he ever seen in her?

'I got what you asked for,' he said.

'What?'

'The name of the cop who arrested Esterhaus last year. You still want it, don't you?'

'Who was it?'

'The name was Ben Fuller, Narcotics detail. A sergeant with eighteen years on the force. He filed the

TESS GERRITSEN

arrest report. Possession of three live marijuana plants.'

'Did Fuller also arrange the release?'

'Nope. Feds did. They stepped in and pulled their ex-witness out of the fire. So you can drop the conspiracy angle. Fuller had nothing to do with it.'

'Can I see his Internal Affairs file?'

'Won't do you any good.'

'Why not?'

The elevator doors slid open. 'Because Ben Fuller's dead,' he said, and walked out.

Kat dashed after him into the first floor lobby. 'Dead? How?'

'Shot to death in the line of duty. He was a good cop, Kat. I've talked to his buddies. He had a wife, three kids, and a whole drawer full of commendations. So lay off the guy, okay? He was a hero. He doesn't deserve anyone mucking up his memory.' With that, Ed went out the front door.

Kat watched her ex-husband stride away down the sidewalk. Then she stalked off to her car.

Traffic was heavy on Dillingham, and she didn't have the patience to deal with it. Every red light, every idiot making a left turn, seemed to jog her irritation up another notch. By the time she got back to the morgue, she felt like a menace to the public.

In her office two dozen long-stemmed roses sat in a vase on her desk. 'What the hell's *this*?'

Clark stuck his head out of his office and called out sweetly: 'So who's the new lover boy, Novak?'

She slammed the door on his laughter. Then she sank into her chair and sat staring at the roses. They were gorgeous. They were blood red, the symbol of love, of passion.

Once, Ed had sent her roses, that very same color. Just before he'd asked for a divorce.

She dropped her head in her hands and wondered morbidly what sort of flowers Adam Quantrell would send to her funeral.

Her dark mood lasted all afternoon, through the processing of a hit-in-the-crosswalk old lady, through hours of paper catch-up and court depositions. By the time she drove through Adam's stone gate that evening, she was good and ready for a warm hug and some pampering. Or at the very least, a stiff drink.

What she found instead was Isabel's Mercedes parked in the driveway.

Kat got out of her car and stood for a moment by the Mercedes, gazing in at the leather upholstery, the kidskin gloves lying on the front seat. Then, in an even blacker mood, she went to the front door and rang the bell.

Thomas opened the door and regarded her with surprise. 'Oh dear! Did Mr. Q. neglect to give you a key, Dr. Novak?'

Kat cleared her throat. It had never occurred to her to simply walk in the door. After all, she was a guest and would always feel like one. 'Well, yeah,' she said. 'I guess he did give me a key.'

Thomas stepped aside to usher her in.

'I thought I should ring first,' she added as he took her jacket.

'Of course,' he said. He reached into the closet for a hanger. 'Mr. Q. hasn't arrived yet. But Miss Calderwood dropped by for a visit. She's in the parlor, if you'd care to join her for tea.'

Joining Isabel was the last thing she felt like doing, but she couldn't think of a graceful way to avoid it. So, hoisting a socially acceptable smile onto her lips, she entered the parlor.

Isabel was seated on the striped couch. Her sweater, a fluffy cashmere, hung fetchingly off the shoulder. She seemed unsurprised to see Kat; in fact, she appeared to have expected her.

'Hope you haven't been waiting long,' said Kat. 'I don't know when Adam's expected home.'

'He gets home at six o'clock,' said Isabel.

'Did he call?'

'No. That's when he always gets home.'

'Oh.' Kat sat down in the Queen Anne chair and wondered what else Isabel knew about Adam's habits. *Probably more than I ever will.* She glanced at the end table and saw the empty teacup, the plate of biscuits. The book Isabel had been reading lay beside her on the couch – the title was in French. The very air held the scent of her perfume – something cool, something elegant; no drugstore florals for her.

'Six o'clock is his usual time,' Isabel went on, pouring more tea into her cup. 'Unless it's Wednesday, when he kicks off early and gets home around five. He occasionally has a drink before supper – Scotch, heavy on the soda – and perhaps a glass of wine with his meal, but only one glass. After supper, he reads. Scientific journals, the latest pharmaceuticals, that sort of thing. He takes his work seriously, you see.' She set the teapot back down. 'And then he makes time for fun. Which normally includes me.' She looked at Kat and smiled.

'Look, if you're telling me all this because you feel threatened, Isabel, don't bother. With me, what you see is what you get. No blue blood, no pedigree.' She laughed. 'Definitely no class.'

'I didn't mean to put you down,' said Isabel hastily. 'I simply thought I could clear up a few things about Adam.'

'Such as?'

'Oh, I don't know . . .' Isabel shrugged. 'Aspects of his life you may not be familiar with. It must seem quite disorienting. Being thrust into this huge old house. All these portraits of strangers hanging on the walls. And then there's a whole circle of his friends you've never met.'

'I guess you know them all.'

'We grew up in that same circle, Adam and I. I knew Georgina. I watched the whole sad affair. And I was there when he needed a friend.' She paused, and added significantly, 'I'm still here.' *And I'll be here long after you're gone*, was the unspoken message. Isabel took a sip of tea and set the cup and saucer back down on the end table. 'I just wanted you to think about this. So you know what to expect.'

Kat did think about it. She thought about it as Isabel walked out the front door, as the Mercedes drove down the driveway. She thought about the gap between Surry Heights and South Lexington – a distance measured not in miles but in universes. She thought about country clubs and back alleys, picket fences and barbed wire.

And she thought about her heart, recently healed, and how long it takes to put the pieces back together once it's broken.

She went upstairs, collected her toothbrush and underwear, and came back down again.

Thomas, carrying a tray of fresh tea and biscuits, met her in the hall. 'Dr. Novak,' he said. 'I was just bringing this in to you.'

'Thanks. But I'm on my way out.'

He frowned when he saw the car keys she'd already removed from her purse. 'When shall I tell Mr. Q. you'll be returning?'

'Tell him . . . tell him I'll be in touch,' she said, and walked out of the house.

'But, Dr. Novak—'

She got into her car and started the engine. 'You've been great, Thomas!' she called through the car window. 'Don't let Miss Calderwood push you around.' As she drove off, she could see him in her rearview mirror, still staring after her.

The stone pillars lay ahead. She was in such a hurry to get away, she almost crashed into Adam's Volvo, driving in through the gate. He skidded to a stop at the side of the road.

'Kat?' he yelled. 'Where are you going?'

'I'll call you!' she yelled back, and kept on driving.

A half mile later, she glanced in her mirror and saw, through a film of tears, that the road behind her was empty. He hadn't followed her. She blinked the tears away and, gripping the steering wheel more tightly, drove on, toward the city.

Away from Adam.

I'll call you. What the hell did that mean?

Adam watched Kat's taillights disappear into the dusk and wondered when she'd be back. Had there been a call from the morgue? Some urgent reason for her to rush to work? An emergency autopsy?

He pulled in front of the house and parked. Even before he'd climbed the front steps, Thomas had appeared in the doorway.

'Evening, Thomas. What's up?'

'I was about to ask you. Dr. Novak just left.'

'Yes, I passed her at the gate.'

'No, I mean she's *left*. Taken her things with her.'

'What?' Adam turned and stared up the driveway. By now, she would be a good mile or more away, perhaps already turning onto the freeway. He'd never be able to catch up with her in time.

He looked back at Thomas. 'Did she say why she was leaving?'

Thomas shrugged. 'Not a word.'

'Did she say *anything*?'

'I never had the opportunity to speak with her. She and Miss Calderwood were taking tea, and—'

'*Isabel* was here?'

'Why, yes. She left a short time before Dr. Novak did.'

At once, Adam turned and headed to his car.

Isabel was home. He saw her Mercedes parked in the garage, the groundsman busy polishing the flanks to a gleaming finish. Adam took the front steps two at a time. He didn't bother to knock; he just walked in the door and yelled: 'Isabel!'

She appeared, smiling, at the top of the stairs.
'Why, Adam. How unexpected—'

'What did you say to her?'

Isabel shook her head innocently. 'To whom?'

'Kat.'

'Ah.' With new comprehension in her gaze, Isabel
glided down the stairs. 'We spoke,' she admitted. 'But
nothing of earth-shattering significance.'

'*What did you say?*'

She came to a stop on the bottom step. The crystal
chandelier above spilled its pool of sparkling light
onto her hair. 'I only told her that I understood the
difficulties she must be having. The transition to a
large house. A new circle of friends. She's not having
an easy time of it, Adam.'

'Not with friends like you.'

Her chin jutted up. 'I was only offering her my
advice. And sympathy.'

'Isabel.' He sighed. 'I've known you a long time.
We've shared some . . . reasonably enjoyable
moments together. But I've never known you to be, in
any way, shape, or form, sympathetic to anyone.
Except maybe yourself.'

'But Adam! Look at who she is, where she comes
from! I'm telling you this as a friend. I don't want to
see you make a mistake.'

'The only mistake I ever made,' he said, walking
out of the house, 'was calling you a *friend*.' He

slammed the door shut behind him, got back in his car, and drove home.

He spent all evening trying to locate Kat. He called her cell phone. It was switched off. He called the city morgue. He called Lou Sykes. He even called Ed Novak. No one knew where she'd gone, where she was spending the night. Or, if they knew, they weren't telling him.

At well past midnight, he went up to bed in frustration. There, lying in the darkness, Isabel's words came back to assail him. *Look at who she is, where she comes from.* He asked himself over and over if it made a difference to him.

And the honest answer was: *no.*

He'd already had a 'proper' marriage, to a proper woman. Georgina was everything the social register required: blue-blooded, wealthy, well-glossed by finishing school. Together they were, by the standards of their social set, the perfect couple.

They had been miserable.

So much for proper partners.

Kat Novak's origins, her hardscrabble youth, were, if anything, an asset. She was a survivor, a woman who'd wrestled the challenges life had thrown at her and come out the stronger for it. Could any of his friends, with their money and their platinum exteriors, have done the same? he wondered.

And then, even more troubling, was the next thought: Could he have?

The phone was ringing when Kat walked into her office the next morning. She ignored it. Calmly she hung up her coat, slid her purse in the desk drawer, revved up the coffee machine for a six-cup pot. An IV infusion of caffeine was what she really needed this morning. It had been a sleepless night on a lumpy motel bed, and she was feeling as alert as a grizzly bear in January and just about as cheerful.

She found her desk littered with pink message slips, taped in a haphazard collage. Calls from her overwhelmed insurance agent, from the DA's, from defense attorneys, from a mortuary. And from Adam, of course – five calls, judging by the number of slips. On the last slip, the night tech had scrawled in frustration: '*Call* this guy!' Kat crumpled up all the message slips from Adam and tossed them in the trash can.

The phone rang. She frowned at it, watched it ring once, twice, three times. Wearily she picked it up. 'Kat Novak.'

'Kat! I've been trying to reach you—'

'Morning, Adam. How're things?'

There was a long pause. 'Obviously,' he said, 'we have to talk.'

'About what?'

'About why you left.'

'Simple.' She leaned back and propped her feet up on a chair. 'It was time to leave. You've been great to me, Adam. You really have. But I didn't want to wear out the welcome. And I had to find my own place eventually, so I—'

'So you ran.'

'No. I walked.'

'You *ran*.'

Her spine stiffened. 'And what, exactly, am I supposed to be running from?'

'From me. From the chance it might not work.'

'Look, I have things to do right now—'

'Is it so hard for you, Kat, to stick your neck out? It's not easy for me, either. I take a step toward you, you take a step back. I say the wrong thing, look at you the wrong way, and you're off like a shot. I don't know how to deal with it.'

'Then don't.'

'Is that what you really want?'

She sighed. 'I don't know. Honestly, I don't know what I want.'

'I think you do. But you're too scared to follow your heart.'

'How the hell do you know what's in my heart?'

'Wild guess?'

'It's not like Cinderella, okay?' she snapped. 'Girls from the Projects don't have fairy godmothers to spiff them up. And they don't find happily-ever-afters in Surry Heights. Isabel gave me the straight scoop and I appreciate that. I'd be out to sea with your country club set. Too many damn forks on the table. Too many cute French words. Face it, I can't ski, I can't ride a horse, and I can't tell the difference between Burgundy and Beaujolais. It's all red wine to me. I don't see any way of getting past that. No matter how much you may lust after my body, you'll find after a while that it isn't enough. You'll want a fancier package. And I'll just want to be *me*.'

'I never took you for a coward before.'

She laughed. 'Go ahead, insult me if it makes you feel better.'

'You'll risk your neck for an old car. You'll march into a damn combat zone without blinking. But you're too scared to take a chance on *me*.'

She looked down at one of the message slips taped to her desk, and noticed it was from the Greenwood Mortuary, in response to a call she'd made to them yesterday.

'Kat?' Adam asked. 'Are you listening?'

'I can't talk now,' she said, and folded the slip in half. 'I have to go to a burial.'

Grim affairs, burials. Grimmer still is a pauper's burial. There are no gaudy sprays of gladioli, no wreaths, no sobbing family and friends. There is just a coffin and a muddy hole in the ground. And the burial crew, of course: in this case, two sallow-faced grave-diggers, their hats dripping with rain, and a blacksuited official from the Greenwood Mortuary, huddled beneath an umbrella. Mandy Barnett was being laid to her everlasting rest in the company of total strangers.

Kat stood in the shelter of a nearby maple tree and sadly watched the proceedings. It was the starkest of ceremonies, words uttered tonelessly under gray skies, rain splattering the coffin. The official kept glancing around, as though to confirm that he was playing to an audience – any audience. *At least I'm here*, thought Kat. *Even if I am just another stranger at her graveside*. A short distance away, Vince Ratchet also stood watching the scene. Cemeteries were routine stops for the boys from Homicide. They knew that two types of people attended victims' funerals: those who came to mourn, and those who came to gloat.

In Mandy Barnett's case, no one at all appeared. Those who passed through the cemetery this after-noon seemed intent on their own business: a couple bearing flowers to a loved one; an elderly woman, picking dead leaves off a grave; a groundskeeper, rattling by in a golf cart filled with tools. They all glanced at the coffin, but their looks were only mildly curious.

The rain let up to a fine drizzle. In a still mist, the

burial crew set to work, shoveling earth into the trench. Ratchet came over to Kat and muttered, 'This was a bust. Not a goddamn soul.' He fished a hand-kerchief out of his pocket and blew his nose. 'And I'll probably catch pneumonia for my trouble.'

'You'd think there'd be someone,' said Kat.

'Weather might have something to do with it.' Ratchet glanced up at the sky and pulled his raincoat closer. 'Or maybe she didn't have any friends.'

'Everyone has a connection. To someone.'

'Well, I think we got us a dead end.' Ratchet looked back at the grave. 'Real dead.'

'So there's nothing new?'

'Nada. Lou's ready to call it quits. Told me not to bother coming out here today.'

'But you came.'

'Hate to walk away from a case. Even if Lou thinks it's a waste of time.'

They watched as the last shovelful of dirt was tossed onto the grave. The crew patted it down, gave their handiwork one final inspection, and walked away.

After a while, so did Ratchet.

Kat was left standing alone under the tree. Slowly she crossed the wet grass to the grave and stared down at the mound. There was no headstone yet, no marker. Nothing to identify the woman who lay beneath this bare pile of dirt. *Who were you, Mandy*

Barnett? Were you so alone in this world that no one even noticed when you left it?

'It's not as if you can do anything about it,' said a voice behind her.

She turned and saw Adam. He was standing a few feet away, mist sheening his hair.

She looked back down at the grave. 'I know.'

'So why did you come?'

'I guess I feel sorry for her. For anyone who doesn't have a mourner to her name.'

Adam came to stand beside her. 'You don't know a thing about her, Kat. Maybe she didn't want any friends. Or deserve any friends. Maybe she was a monster.'

'Or just a victim.'

He took her arm. 'We'll never know. So let's just go inside somewhere. Get warm and dry.'

'I have to go back to work.' She paused as a flicker of movement drifted through her peripheral vision. She focused on two figures, a woman and a child, both dressed in black, standing beneath a distant tree. It was an eerie apparition, almost ghostly through the mist. They seemed to be gazing in her direction, their faces very still and solemn. Or was it Mandy Barnett's grave they were looking at?

Suddenly the woman noticed that Kat had spotted them. At once the woman grabbed the child's hand and began to lead her away, across the grass.

'Wait!' called Kat.

The woman was moving quickly now, almost dragging the child after her.

Kat started after them. 'I have to talk to you!'

The woman and child were already scurrying towards a parked car. Kat dashed across the last patch of lawn, reaching the blacktop just as the woman slammed her car door shut.

'Wait!' said Kat, rapping on the window. 'Did you know Mandy Barnett?'

She caught a glimpse of the woman's frightened face, staring at her through the glass, and then the car jerked away. Kat was flung backwards. The car made a sharp U-turn, spun around in the parking lot, and took off toward the cemetery gates.

Footsteps thudded toward her across the pavement. 'What's going on?' said Adam.

Without a word, Kat turned and made a dash for her car.

'Kat?' he yelled. 'What the hell—'

'Get in!' she snapped, sliding into the driver's seat.

'Why?'

'Okay, *don't* get in!'

He got in. At once, Kat turned the ignition and hit the gas pedal. They screeched across the slick blacktop and through the cemetery gates.

'We've got a choice,' said Kat as they approached the first intersection. 'East or west. Which way?'

271

TESS GERRITSEN

'Uh . . . east is back to town. She'd probably go that way.'

'Then we go west.'

'What?'

'Just a hunch. Trust me.' Kat turned west.

The road took them past a shopping mall, past a Pizza Hut, an Exxon gas station, a Burger King – the institutional underpinnings of Anytown, U.S.A. At the first red light, Kat pulled to a stop behind a line of cars. The windshield filmed over with mist. She turned on the wipers.

A block ahead, a dark green Chevy pulled out of a Dunkin' Donuts parking lot.

'There they are,' said Kat.

Adam shook his head in amazement. 'You were right.'

'First rule of escape: Never move in a straight line. See? She's heading north. I bet she'll circle back towards town. The long way around.'

The light turned green. Kat turned north, in pursuit of the Chevy. She kept her distance, with two cars between them. A half mile along, the Chevy turned east. As she'd predicted, her quarry was moving in a wide circle, taking secondary roads back to town.

'Is this why you went to the burial?' asked Adam.

'The same reason the cops went. To see who'd turn up to pay their last respects. I figured someone would. The same anonymous person who slipped

272

Greenwood Mortuary the cash for that coffin. It was just bottom-of-the-line plywood and veneer, but it was paid for. Our mystery lady in that Chevy must've been the one.'

'Did you get a look at her?'

'Just a glimpse. Late twenties, maybe. And a kid about six years old.'

They followed the Chevy to the Stanhope district, a bluecollar suburb of single family homes lined up on postage-stamp lots. From a block away, they saw the Chevy pull into a driveway. The woman got out and helped the child from the car, and together they climbed the porch steps into a house. It was a pink stucco box, irredeemably ugly, with cast-iron bars on the windows and a TV antenna the size of an oil rig on the roof.

Kat parked. For a moment they sat studying the house. 'What do you think?' she said.

'It's like approaching a trapped animal. She could be dangerous. Why don't we just call the police?'

'No, I think she's afraid of the police. Otherwise she'd have called *them*.'

After a pause, he nodded. 'All right, we can try talking to her. But the first sign of trouble and we're *out* of there. Is that clear?'

They got out of the car and she smiled across the roof at him. 'Absolutely.'

They could hear the sound of the TV as they

approached the front door. Some kids' show – cartoon voices, twinkly music. Kat stood off to the side of the porch, and Adam knocked.

A little girl appeared at the screen door.

Adam flashed his million-dollar smile. 'Can I talk to your mommy?' he said.

'She's not here.'

'Can you call her, then?'

'She's not here.'

'Well, is she in another room or something?'

'No.' The voice wavered, dropped to a whisper. 'She went away to heaven.'

Adam stared at her pityingly. 'I'm sorry.'

There was a silence, then the girl said, 'You wanna talk to my Auntie Lila?'

'Missy? Who's out there?' called a voice.

'Just a man,' said the girl.

Bare feet slapped across the floor and a woman came to the screen door. She peered out blankly at Adam. Then her gaze shifted and she caught sight of Kat, standing off to the side. The woman froze in recognition.

'It's all right,' said Kat. 'My name's Dr. Novak. I'm with the medical examiner—'

'It was you. At the cemetery . . .'

'I've been trying to find someone who knew Mandy Barnett.'

'My mommy?' said the child.

The woman looked down at the girl. 'Go on, honey. Go watch TV.'

'But she's talking about my mommy.'

'Just grownup stuff. Listen! I think *Spongebob* is on! Go on, you watch it.'

The girl, faced with the choice of adult conversation or her favorite cartoon, chose the latter. She scampered off into the next room.

The woman looked back at Kat. 'Why're you asking about Mandy? You with the police?'

'I told you, I'm with the medical examiner's office.' She paused. 'I think Mandy Barnett was murdered.'

The woman was silent as she considered her next move. 'It's not like I know anything,' she said.

'Then why are you afraid?'

'Because people might think I know more than I do.'

'Tell us what you know,' said Adam. 'Then we'll all know it. And you won't have to be afraid.'

The woman glanced toward the sound of the TV, now blaring out a cereal commercial. She looked back at Kat. Then, slowly, she unlatched the screen door and motioned them to come in.

14

They sat in the dining room, in chairs upholstered in green and yellow plaid. There was a bowl of plastic fruit on the table and on the wall hung a picture of a soulful young Elvis, gazing like some patron saint from an oil and canvas eternity. Lila lit a cigarette, blew out tendrils of smoke that wreathed her close-cropped hair.

'I was just a friend of hers,' said Lila. 'I mean, a good friend, but that's all. We used to hang out together, cruise the bars. You know, girl stuff.' She flicked off her ash. 'Then I got married, and we sort of drifted apart. I knew she was having a hard time of it. Kept trying to borrow money from me till I just didn't have any to give her. See, Mandy, she liked to party, and she wasn't exactly responsible. Had this kid at home and she'd just go out and leave her.'

'Is that Mandy's child?' asked Kat, nodding toward the TV room.

'Yeah. That's Missy. Anyway, I got tired of Mandy coming around for cash, so we had this falling out. It was her fault. I mean, she was working and all, but she just couldn't manage her wallet.'

'She had a job?'

'She worked the phones in some boiler room. A company called Peabody or Peabrain, over on Radisson and Hobart. They do telemarketing. You know, sell Florida vacations to poor shmucks in Jersey. Easy work, sitting all day on your tush. It wasn't bad money, either. But Mandy, she liked nice stuff. She couldn't keep any money in the bank.'

'We never heard she had a job,' said Adam.

Lila's brown eyes focused admiringly on Adam. Married or not, the woman still had an appreciation for the masculine form. She exhaled a lungful of smoke. 'It was under the table. You know, no taxes, that kind of thing. Anyway, she quit about six months ago.'

'Then how did she support herself?'

'Hell if I know.' Lila laughed. 'Girls like Mandy, they survive. One way or another, they do okay. If they can't bum off friends, then they pick up cash somewhere else. Maybe she found herself a sugar daddy.'

'She mention any names?' asked Kat.

'No. But I figure there must've been someone, 'cause she suddenly had money to burn. All she'd say was, she got lucky, that she was set up for life. I'd babysit Missy once in a while, see, and Mandy'd drop her off here. God, she'd come back high as a kite.'

'You mean on drugs?'

'Oh, yeah. She liked a hit once in a while. Not all the time. She wasn't *that* irresponsible.'

'So this started when?' asked Kat. 'The money, the drugs?'

'About six months ago.'

'The same time she quit her job.'

'Yeah. About.'

'And then what happened?'

Lila shrugged. 'She started getting . . . weird.'

'How?'

'Looking over her shoulder. Closing all my curtains. I figured it was the drugs. You know, they make you a little crazy after a while. I tried talking to her about it, but all she'd say was, things were fine. Then, a couple of weeks ago, she dropped Missy off and told me to keep her for a while. Said she was gonna party seriously.'

'Meaning?'

'Get high. She was going to try out some new stuff she'd bought off a kid in the neighborhood.' Lila crushed out her cigarette butt. 'And that was the last time I saw her.'

'Why didn't you call the police?' asked Adam. 'Report her missing?'

Lila paused and looked away. 'I didn't want to get involved.'

There's more to it than that, thought Kat, watching the woman's eyes, noting how she looked everywhere but at *them*.

'Why are you afraid of the police?' asked Kat.

'Get busted a few times,' Lila muttered, 'and *you* wouldn't be a fan either.'

'No, you're actually *afraid* of them.'

Lila looked up at Kat. 'So was *she*. The last thing she says to me – the last time I saw her – she tells me, any cop comes around, it was real important I play stupid. Tell 'em the kid's mine and I don't know any Mandy. She says I could get hurt if I start blabbing. That's why you scared me, at the cemetery. I thought maybe you were one of *them*.'

In the next room, Missy was flipping channels. They could hear the clack-clack of the dial, the intermittent blasts of music.

'What about Missy?' Adam asked. 'What happens to her now?'

Lila thought about it for a moment. 'I guess she'll stay with me.' She sighed. 'I sort of like the kid. And my old man, he doesn't mind.' Lila gave a shrug and lit up another cigarette. 'After all,' she said, blowing out a cloud of smoke, 'where else is the kid gonna go?'

*   *   *

'So Mandy Barnett turns out to be a major screwball,' said Kat as she drove north on Sussex.

'You almost sound disappointed.'

'I don't know why. I guess I kept thinking of her as a victim. And I felt sorry for her. No one at the burial, no one even asking about her. A sort of . . . lost soul.' She sighed. 'Maybe I identified with her.'

'You're not a lost soul. You never were.'

She glanced at him, saw he was watching her with that penetrating gaze of his. Quickly she looked back at the road. 'Oh yeah, I'm tough,' she said with a laugh. 'No chinks in my armor.'

'I didn't say you were invulnerable.'

One look at you, and I know just how vulnerable I am, she thought. The old temptation was back, to give it a chance, to let this relationship take root. She was feeling brave and scared at the same time, one minute certain it would work, the next minute just as certain it would be a disaster. This was someone she could love far too much, and for that sin of recklessness, there was a special place reserved in hell. Or heaven.

She concentrated on her driving, navigating the stop-and-go traffic along Sussex.

'Where are we going?' he asked.

'Just a detour. To Bellemeade.'

'Why?'

'I have this hunch. Something that might pull together some loose ends.'

'And which of the dozen-plus loose ends are we talking about?'

'Nicos Biagi.'

She turned onto Flashner Boulevard. A half mile up, they came to the intersection of Flashner and Grove. On one corner stood La Roma Arms, a white stucco apartment building with wrought-iron verandas. From its name, Kat assumed it was designed to resemble an Italian villa; it looked more like a crumbling version of the Alamo. She pulled into the Roma driveway and parked next to the pool area. The pool itself was empty, and a sign was posted on the fence: *Temporarily closed for maintenance*. About two years' worth of dead leaves were rotting at the bottom.

'Mandy's apartment?' asked Adam.

'This is it. Flashner and Grove.'

'Why are we here?'

'I just wanted to take a look at the neighborhood.' She glanced up and down the street, her gaze tracing Grove Avenue. 'There it is.'

'There *what* is?'

'The Big E Supermarket.' She pointed up the street to the grocery store, looming at the next corner. 'Only a block away.'

'The Big E,' muttered Adam, frowning. 'Isn't

that where Nicos Biagi worked? As a stockboy?'

'You got it. A convenient location, wouldn't you say? All Mandy had to do was walk down to the Big E, pick up her purchase, and she's ready to party. And Nicos goes home with a nice delivery fee. And his own private sample of the drug.'

'Which kills all of them.'

'But see, that's the part that doesn't add up,' she said. 'Business-wise, I mean. Here you've got a new drug that could make you millions on the street. What supplier would hand out a poisonously pure sample, thereby killing off his market?'

'A supplier who's out to kill one buyer in particular,' said Adam. 'Mandy Barnett.'

'But why Mandy?' Kat frowned, trying to pull the pieces together. She knew Mandy was a party girl, a flake. A loser on a permanent downhill slide. Then, six months ago, her fortunes had changed. Suddenly she had money to burn. She'd quit her job and embarked on a spree of spending and partying. *Was* there a sugar daddy, as Lila had suspected? Or some new job with high rewards – and high risks?

'We're missing something entirely,' said Adam. 'Where did all her money come from? She was getting a steady supply of cash from *somewhere*. And that was *after* she quit her job . . .'

Kat suddenly popped the car into gear. 'That's our next stop. Radisson and Hobart.'

'What, her old job?'

Kat grinned at him. 'Your synapses are finally catching up.'

'Whatever happened to solving crimes the old-fashioned way? Letting the police do it?'

'Under normal circumstances, yeah. I'd take the lazy gal's way out and dump this mess in their laps.'

'Under normal circumstances?'

'When alarm bells aren't going off in my head. But I'm hearing enough bells to give me a splitting headache. First, Maeve swears it's the city elite that's killing off junkies – meaning, the authorities. Then we hear Mandy was afraid of the cops. So afraid, in fact, that she hid her kid from them, and told the babysitter Lila to play dumb. And finally, there's Esterhaus. Okay, so maybe he *did* steal the Zestron and have it delivered to Mandy. But *why*? Who could've pushed him into it?'

'Someone who knew about his old connections with the mob. And could blackmail him.'

Kat nodded. 'The authorities.'

'Good Lord.' Adam sat back, shaken by the thought. 'A revolutionary method to mop up crime.'

'I'm not going to jump to conclusions here. Let's just say I'm not quite ready to take this to the cops.'

It was a good twenty-minute drive to the Watertown district. Along the way, they stopped at a phone booth to check the yellow pages. There was no listing for Peabody under Telemarketing. In fact, there were no *p*s listed at all. Directory Assistance likewise came up with a blank.

They drove on anyway, to Watertown.

It was a section of the city Kat seldom had reason to visit. Situated at the southeast corner of Albion, it had evolved over a half century from a thriving port to a malodorous district of fish processing plants, decaying piers, and ramshackle warehouses. At least there was still evidence of economic life in the neighborhood, mostly dockside bars and army surplus outlets. In fact, standing at the intersection of Radisson and Hobart, Kat could spot three surplus stores. Across the street, a sign hung in the window: *Guns and ammo – for the sake of those you love.* The Atlantic Ocean was only a block away, but the sea wind couldn't wash the smells of diesel and processed fish from the air.

The name of the company, it turned out, was Piedmont, not Peabody. They had to ask at a corner bar to find it, as the name itself appeared on none of the buildings. The company occupied a third-floor office in the Manzo Building on Hobart Street. The sign on the door said simply: *Piedmont.* From the room inside came the whine of a printer.

They knocked.

'Yeah, who is it?' a man called.

Kat hesitated and then said, 'We're friends of Mandy Barnett.'

An instant later the door opened and a man appeared, looking cross. 'Where the hell has she been?' he demanded.

'Maybe we can talk about it?' said Kat.

The man waved them inside, then shoved the door shut. It was a dismal office, if one could even call it that. Bare walls, a steel desk. In the corner sat a computer, its printer spewing out a list of names and telephone numbers. Another doorway led to an adjoining room, equally dismal.

'So what's going on?' said the man. 'She wanna come back to work or something? Well, you can tell her, forget it. And by the way, she still owes me.'

'For what?' asked Kat.

'Two weeks' salary. I give her an advance, and she skips out.'

'Excuse me, Mr. . . .'

'Rick. Just Rick.'

'Rick. I guess you haven't heard. Mandy Barnett's dead.'

He stared at her, looked at Adam, then back at her. 'Aw, Christ. Now I'll *never* get the three hundred back.' The phone rang. He went over to the desk, picked up the receiver, and slammed it down again. 'That's what I get for being Mr. Nice Guy.'

'You're not the least bit interested in how

she died?' said Adam with undisguised disgust.

'Okay,' Rick sighed. 'How'd the bitch die?'

'A drug overdose.'

'I'm *real* surprised.' Rick dropped into a chair and looked at them with utter disinterest. 'So why're you here? She leave me something in her will?'

'Rick, my friend,' said Kat, pulling up a chair. 'We have to talk. I'm from the medical examiner's office, see, and I have to ask you some questions.'

'You and what cop?'

'Take your pick. There's my buddy in Homicide, Lieutenant Sykes. Or maybe you'd like to meet the guys in Fraud. They'd probably like to meet *you*.' She glanced around the office. 'What *is* it you sell here, by the way? Bargain vacations?'

Rick sank, glowering, into his chair.

'We're in the right mood now, are we?' said Kat.

'I don't know nothing.'

'Mandy quit her job six months ago. Is that right?'

Rick grunted, a sound Kat took to be a yes.

'Why did she quit?'

Another grunt, coupled with a sullen shrug. Communication worthy of a caveman.

'Was she mad about something?' asked Adam. 'Did she give you a reason?'

Maybe it was the fact a man was now asking the questions; Rick finally decided to answer. 'She didn't tell me anything. She just walked off the job. Called a few days later to say she wasn't coming back. She had something better going.'

'Another job?'

'Who knows? The bitch was flaky, you know? One minute she's at her desk, working the phone. Then I get back from lunch and there's a note on the door sayin' she's out of here. No explanation, just – poof! Here I am, paying rent on two rooms, and I can't get anyone to man the other desk.'

'She had her own office?' said Adam.

'That room over there.' He pointed to a doorway. 'Her own private space. Didn't appreciate it none.'

'May we see the office?' asked Adam.

'Go ahead. Won't tell ya nothin'.'

The adjoining room was like the first, but without a computer. There was a window that looked down on a grim back-alley view of broken glass, trash cans.

Adam opened and closed a desk drawer. 'Not much in here,' he said.

'She took it all with her,' said Rick. 'Even the pencils. *My* pencils.'

'No papers, no notes.' Adam pulled out the last drawer. 'Nothing.' He shut it.

'See?' said Rick. 'I told ya there wasn't anything to look at. Just a desk and a telephone.' He glanced at Kat, who was gazing down at the alley. 'And a window,' Rick pointed out. 'I was generous. I let *her* have the view.'

'And a lovely view it is,' said Kat dryly.

'Okay, so it's not the seaside. But it faces south and you get some sun. And Bolton's a quiet street so you don't get blasted away by traffic noise.'

'Well,' said Adam. 'I guess there's not much more to see in here.'

'That's what I said. You satisfied now?'

Kat was still gazing out the window. In the alley below, a man appeared, lugging a trash bag. He dumped it in a can, slammed down the lid, and retreated back up the alley. Something was still bothering her. It had to do with this window, with Mandy Barnett and the reason she'd left her job so abruptly six months ago.

She turned to Rick. 'Did you say that was Bolton Street out there?'

'Yeah. Alley comes off it.'

'What are the nearest cross streets?'

'To Bolton?' Rick shrugged. 'Radisson's to the east. And west, that'd be, uh . . .'

'Swarthmore,' said Kat softly. It came to her like a lightning flash of memory: the name of the street. Its significance.

Bolton and Swarthmore. That's where my partner went down. Drug bust went sour, got boxed in a blind alley . . .

Kat swung around to look at Adam. 'My God, that's *it*. That has to be it!'

Adam shook his head. 'What are you talking about?'

'There was a cop killed there! In that alley!' She glanced at Rick. 'When did Mandy quit her job?'

'I told ya. Six months ago—'

'I need the exact date!'

Rick went into the front office, pulled out a ledger book. 'Let's see. Last call she logged was October second.'

'I have to make a call,' snapped Kat, pulling out her cell phone.

Adam was shaking his head, trying to catch up with her leaps of logic. 'A dead cop? How does that fit in?'

'It was blackmail,' she said, punching in the phone number. 'That's where Mandy's money was coming from. She saw a cop get killed in that alley. And she was squeezing the killer for cash . . .'

'Until he refused to be squeezed any longer,' Adam finished for her.

'Right. So he arranges to have a little poison slipped her way. Courtesy of the local drug dealer, Nicos . . . Hello? Ed?'

The voice on the other end of the line sounded harassed. 'Kat? I'll call you back, I'm already late—'

'Ed, one question. That cop, Ben Fuller. The one who arrested Esterhaus. Where was he killed?'

'Somewhere out in Watertown.'

'The date?'

'That's two questions.'

'The *date*, Ed!'

'I don't know. October sometime. Look, the parade starts in twenty minutes and I gotta get out to the limo—'

'Was it October second, Ed?'

A pause. 'Could've been.'

'I want you to find out one more thing.'

'*Now* what?'

'The name of Ben Fuller's partner.'

'I'd have to check—'

'Then *do* it.'

'Yes, *ma'am*!' growled Ed and hung up.

She looked at Adam. 'It *was* Ben Fuller who died in that alley. The police called it a drug bust gone sour. I think he was murdered. By another cop.'

They stared at each other, both of them shaken by their conclusions. By what they had to do next.

Adam took her arm. 'Let's go. We're taking this straight to the police commissioner.'

'He'll be in the parade. So will everyone else.'

'Then we head for City Hall. The sooner we unload this bomb, the sooner we can stop watching our backs.'

'You think he knows we're on to him?'

'Are you kidding? Ed's probably griping to

everyone in earshot about his ex-wife and her wild theories. The word'll be out.'

'Hey!' called Rick, as they headed out the door. 'What's all this with the cops? Am I gonna have trouble?'

'Not to worry,' said Adam. 'You, Rick, are of absolutely *no* interest to anyone.'

'Oh. Well, that's good,' said Rick.

They left the office and headed down the stairs. Their descent had suddenly taken on the panic of flight. *We know too much*, Kat thought. *And it could get us killed.*

By the time they reached the ground floor, her hand was sweaty against the banister. They emerged from the building, into the gloom of an impending storm. From the Atlantic, black clouds were roiling in, and the very air smelled of brine and violence.

Adam glanced up and down Bolton Street, his gaze quickly surveying the shabby buildings, the wind-blown sidewalks. Across the street, a man emerged from a bar, hugged his coat, and trudged away. At the intersection, a car stood idling, music booming from its radio. So far there was no sign of danger. Still, she was glad when Adam reached for her hand; the warmth of his grasp was enough to steady her nerves.

They started up the street. Her car was right around the corner, on Radisson. As they reached it, the first fat drops of rain were beginning to fall.

Kat pulled out her keys; Adam reached over and took them out of her hand. 'I'll drive,' he said. 'You look shaken up.'

She nodded. 'Thanks.'

He unlocked the passenger door and helped her in. Then he circled around and slid into the driver's seat, bringing in with him the comforting scents of damp wool, of skin-warmed after-shave. He pulled the door shut. 'We'll get this over with,' he said, 'and then I'm taking you home.'

She looked at him. 'I think I'd like that,' she said softly. 'I'd like that very much.'

They smiled at each other. He reached down to put the key in the ignition. Her gaze was still focused on his face. Only vaguely did she register the shadow moving alongside the car, closing in on her window. She glanced to her right just as the door was yanked open.

A blast of chilly air swept across her face; colder still was the icy gun barrel pressed against her temple.

Kat jerked taut. 'No! Vince—'

'Not a muscle,' growled Ratchet. 'Got that, Quantrell?'

Adam sat frozen behind the wheel, his gaze locked on Kat. 'Don't,' he said, panic seeping into his voice. 'Don't hurt her.'

'Into the back seat,' Ratchet ordered. '*Move it, Novak.*'

On wobbly legs, Kat stepped out of the car and climbed through the rear door into the back seat. Ratchet slid in beside her and slammed the door shut. The gun barrel was still pressed to her head.

'Okay,' said Ratchet. 'Drive.'

Adam turned to look at them. 'Leave her alone! There's no reason for this—'

'She knows. So do you.'

'So does the DA!'

'He doesn't know crap. Far as he's concerned, it's a nuisance case. And his ex-wife's a pain.' Ratchet clicked back the gun hammer. 'Which she is.'

'No!' cried Adam. 'Please—'

'Then *drive*.'

'Where?'

'Up Radisson.'

Adam threw Kat a desperate look. He had no choice. Then he turned and started the engine. As they pulled into traffic, she could see his knuckles were white on the steering wheel. There was nothing he could do; one false move and Ratchet would blow her away.

She said, 'They'll figure it out, Vince. Ed knows you were Ben Fuller's partner. He's already wondering what really happened to Fuller. How could you do it to your own partner?'

'He wasn't a good sport.'

'Meaning what? He wouldn't play along? Wouldn't take the payoffs?'

'Goddamn Boy Scout. God, honor, country. That stuff doesn't pay the bills. Ben and I, we just never came to an understanding. No common ground, see.'

'Not like you and Mandy Barnett,' said Adam.

'Hey, Mandy, I could sorta understand. Bitch saw an opportunity, she grabbed it. Trouble is, she started getting greedy. More money, always more.'

'So you had Esterhaus pass along some poison. Something you thought couldn't be identified,' said Adam.

Ratchet gave a grunt of surprise. 'He talked?'

'He didn't have to,' said Kat. 'We knew about his arrest. You were Fuller's partner at the time, weren't you? You would've heard all about Esterhaus. And his troubles.'

'Yeah. Those Miami boys.' Ratchet laughed. 'He was scared to death of them.'

'So you two cut a deal. He got you the drug. And you didn't call Miami.'

'Hey, it worked.'

'Except for one detail, Vince. Zestron-L killed a few too many victims. One body, the ME might overlook. But four? That was a trend.'

They pulled to a stop at a red light. Ratchet glanced at the street sign. 'Turn right,' he said.

'Where are we going?' asked Adam.

'The docks.'

Adam flashed Kat a backward glance. *Keep your cool*, it said. *I'll get us out of this somehow*.

He turned right.

Three blocks east took them to the wharf. The rainswept docks were deserted. A series of piers jutted out, most of them long since abandoned to disuse. A single fishing trawler rocked in the gray water, straining at its moorings.

'That warehouse up ahead,' said Ratchet. 'Drive there.'

'The pier won't hold the weight,' said Adam.

'Yes it will. *Go*.'

Adam pulled off the pavement and slowly guided the car onto the pier. They could hear the wood creak under the weight, could feel the thump of the tires over the boards. At the warehouse entrance, they rolled to a stop.

'Okay,' said Ratchet. 'Out of the car.'

Kat stepped out. The wind whipped her hair and lashed her face with sea spray. She stood with the gun shoved against her back, her heart pounding.

'Quantrell! Open the warehouse door,' ordered Ratchet.

'Two more murders,' said Adam. 'What's it going to get you, Vince?'

'My freedom, maybe? Open the door.'

Adam reluctantly set his shoulder against the

295

sliding panel. 'You killed Fuller,' he grunted, pushing against the door. 'And Esterhaus. And Mandy Barnett.' Slowly the panel slid open, revealing a seemingly impenetrable darkness. 'Where's it going to end?'

'With you two.' Ratchet waved the gun. 'Inside.'

There was no arguing with a bullet. They stepped out of the wind's assault, into the gloom. The darkness smelled of dust and sea rot.

'Sykes will figure it out,' said Adam. 'He'll find us—'

'Not for a while. See, this particular warehouse belongs to Vito Scalisi. And his sentence runs another eight years. By the time they open the building again, the rats'll have taken care of things. If you catch my drift.'

Meaning our bodies, thought Kat with a rush of nausea. Quickly she glanced around and saw, through the shadows, a jumble of old crates, wooden pallets. Overhead, ropes dangled from a catwalk. And high above, rainwater dripped steadily through a hole in the roof. There were no other exits, no way out.

Adam was still trying to buy time. 'People saw you at the burial, Vince—'

'I was there in the line of duty.'

'They saw us, too! They'll put it together – know you followed us—'

'Me? I went home to bed. This damn virus, you see.' He raised his gun. 'Both of you, against the wall. Don't want to have to drag you. Not with my bad back.'

Adam moved close to Kat and wrapped his arms around her. She felt his breath warm her hair, felt his lips brush the top of her head. 'Get ready,' he whispered. 'When I move, you *run*.'

In bewilderment she stared up at him, and saw the unbending command in his gaze: *Don't argue. Just do it.*

'Skip the tender farewells, okay?' barked Ratchet. 'Against the wall.'

With a nudge, Adam pushed her away, placing himself between her and Ratchet. Calmly, he turned to face the gun.

'You know, Vince,' said Adam. 'You've neglected a few vital details. The car, for instance.'

'Getting rid of the car's easy.'

'I'm talking about *my* car.' Adam took a step forward, so small it was scarcely noticeable. 'An abandoned Volvo at the cemetery . . .' He took another step toward Ratchet. Toward the gun. 'It'll raise a lot of questions.'

'I can take care of that, too.'

'And then there's the matter of Mandy Barnett's boyfriend.'

'What?'

'You think she kept her little gold mine a secret?' Another step. 'You think he didn't ask where all her drugs, all her cash, was coming from?'

Ratchet was poised on the verge of finishing off the whole bloody business, but new doubts had been stirred. His hand wavered, the gun barrel dropping a fraction of an inch.

Adam was still ten feet away, too far to make his move. But he might not get a better chance.

Kat, standing behind Adam, could almost sense the tensing of his muscles, the last coiling up before the spring. *Dear God, he's going to do it.*

Adam's body would take the first bullet, and probably the second as well. By that time she could be on Ratchet. It was a last-chance gamble, one they were almost certain to lose, but the alternative was to go down like sheep in a slaughterhouse.

She leaned forward, poised like a sprinter on the balls of her feet, waiting for Adam's move. Any second now . . .

The ringing of Ratchet's cell phone suddenly seemed to trap them in an instant's freeze-frame. Pure force of habit made Ratchet glance down at the phone on his belt. In that split second of inattention, Adam sprang.

He was halfway to Ratchet when the first shot exploded. The thud of the bullet into his flesh scarcely slowed his momentum. Before Ratchet could even squeeze off a second shot, Adam hurtled against him. Both men toppled to the ground.

Kat scrambled forward to help, but the men were rolling over and over in a confusing tangle of limbs, grappling for the gun. Another shot went off, this one wild – the bullet whistled past Kat's cheek. Adam's hand shot out to grab Ratchet's wrist. He managed to grunt out: '*Run!*' before Ratchet, roaring like a bull, flung him aside.

Kat attacked, clawing for the gun, but Ratchet had too firm a grip. Enraged, he swung at her, his fist slamming into her jaw. The blow sent her flying. She tumbled across the floor to land in a pile of damp burlap. Through eyes half blinded by pain, she saw Ratchet turn and walk over to look at Adam, who now lay motionless.

He's dead, she thought. *He's dead.* Fueled by grief, by rage, she staggered to her feet. Even as blackness gathered before her eyes, she struggled desperately toward the warehouse door, toward the far-off rectangle of daylight.

Just as she reached the doorway, Ratchet turned to her, raised his gun, and fired.

The bullet splintered the frame, and fragments of wood stung her cheek. She flung herself through the doorway, into the driving wind.

With Ratchet right behind her, a few seconds' head start was all she had. Still dizzy from the blow, she was moving like a drunken woman. The car was parked a few feet ahead. Beyond it stretched the pier, barren of any cover. Running was futile. It would be a single shot, straight into her back.

No escape, she thought. *I can't even see straight.*

Just as Ratchet came tearing out of the warehouse, Kat ducked around the rear of the car. He fired; the bullet pinged off the rear fender. Kat scurried alongside the car and yanked the passenger door open. One glance told her the keys weren't in the ignition. No escape in there, either – the car would be a trap.

Ratchet was moving in for the kill.

She heard the creak of the planks as he moved along the other side of the car, circling to the rear. Ahead there was only the warehouse, another dead end.

She took a deep breath, pivoted away from the car, and leaped off the pier.

15

The stomach-wrenching plunge hurled her into icy water. She sank in over her head, into a frightening swirl of brine. She floundered to the surface, gasping, her eyes and throat stung by the salt. One breath was all she managed; the zing of a bullet through the water sent her diving once again into the depths.

Frantically she stroked her way under the pier and surfaced again to cling at the foundation post. Windblown waves churned and thrashed against her face. Her hands had already gone numb from cold and fear, but at least her head was now clear. She glanced toward land, saw that the only way to shore would mean a clamber across exposed rocks. In other words, suicide.

She looked up through the gaps in the planks, and she spied Ratchet at the other edge of the pier, scanning the water. He knew she wouldn't swim away from the cover of the pier. He also knew the water was frigid. Fifteen minutes, a half hour – eventually she'd die of hypothermia. For him it was a simple waiting game. One she was sure to lose.

Numbness was creeping up her feet. She couldn't bob in this icy bath forever. Neither could she risk climbing those rocks. She had no choice – she had to do the unexpected.

Treading water with her legs, she managed to pull off her jacket. She tied the sleeves together, trapping air in the body, and tossed the jacket away, towards the edge of the pier where Ratchet was crouched. Then she dove and began to swim frantically in the other direction, into open water.

The sound of gunshots told her the ruse had worked. Ratchet was too busy firing at her jacket to see that she was swimming away from the cover of the pier. She surfaced for another breath, dove, and kept swimming an underwater course parallel to shore, surfacing, diving again. She could hear Ratchet still shooting. Sooner or later, though, he'd realize he was aiming at an empty jacket and he'd turn to scan the open water; she had only a few precious seconds to put as much distance as possible between her and the warehouse pier.

She surfaced a fifth time and saw that she'd pulled even with the next pier, where the trawler was moored. She turned toward shore and began to stroke for all she was worth, aiming for the trawler.

The gunshots had ceased. She came up for air and glanced in Ratchet's direction. He was pacing the pier now, his gaze scanning an ever-growing perimeter. She ducked under the surface and kicked wildly. When she came up again, the stern of the trawler was only twenty feet away. From the gunwale hung a rusty chain ladder – she could pull herself aboard! With escape so near at hand, she began to swim with abandon across the surface, drawing closer and closer to the trawler. Finally she reached up; her fingers closed around the first steel rung.

A gunshot rang out, ricocheted off the trawler's hull. He had spotted her!

Soaked, exhausted, she could barely pull herself up onto the next rung. So little time – already, Ratchet was dashing back up the warehouse pier, toward shore. Another few seconds and he'd be on the next pier, cutting off her escape. She reached for the next rung, and the next. Water streamed off her clothes. The wind kept banging the ladder against the hull, bruising her fingers. She grabbed the edge of the gunwale and hauled herself up and over.

She tumbled, gasping, onto the deck. *No time, no time!* She struggled to her feet and dashed to the starboard side, ready to leap off onto the pier.

Too late. Ratchet was already running along the

shore. He'd reach the head of the pier before she could. Her escape route was cut off.

She scrambled to the ship's pilot house, yanked at the door. It was locked. *What now? Back in the water?*

She ran back to the stern and gazed down at the roiling waves, preparing herself for another dive. But she knew she didn't have the strength to swim any longer. Her whole body was shaking from the cold. Another ten minutes in the sea would finish her.

She looked toward shore: Ratchet was on the pier now, and coming her way.

Her gaze shifted back to the stern, and two words stenciled in red on a deck locker caught her eye: *Emergency Supplies.*

She threw open the lid. Inside were life jackets, blankets, tools.

And a flare gun.

She reached for it. With trembling hands, she slipped a flare in the barrel, cocked the gun. One shot – that was the only chance she'd have.

Ratchet's footsteps thudded closer across the pier.

Kat swiveled, ducked around to the port side of the pilot house. There she crouched, waiting, listening. She heard his footsteps come to a stop on the pier somewhere along the starboard side. Then she heard the soft metallic thump as he stepped aboard.

Which way was he coming? Fore or aft?

She took a gamble – maybe the last she'd ever take – and moved toward the bow. There she crouched at the edge of the pilot house. Not a sound reached her. Not a footstep, nothing. There was only the roar of her own blood through her ears.

Then, suddenly, there he was. He stepped around the corner of the pilot house, right in front of her. There was no pity in his gaze, no expression at all. He raised the pistol.

She brought the flare gun up and fired.

His shriek was like a wild animal's, cutting through the roar of the wind. He staggered backward, his chest hissing with phosphorescent sparks. His gun clattered to the deck. Kat scrambled forward and grabbed it. Ratchet fell on his back and lay jerking in agony, screaming, tearing at his clothes. Kat clutched the pistol and stood over him, the barrel pointed at his head. *I could pull this trigger*, she thought. *I could blow you away. I want to blow you away.*

But she only stood there, watching him twitch. The terror, the exhaustion, had drained her of the ability to move. She was afraid to turn her back on him, even for an instant, afraid he'd suddenly rise up like a monster from the grave. So she kept the gun pointed at him, even as the sound of sirens wailed closer, even as the wind shrieked in her ears. She heard car doors slam, heard footsteps pounding up the pier. Only when they'd twice yelled the command: 'Drop it!' did she finally look up.

Two cops stood on the pier, their guns pointed at her.

'Drop it or we shoot!' one of them shouted.

She dropped the gun and kicked it away, where Ratchet wouldn't reach it, even if he could. Then, slowly, she turned to the cops and staggered toward them.

'Help me,' she said. She stretched her hands to them, and her voice dissolved into a moan of grief. *'Help me . . .'*

He still had a pulse. Crouching beside him in the darkness of the warehouse, Kat felt the faint throb of Adam's carotid artery. 'He's alive!' she cried.

The cop shone his flashlight, and the beam came down on Adam's blood-soaked shirt. 'Jesus,' he muttered, and turned to yell at his partner. 'Get the ambulance crew in here first!'

'Adam,' whispered Kat. She brushed back his hair, cradled his face in her lap. 'Adam, you have to live. Do you hear me? Damn you, *you have to live!*'

He didn't answer. All she heard was the sound of his breathing. It came in short, unsteady gasps, but at least his lungs were working.

She was still holding him in her arms when the EMTs arrived. They swept in with their stretcher, their IV bottles, their bag of tricks. As she stood by uselessly, they bundled him up and away, into the ambulance. She was left standing in the buffeting wind as the wail of sirens faded into the distance.

'You have to live,' she whispered. 'Because I love you.'

Footsteps creaked across the pier. Dazed, she turned to see Lou Sykes, holding out a blanket. 'Blue lips aren't very becoming,' he said, and slipped the blanket over her shoulders. 'You okay, Novak?'

'Just . . . cold.' She shuddered, and the tears suddenly flooded her eyes. 'He saved my life.'

'I know.'

'And I didn't believe in him. I was afraid to believe in him . . .'

'Maybe it's time you did.'

She looked up at Sykes's gleaming face. *Leave it to a homicide cop*, she thought. An old hand at death dishing out advice to the living.

She turned to his car. 'Take me to the hospital.'

'Right now?'

'Right now,' she said, and climbed into the car. 'When he wakes up, I want to be there.'

She was there when he came out of surgery. She stayed at his bedside as he slept all night. Other visitors came and went, but she remained. He slept most of the next morning as well, kept under by narcotics. The bullet had passed through his left lung, nicked his pericardium, and missed his ventricle by a fraction of an inch. He'd lost massive amounts of blood, his lung was collapsed, and he had plastic tubes gurgling out of his chest, but he was a lucky man.

At 10:00 A.M., Sykes appeared to fill her in on the latest. Ratchet had massive phosphorus burns on his chest, but he would be okay – certainly well enough to stand trial for murder times three. Ed Novak was telling the press he'd long had suspicions about Ben Fuller's death, and only his tireless efforts had broken the case. He was going to come out smelling like a rose, but Kat didn't care. She figured that if the voters of Albion chose to elect Ed Novak and Mayor Sampson, then mediocrity was exactly what they deserved.

At noon, another visitor showed up. There was a knock, and then Maeve appeared. She didn't come in at first; she just stood in the doorway, staring across the room at her sleeping father. She was stuffed tight as a sausage into a black leather dress, but her rainbow-tinted hair had been gathered almost demurely into a ponytail, and her face was white with fear.

'Is he gonna be all right?' she said.

'I think so,' said Kat. 'Why don't you come in?'

Maeve crept almost timidly to the bedside. She said, 'Dad?' Adam didn't stir.

'Sleeping meds,' said Kat. 'He's out cold.'

Maeve touched her father's face, then pulled away, as though embarrassed.

'He almost died,' said Kat.

For a moment Maeve didn't respond; she just stared at Adam. Softly she said, 'He drove me crazy, y'know? Telling me what to do, what not to do. But he was always there. I have to say that for the old man. He was always there . . .' She wiped her hand over her eyes. Then, abruptly, she turned and walked toward the door.

'Maeve?'

Maeve stopped, looked back. 'Yeah?'

'Come back. When he's awake.'

Maeve shrugged. 'Maybe,' she said, and left the room.

You'll be back, Kat thought with a smile.

It was late afternoon when Adam finally stirred and opened his eyes. The first face he saw was Kat's, gazing down at him.

'Hello, hero,' she said.

He groaned. 'Who are you talking to?'

'To you.' She leaned forward and kissed him. As she pulled back, his face blurred away through her tears. She shook her head and laughed. 'You are one crazy man. Do you know what you did?'

'What?'

'You saved my life.'

'If that's what it takes,' he whispered. 'To keep you around.'

She smiled. He smiled.

And they both knew that, this time, she would be staying.

KEEPING THE DEAD

Confront your darkest fears in Tess Gerritsen's new RIZZOLI and ISLES bestseller

He hides...

He kills...

He keeps...

'A seamless blend of good writing and pulse-racing tension' *Independent*

Here's a sample to whet your appetite...

Dr. Maura Isles could not decide whether to stay or to flee.

She lingered in the shadows of the Pilgrim Hospital parking lot, well beyond the glare of the klieg lights, beyond the circle of TV cameras. She had no wish to be spotted, and most local reporters would recognize the striking woman whose pale face and bluntly cut black hair had earned her the nickname Queen of the Dead. As yet no one had noticed Maura's arrival, and not a single camera was turned in her direction. Instead, the dozen reporters were fully focused on a white van that had just pulled up at the hospital's lobby entrance to unload its famous passenger. The van's rear doors swung open and a lightning storm of camera flashes lit up the night as the celebrity patient was gently lifted out of the van and placed onto a hospital gurney. This patient was a media star whose new-found fame far outshone any mere medical examiner's. Tonight Maura was merely part of the awestruck audience, drawn here for the same reason the reporters had converged like frenzied groupies outside the hospital on a warm Sunday night.

All were eager to catch a glimpse of Madam X.

Maura had faced reporters many times before, but the rabid hunger of this mob alarmed her. She knew that if some new prey wandered into their field of vision, their attention could shift in an instant, and tonight she was already feeling emotionally bruised and vulnerable. She considered escaping the scrum by turning around and climbing back into her car. But all that awaited her at home was a silent house and perhaps a few too many glasses of wine to keep her company on a night when Daniel Brophy could not. Lately there were far too many such nights, but that was the bargain she had struck by falling in love with him. The heart makes its choices without weighing the consequences. It doesn't look ahead to the lonely nights that follow.

The gurney carrying Madam X rolled into the hospital, and the wolf pack of reporters chased after it. Through the glass lobby doors, Maura saw bright lights and excited faces, while outside in the parking lot she stood alone.

She followed the entourage into the building.

The gurney rolled through the lobby, past hospital visitors who stared in astonishment, past excited hospital staff waiting with their camera phones to snap photos. The parade moved on, turning down the hallway and toward Diagnostic Imaging. But at an inner doorway, only the gurney was allowed through. A hospital official in suit and tie stepped forward and blocked the reporters from going any farther.

"I'm afraid we'll have to stop you right here," he said. "I know you all want to watch this, but the room's very small." He raised his hands to silence the disappointed grumbles. "My name is Phil Lord. I'm the public relations officer for Pilgrim Hospital, and we're thrilled to be part of this study, since a patient like Madam X comes along only every, well, two thousand years." He smiled at the expected laughter. "The CT scan won't take long, so if you're willing to wait, one of the archaeologists will come out immediately afterward to announce the results." He turned to a pale man of about forty who'd retreated into a corner, as though hoping he would not be noticed. "Dr. Robinson, before we start, would you like to say a few words?"

Addressing this crowd was clearly the last thing the bespectacled man wanted to do, but he gamely took a breath and stepped forward, nudging his drooping glasses back up the bridge of his beakish nose. This archaeologist bore no resemblance at all to Indiana Jones. With his receding hairline and studious squint, he looked more like an accountant caught in the unwelcome glare of the cameras. "I'm Dr. Nicholas Robinson," he said. "I'm curator at—"

"Could you speak up, Doctor?" one of the reporters called out.

"Oh, sorry." Dr. Robinson cleared his throat. "I'm curator at the Crispin Museum here in Boston. We are immensely grateful that Pilgrim Hospital has so generously offered to perform this CT scan of Madam X. It's an extraordinary opportunity to catch an intimate glimpse into the past, and judging by the size of this crowd, you're all as excited as we are. My colleague Dr. Josephine Pulcillo, who is an Egyptologist, will come out to speak to you after the scan is completed. She'll announce the results and answer any questions then."

"When will Madam X go on display for the public?" a reporter called out.

"Within the week, I expect," said Robinson. "The new exhibit's already been built and—"

"Any clues to her identity?"

"Why hasn't she been on display before?"

"Could she be royal?"

"I don't know," said Robinson, blinking rapidly under the assault of so many questions. "We still need to confirm it's a female."

"You found it six months ago, and you still don't know the sex?"

"These analyses take time."

"One glance oughta do it," a reporter said, and the crowd laughed.

"It's not as simple as you think," said Robinson, his glasses slipping down his nose again. "At two thousand years old, she's extremely fragile and she must be handled with great care. I found it nerveracking enough just transporting her here tonight, in that van. Our first priority as a museum is preservation. I consider myself her guardian, and it's my duty to protect her. That's why we've taken our time coordinating this scan with the hospital. We move slowly, and we move with care."

"What do you hope to learn from this CT scan tonight, Dr. Robinson?"

Robinson's face suddenly lit up with enthusiasm. "Learn? Why, everything! Her age, her health. The method of her preservation. If we're fortunate, we may even discover the cause of her death."

"Is that why the medical examiner's here?"

The whole group turned like a multi-eyed creature and stared at Maura, who had been standing at the back of the room. She felt the familiar urge to back away as the TV cameras swung her way.

"Dr. Isles," a reporter called out, "are you here to make a diagnosis?"

317

"Why is the ME's office involved?" another asked.

That last question needed an immediate answer, before the issue got twisted by the press.

Maura said, firmly: "The medical examiner's office is not involved. It's certainly not paying me to be here tonight."

"But you are here," said Channel 5's blond hunk, whom Maura had never liked.

"At the invitation of the Crispin Museum. Dr. Robinson thought it might be helpful to have a medical examiner's perspective on this case. So he called me last week to ask if I wanted to observe the scan. Believe me, any pathologist would jump at this chance. I'm as fascinated by Madam X as you are, and I can't wait to meet her." She looked pointedly at the curator. "Isn't it about time to begin, Dr. Robinson?"

She'd just tossed him an escape line, and he grabbed it. "Yes. Yes, it's time. If you'll come with me, Dr. Isles."

She cut through the crowd and followed him into the Imaging Department. As the door closed behind them, shutting them off from the press, Robinson blew out a long sigh.

"God, I'm terrible at public speaking," he said. "Thank you for ending that ordeal."

"I've had practice. Way too much of it."

They shook hands, and he said: "It's a pleasure to finally meet you, Dr. Isles. Mr. Crispin wanted to meet you as well, but he had hip surgery a few months ago and he still can't stand for long periods of time. He asked me to say hello."

"When you invited me, you didn't warn me I'd have to walk through that mob."

"The press?" Robinson gave a pained look. "They're a necessary evil."

"Necessary for whom?"

"Our survival as a museum. Since the article about Madam X, our ticket sales have gone through the roof. And we haven't even put her on display yet."

Robinson led her into a warren of hallways. On this Sunday night, the Diagnostic Imaging Department was quiet and the rooms they passed were dark and empty.

"It's going to get a little crowded in there," said Robinson. "There's hardly space for even a small group."

"Who else is watching?"

"My colleague Josephine Pulcillo; the radiologist, Dr. Brier; and a CT tech. Oh, and there'll be a camera crew."

"Someone you hired?"

"No. They're from the Discovery Channel."

She gave a startled laugh. "Now I'm *really* impressed."

"It does mean, though, that we have to watch our language." He stopped outside the door labeled CT and said softly: "I think they may be already filming."

They quietly slipped into the CT viewing room, where the camera crew was, indeed, recording as Dr. Brier explained the technology they were about to use.

"*CT* is short for 'computed tomography.' Our machine shoots X-rays at the subject from thousands of different angles. The computer then processes that information and generates a three-dimensional image of the internal anatomy. You'll see it on this monitor. It'll look like a series of cross sections, as if we're actually cutting the body into slices."

As the taping continued, Maura edged her way to the viewing window. There, peering through the glass, she saw Madam X for the first time.

In the rarefied world of museums, Egyptian mummies were the undisputed rock stars. Their display cases were where you'd usually find the schoolchildren gathered, faces up to the glass, every one of them fascinated by a rare glimpse of death. Seldom did modern eyes encounter a human corpse on display, unless it wore the acceptable countenance of a mummy. The public loved mummies, and Maura was no exception. She stared, transfixed, even though what she actually saw was nothing more than a human-shaped bundle resting in an open crate, its flesh concealed beneath ancient strips of linen. Mounted over the face was a cartonnage mask— the painted face of a woman with haunting dark eyes.

But then another woman in the CT room caught Maura's attention. Wearing cotton gloves, the young woman leaned into the crate, removing layers of Ethafoam packing from around the mummy. Ringlets of black hair fell around her face. She straightened and shoved her hair back, revealing eyes as dark and striking as those painted on the mask. Her Mediterranean features could well have appeared on any Egyptian temple painting, but her clothes were thoroughly modern: skinny blue jeans and a Live Aid T-shirt.

"Beautiful, isn't she?" murmured Dr. Robinson. He'd moved beside Maura, and for a moment she wondered if he was referring to Madam X or to the young woman. "She appears to be in excellent condition. I just hope the body inside is as well preserved as those wrappings."

"How old do you think she is? Do you have an estimate?"

"We sent off a swatch of the outer wrapping for carbon fourteen analysis. It just about killed our budget to do it, but Josephine insisted. The results came back as second century BC."

"That's the Ptolemaic period, isn't it?"

He responded with a pleased smile. "You know your Egyptian dynasties."

"I was an anthropology major in college, but I'm afraid I don't remember much beyond that and the Yanomamo tribe."

"Still, I'm impressed."

She stared at the wrapped body, marveling that what lay in that crate was more than two thousand years old. What a journey it had taken, across an ocean, across millennia, all to end up lying on a CT table in a Boston hospital, gawked at by the curious. "Are you going to leave her in the crate for the scan?" she asked.

"We want to handle her as little as possible. The crate won't get in the way. We'll still get a good look at what lies under that linen."

"So you haven't taken even a little peek?"

"You mean have I *unwrapped* part of her?" His mild eyes widened in horror. "God, no. Archaeologists would have done that a hundred years ago, maybe, and that's exactly how they ended up damaging so many specimens. There are probably layers of resin under those outer wrappings, so you can't just peel it all away. You might have to chip through it. It's not only destructive, it's disrespectful. I'd never do that." He looked through the window at the dark-haired young woman. "And Josephine would kill me if I did."

"That's your colleague?"

"Yes. Dr. Pulcillo."

"She looks like she's about sixteen."

"Doesn't she? But she's smart as a whip. She's the one who arranged this scan. And when the hospital attorneys tried to put a stop to it, Josephine managed to push it through anyway."

"Why would the attorneys object?"

"Seriously? Because this patient couldn't give the hospital her informed consent."

Maura laughed in disbelief. "They wanted informed consent from a *mummy*?"

"When you're a lawyer, every *i* must be dotted. Even when the patient's been dead for a few thousand years."

Dr. Pulcillo had removed all the packing materials, and she joined them in the viewing room and shut the connecting door. The mummy now lay exposed in its crate, awaiting the first barrage of X-rays.

"Dr. Robinson?" said the CT tech, fingers poised over the computer keyboard. "We need to provide the required patient information before we can start the scan. What shall I use as the birth date?"

The curator frowned. "Oh, gosh. Do you really need a birth date?"

"I can't start the scan until I fill in these blanks. I tried the year zero, and the computer wouldn't take it."

"Why don't we use yesterday's date? Make it one day old."

"Okay. Now the program insists on knowing the sex. Male, female, or other?"

Robinson blinked. "There's a category for *other*?"

The tech grinned. "I've never had the chance to check that particular box."

"Well then, let's use it tonight. There's a woman's face on the mask, but you never know. We can't be sure of the gender until we scan it."

"Okay," said Dr. Brier, the radiologist. "We're ready to go."

Dr. Robinson nodded. "Let's do it."

They gathered around the computer monitor, waiting for the first images to appear. Through the window, they could see the table feed Madam X's head into the doughnut-shaped opening, where she was bombarded by X-rays from multiple angles. Computerized tomography was not new medical technology, but its use as an archaeological tool was relatively recent. No one in that room had ever before watched a live CT scan of a mummy, and as they all crowded in, Maura was aware of the TV camera trained on their faces, ready to capture their reactions. Standing beside her, Nicholas Robinson rocked back and forth on the balls of his feet, radiating enough nervous energy to infect everyone in the room. Maura felt her own pulse quicken as she craned for a better view of the monitor. The first image that appeared drew only impatient sighs.

"It's just the shell of the crate," said Dr. Brier.

Maura glanced at Robinson and saw that his lips were pressed together in thin lines. Would Madam X turn out to be nothing more than an empty bundle of rags? Dr. Pulcillo stood beside him, looking just as tense, gripping the back of the radiologist's chair as she stared over his shoulder, awaiting a glimpse of anything recognizably human, anything to confirm that inside those bandages was a cadaver.

The next image changed everything. It was a startlingly bright disk, and the instant it appeared, the observers all took in a sharply simultaneous breath.

Bone.

Dr. Brier said, "That's the top of the cranium. Congratulations, you've definitely got an occupant in there."

Robinson and Pulcillo gave each other happy claps on the back. "This is what we were waiting for!" he said.

Pulcillo grinned. "Now we can finish building that exhibit."

"Mummies!" Robinson threw his head back and laughed. "Everyone loves mummies!"

New slices appeared on the screen, and their attention snapped back to the monitor as more of the cranium appeared, its cavity filled not with brain matter but with ropy strands that looked like a knot of worms.

"Those are linen strips," Dr. Pulcillo murmured in wonder, as though this was the most beautiful sight she'd ever seen.

"There's no brain matter," said the CT tech.

"No, the brain was usually evacuated."

"Is it true they'd stick a hook up through the nose and yank the brain out that way?" the tech asked.

"Almost true. You can't really yank out the brain, because it's too soft. They probably used an instrument to whisk it around until it was liquefied. Then they'd tilt the body so the brain would drip out the nose."

"Oh man, that's gross," said the tech. But he was hanging on Pulcillo's every word.

"They might leave the cranium empty or they might pack it with linen strips, as you see here. And frankincense."

"What *is* frankincense, anyway? I've always wondered about that."

"A fragrant resin. It comes from a very special tree in Africa. Valued quite highly in the ancient world."

"So that's why one of the three wise men brought it to Bethlehem."

Dr. Pulcillo nodded. "It would have been a treasured gift."

"Okay," Dr. Brier said. "We've moved below the level of the orbits. There you can see the upper jaw, and . . ." He paused, frowning at an unexpected density.

Robinson murmured, "Oh my goodness."

"It's something metallic," said Dr. Brier. "It's in the oral cavity."

"It could be gold leaf," said Pulcillo. "In the Greco-Roman era, they'd sometimes place gold-leaf tongues inside the mouth."

Robinson turned to the TV camera, which was recording every remark. "There appears to be metal inside the mouth. That would correlate with our presumptive date during the Greco-Roman era—"

"Now what is *this*?" exclaimed Dr. Brier.

Maura's gaze shot back to the computer screen. A bright starburst had appeared within the mummy's lower jaw, an image that stunned Maura because it should not have been present in a corpse that was two thousand years old. She leaned closer, staring at a detail that would scarcely cause comment were this a body that had arrived fresh on the autopsy table. "I know this is impossible," Maura said softly. "But you know what that looks like?"

The radiologist nodded. "It appears to be a dental filling."

Maura turned to Dr. Robinson, who appeared just as startled as everyone else in the room. "Has anything like this ever been described in an Egyptian mummy before?" she asked. "Ancient dental repairs that could be mistaken for modern fillings?"

Wide-eyed, he shook his head. "But it doesn't mean the Egyptians were incapable of it. Their medical care was the most advanced in the ancient world." He looked at his colleague. "Josephine, what can you tell us about this? It's your field."

Dr. Pulcillo struggled for an answer. "There—there are medical papyri from the Old Kingdom," she said. "They describe how to fix loose teeth and make dental bridges. And there was a healer who was famous as a maker of teeth. So we know they were ingenious when it came to dental care. Far ahead of their time."

"But did they ever make repairs like *that*?" said Maura, pointing to the screen.

Dr. Pulcillo's troubled gaze returned to the image. "If they did," she said softly, "I'm not aware of it."

On the monitor, new images appeared in shades of gray, the body viewed in cross section as though sliced through by a bread knife. She could be bombarded by X-rays from every angle, subjected to massive doses of radiation, but this patient was beyond fears of cancer, beyond worries about side effects. As X-rays continued to assault her body, no patient could have been more submissive.

Shaken by the earlier images, Robinson was now arched forward like a tightly strung bow, alert for the next surprise. The first slices of the thorax appeared, the cavity black and vacant.

"It appears that the lungs were removed," the radiologist said. "All I see is a shriveled bit of mediastinum in the chest."

"That's the heart," said Pulcillo, her voice steadier now. This, at least, was what she'd expected to see. "They always tried to leave it in situ."

"Just the heart?"

She nodded. "It was considered the seat of intelligence, so you never separated it from the body. There are three separate spells contained in the Book of the Dead to ensure that the heart remains in place."

"And the other organs?" asked the CT tech. "I heard those were put in special jars."

"That was before the Twenty-first Dynasty. After around a thousand BC, the organs were wrapped into four bundles and stuffed back into the body."

"So we should be able to see that?"

"In a mummy from the Ptolemaic era, yes."

"I think I can make an educated guess about her age when she died," said the radiologist. "The wisdom teeth were fully erupted, and the cranial sutures are closed. But I don't see any degenerative changes in the spine."

"A young adult," said Maura.

"Probably under thirty-five."

"In the era she lived in, thirty-five was well into middle age," said Robinson.

The scan had moved below the thorax, X-rays slicing through layers of wrappings, through the shell of dried skin and bones, to reveal the abdominal cavity. What Maura saw within was eerily unfamiliar, as strange to her as an alien autopsy. Where she expected to see liver and spleen, stomach and pancreas, instead she saw snake-like coils of linen, an interior landscape that was missing all that should have been recognizable. Only the bright knobs of vertebral bone told her this was indeed a human body, a body that had been hollowed out to a mere shell and stuffed like a rag doll.

Mummy anatomy might be alien to her, but for both Robinson and Pulcillo this was familiar territory. As new images appeared, they both leaned in, pointing out details they recognized.

"There," said Robinson. "Those are the four linen packets containing the organs."

"Okay, we're now in the pelvis," Dr. Brier said. He pointed to two pale arcs. They were the top edges of the iliac crests.

Slice by slice, the pelvis slowly took shape, as the computer compiled and rendered countless X-ray beams. It was a digital striptease as each image revealed a tantalizing new peek.

"Look at the shape of the pelvic inlet," said Dr. Brier.

"It's a female," said Maura.

The radiologist nodded. "I'd say it's pretty conclusive." He turned and grinned at the two archaeologists. "You can now officially call her Madam X. And not *Mister* X."

"And look at the pubic symphysis," said Maura, still focused on the monitor. "There's no separation."

Brier nodded. "I agree."

"What does that mean?" asked Robinson.

Maura explained. "During childbirth, the infant's passage through the pelvic inlet can actually force apart the pubic bones, where they join at the symphysis. It appears this female never had children."

The CT tech laughed. "Your mummy's never been a mommy."

The scan had moved beyond the pelvis, and they could now see cross sections of the two femurs encased in the withered flesh of the upper thighs.

"Nick, we need to call Simon," said Pulcillo. "He's probably waiting by the phone."

"Oh gosh, I completely forgot." Robinson pulled out his cell phone and dialed his boss. "Simon, guess what I'm looking at right now? Yes, she's gorgeous. Plus, we've discovered a few surprises, so the press conference is going to be quite the—"

In an instant he fell silent, his gaze frozen on the screen.

"What the hell?" blurted the CT tech.

The image now glowing on the monitor was so unexpected that the room had fallen completely still. Were a living patient lying on the CT table, Maura would have had no difficulty identifying the small metallic object embedded in the calf, an object that had shattered the slender shaft of the fibula. But that bit of metal did not belong in Madam X's leg.

A bullet did not belong in Madam X's millennium.

"Is that what I think it is?" said the CT tech.

Robinson shook his head. "It has to be post-mortem damage. What else could it be?"

"Two thousand *years* postmortem?"

"I'll—I'll call you back, Simon." Robinson disconnected his cell phone. Turning to the cameraman, he ordered: "Shut it off. Please shut it off *now*." He took a deep breath. "All right. All right, let's—let's approach this logically." He straightened, gaining confidence as an obvious explanation occurred to him. "Mummies have often been abused or damaged by souvenir hunters. Obviously, someone fired a bullet into the mummy. And a conservator later tried to repair that damage by rewrapping her. That's why we saw no entry hole in the bandages."

"That isn't what happened," said Maura.

Robinson blinked. "What do you mean? That has to be the explanation."

"The damage to that leg wasn't postmortem. It happened while this woman was still alive."

"That's impossible."

"I'm afraid Dr. Isles is right," said the radiologist. He looked at Maura. "You're referring to the early callus formation around the fracture site?"

"What does that mean?" asked Robinson. "Callus formation?"

"It means the broken bone had already started the process of healing when this woman died. She lived at least a few weeks after the injury."

Maura turned to the curator. "Where did this mummy come from?"

Robinson's glasses had slipped down his nose yet again, and he stared over the lenses as though hypnotized by what he saw glowing in the mummy's leg.

It was Dr. Pulcillo who answered the question, her voice barely a whisper. "It was in the museum basement. Nick—Dr. Robinson found it back in January."

"And how did the museum obtain it?"

Pulcillo shook her head. "We don't know."

"There must be records. Something in your files to indicate where she came from."

"There are none for her," said Robinson, at last finding his voice. "The Crispin Museum is a hundred thirty years old, and many records are missing. We have no idea how long she was stored in the basement."

"How did you happen to find her?"

Even in that air-conditioned room, sweat had broken out on Dr. Robinson's pale face. "After I was hired three years ago, I began an inventory of the collection. That's how I came across her. She was in an unlabeled crate."

"And that didn't surprise you? To find something as rare as an Egyptian mummy in an unlabeled crate?"

"But mummies *aren't* all that rare. In the 1800s, you could buy one in Egypt for only five dollars, so American tourists brought them home by the hundreds. They turn up in attics and antiques stores. A freak show in Niagara Falls even claims they had King Ramses the First in their collection. So it's not all that surprising that we'd find a mummy in our museum."

"Dr. Isles?" said the radiologist. "We've got the scout film. You might want to take a look at it."

Maura turned to the monitor. Displayed on the screen was a conventional X-ray like the films she hung on her own viewing box in the morgue. She did not need a radiologist to interpret what she saw there.

"There's not much doubt about it now," said Dr. Brier.

No. There's no doubt whatsoever. That's a bullet in the leg.

Maura pulled out her cell phone.

"Dr. Isles?" said Robinson. "Whom are you calling?"

"I'm arranging for transport to the morgue," she said. "Madam X is now a medical examiner's case."

**Now read the complete
book – out now in paperback**